SHADOWBRIGHT

STARTING OUT

By Ryan Darkfield
Edited by Christian Edwards
Artwork by Warren McCabe Smith

Acknowledgements

Roger Victor Richards
Glyn, Claire and Lucas Richards
Sarah Baugh
Chris and Donna Edwards
Warren McCabe-Smith
Ash Fowkes
Allan Parson
Rhianna Parsons

and
Gaynor Richards

CHAPTER 1:
THE BIRTH

I first met Craig in the Autumn of 1996, a few months after England were knocked out of the Euros by the infernal Hun.

We were both studying A-Level Psychology at Halesowen College, under the tutelage of a biker-chick named Wendy, who delivered her seminars in leather trousers and knee-high boots.

Being the only two boys in class, we gravitated to each other, soon bonding over a shared love of cheesy 80's horror films.

I'd always been into writing, so one day I showed him a film script I was working on called 'Image of Evil', a cheap rip-off of the movie *Seven*, featuring a serial killer who he thought he was the Devil.

"I love it!" Craig beamed, after reading the

first page. "We should make this into a film!"

"How?" I chuckled.

"Easy," he replied. " My Dad's got a camera. He can edit stuff on his PC. I'm sure he'll help us if we ask him."

"Yeah," I grinned. "Why not?"

After class, we headed back to Craig's house, where we discussed the project with his dad, Colin.

"I'm more than happy to help you, boys," he said. "I was into this kind of thing myself."

"Dad did some stuff for the BBC," Craig declared proudly.

"...Back in the sixties," Colin sighed, "before everything went to video."

He led us upstairs to his editing suite, a box room at the front of the house, where he gave us a videotape that was labelled, 'The Witch'.

"You gotta see this," Craig enthused, leading me into his bedroom.

"Where's the TV?" I asked, looking round the room.

"I've got something better," he grinned, loading the tape into a video-projector that was fixed to the wall above his bed.

The device whirred into life and a grainy image of an old Vauxhall Victor appeared on screen.

"That's Cradley Heath High Street," Craig said, sitting himself down. "...Just around the corner."

The footage cut to a close-up of the car's headlights being pelted with rain.

"No one's actually driving in that shot," he added. "The car's parked up on someone's drive."

"Whose drive?" I asked.

"One of the actors. He was a mate of my dad's. And that's not real rain, either... It's a watering can."

"No way," I laughed.

"Here we go," Craig stated, as the titles appeared on-screen. "This is where it gets good!"

I sat back watching intently as the action cut to a hallway inside a house. A man with a mop-top haircut entered the shot then began making his way up the stairs. The footage then cut to a scene inside one of the bedrooms, where a woman was sitting in front of a mirror, combing her long brown hair.

The door suddenly opened, and the man burst in, shouting at her in a thick Dudley accent.

"Ya'am a witch!" he roared, loudly but flatly. "Ar'm banishing yow, yow eevul cow!"

He grabbed her by the ear, hauled her to her feet, then began slapping her around the face.

I was intrigued.

Also slightly disturbed.

Well, I would have been if it hadn't looked so fake...

"What do you think so far?" Craig asked.

Before I could reply, the door to his room opened and his mom came in with two cups of tea.

"Hello boys," she said sweetly. "I've made you some drinks."

"Bloody hell, mom," Craig snapped. "We're watching a film!"

She dismissed him with a tut, then placed the cups on his bedside cabinet before tootling off.

"Sorry about that," Craig sighed, handing me my drink. "She's always barging in, unannounced. Do you want me to rewind?"

"No," I replied, shaking my head. "I don't think I've missed much..."

Three minutes later, the credits started to roll, and Craig took the tape out of the player.

"So how many films did your dad make in total?" I asked, with a smile.

"Loads," he replied. "But this one's the best! He'll be dead pleased that I'm following in his footsteps. He's always wanted me to carry the torch, and now with this script of yours, I can."

"But how are we going to film it?" I asked. "It's set in Los Angeles.

"We'll write a letter to Granada Studios," he began, grinning broadly. "We'll ask them if we can take my Dad's camcorder up there and shoot the scenes on their sets."

"You really think they'll let us do that?"

"Why wouldn't they?" Craig responded. "This could be massive blockbuster hit."

"What are we going to do about the guns?

And the explosions?"

"We'll use their props," he replied. "And we can do all the explosions digitally. All we need to do is superimpose them on the footage. My dad does it all the time."

His enthusiasm was infectious, and I was soon clapping along to his every beat.

"Maybe we can get some proper actors to be in it too?" I suggested. "Don't they film Coronation Street at Granada?"

"Yeah, but we don't want any of them shitheads," Craig scoffed. "We want proper actors in this, like Brad Pitt and Morgan Freeman."

"That'd be amazing," I said.

"It's only what we deserve," Craig declared.

He pointed to the drawer of his beside cabinet.

"There's a pen and paper in there," he said. "Let's write to them now. The sooner we get started, the better."

"Yeah!" I squealed, seal-clapping, like it was a Thursday evening in 2020.

We spent the rest of the night drafting the letter, re-scribing it several times so that it looked as neat as possible. When it was done, Craig put it inside a brown envelope, which we labelled *Granada Studios, Manchester*.

"Do you not think we'll need a full address?" I asked.

"Nah," he replied, shaking his head. "The Royal Mail'll know where it is. It's famous."

"Yeah," I agreed. "Everyone knows Granada Studios."

"Come on," he said, "There's a shop down the road with a post-box outside. We can buy a stamp and post it straight away. With any luck, it'll be with them by tomorrow morning..."

* * *

After waiting several months for a response, we concluded that Granada were deliberately ignoring us.

"Why won't they take us seriously?" Craig lamented.

"Probably because we're just a couple of kids," I replied.

"We're not kids. We're filmmakers."

"But how can we be filmmakers if they won't let us make our film?" I grumbled. "It's so unfair."

"You're right," Craig nodded, stroking his chin. "We need to show them we mean business."

"How?" I asked.

"By making it ourselves," he replied. "We'll do it on a shoestring budget, guerrilla-style, like my dad."

I glanced at the script in my hand.

The first page alone featured a protracted chase sequence across the rooftops of LA, followed by a gunfight which resulted in an exploding car.

"I don't think it's possible," I said.

"Not that..." Craig snorted, snatching the script from my hands and casually tossing it over his shoulder. "...I'm talking about other projects, short films... Stuff we can do with a couple of a blokes and a camera."

"Oh," I replied. "Like what?"

"I don't know," Criag said. "But I'm sure we can come up with some ideas."

CHAPTER 2: MATTER OF TIME

We took out our exercise books and started scribbling our thoughts on the pages. Most of them were overly outlandish, involving huge casts, exotic locations, space battles, and giant monsters.

But there were a few doable ideas too.

After binning the unfilmable stuff, we were left with an outline for a sci-fi short involving a man who travels back in time to save his mother from a fatal car crash, which would ultimately prevent him from being born.

"I love this," Craig declared. "It's like an episode of *Twilight Zone!*"

"Yeah," I agreed. "...Or *Creepshow*. Have you ever seen that?"

"Seen it?" Craig laughed. "I've got it on Laserdisc!"

Before I could say anything else, he rushed out of the room and grabbed it from his dad's studio.

"Let's watch it now, for inspiration," he said.

He popped it in the Player then then shouted to his mom to make us some tea.

"Is this the first one or the second one?" I asked, taking a seat next to him on the bed.

"The second," Craig answered.

"Excellent," I replied. "I love *The Raft* episode."

"Yeah," he laughed. "Probably cos there's tits in it!"

He wasn't wrong...

* * *

After watching the film, its prequel and sequel, and the movie version of *The Twilight Zone*, we finally started working on our script.

Several hours later, we'd cobbled together five pages of what we considered to be sci-fi gold.

The basic plot revolved around a woman, Tanya, who picks up a hitchhiker whilst driving along a country road during a storm. The hitcher seems familiar to her, but she doesn't know why. He also seems to know things about her life that a stranger shouldn't. When she asks him why, he tells her that he is her son, and has travelled through time to warn her that if she doesn't turn the car around, she will be hit by a lorry and die in the wreckage. Tanya laughs then tells him that he's crazy, but then he starts to fade before her eyes, like Marty McFly. In a state of shock, she turns the steering wheel, and her cars drifts into the path of an oncoming juggernaut. The film ends with Tanya's son reappearing by the side of the road and whispering the words, "this time," implying that he's been trapped in the paradox for years.

"This is amazing!" Craig declared, after we'd done a quick read-through. "Quality stuff! I can see this shit being on Telly!"

"Me too," I agreed. "Now we just need to work out how we're going to film it."

"Piece of piss," Craig chuckled. "We'll use your car for the driving scenes, then film all the dialogue while we're parked up. We can do what my dad did to create the illusion we're moving."

"Cool," I said. "What about the crash at the end?"

"Easy," he replied. "We'll cut away and insert a sound effect."

"Great," I said. "Who's gonna be in it?"

"We'll cross that bridge later. First, we need to do some tests. Are you free tomorrow night?"

"Yeah!"

* * *

The next evening, we drove up to the Clent Hills Nature Reserve to do some test footage in the car park. When we got there, we were met by Craig's mates Pat and Mittsy, who'd offered to help us out.

"What do you want us to do?" Pat asked sheepishly, as Craig got out his dad's camera.

"Stand at the front of my car," I replied. "Then put your hands on the bonnet and shake it from side to side."

"What do you want me to do?" Mittsy asked.

I handed him a torch.

"Stand behind Craig and shine this on my face," I said.

"Is that it?" he asked.

"Yeah," I replied. "You're the lighting unit."

"What unit am I?" Pat asked.

"You're the Chief Grip," Craig answered.

"How come he gets to be a Chief?" Mittsy said.

"You're both chiefs," I replied. "Just in different areas."

I got into my car and sat myself down in the driver's seat. Craig then aimed the camera at me through the passenger-side window.

"Ok," he called, pressing the record button, "Action!"

I took the steering wheel and pretended to drive while Pat bounced the car up and down.

"Cut," Craig said.

"What's wrong?" I asked.

"You'll need to wind down the window," he replied. "The torchlight is reflecting in the glass."

"No worries," I said.

I leant over the passenger seat and wound down the window.

"Do you want me to carry on doing this?" Pat asked. He looked tired. Then again, he always looked tired. Fat people do.

"You can stop when I call 'cut'," Craig answered.

He took his chubby hands off the bonnet and lit up a cigarette.

"What about me?" Mittsy asked. "Do you want this on or off?"

"On," Craig replied. "Just keep it pointed at Dom."

He lifted the camera then pointed the lens through the window.

"More light..." he ordered.

Mittsy crouched down then aimed the beam directly at my face.

"Less light," Craig instructed.

He redirected the beam onto my chest.

"Do you want me to shake the car?" Pat asked.

I gave him the thumbs up.

"Are we ready to roll, Craig?" I asked.

"Two secs," he said. "I'm having a little problem with the autofocus."

Pat stopped was he was doing and took a breather,

"Ok," Craig said. "Action!"

I looked forward and started turning the

wheel, as if I was traversing a chicane.

"Cut!" Craig yelled. "The car's not moving."

"Oh, sorry," Pat replied.

"How's the lighting?" Mittsy asked.

"It's hard to tell," Craig said. "I can't really see much in the viewfinder."

"Can we make the image brighter if it's too dark?" I asked.

"Yeah," Craig said. "We boost the levels in post."

"Cool," I said, not quite knowing what he meant.

"What about the sound?" I asked. "Do we need to test that too?"

"We can do," Craig replied. "Turn on the engine then say a few of the lines."

I looked around for the script, then realised I'd left it at home.

"I'll have to do it from memory," I said. "Is that ok?"

"Yeah," Craig replied. "This is just a test, remember."

He gestured for me to start, and I began improvising the lines as best I could. After several nonsensical utterances, I asked him if it was ok.

"Levels look good," he replied. "All within range."

Just then, the light from the torch began to fade.

"More light," Craig yelled.

"The batteries are going," Mittsy replied. "You got any spares?"

"No," I said.

Chris grunted.

"Just hold it closer," he snapped.

Mittsy pushed his arm further through the window.

"Too close," Craig muttered. "Now you're in the shot."

Mittsy withdrew his arm.

"No, No..." Craig tutted. "You've gone too far. Now I can't see him."

Just then, the torch cut out completely, shrouding the car in complete darkness. Craig swore. Mittsy half-grunted, half-laughed.

I flicked the switched of the inside light so we could see what we were doing.

"Maybe we could use this?" I suggested.

Craig checked the image in the viewfinder.

"No," he sighed. "It's not strong enough."

"Maybe you should have got new batteries?" Pat suggested, somewhat unhelpfully.

"They were new," Craig snorted, clearly annoyed.

"And they lasted barely half an hour..." I added. "We're gonna need loads when we're shooting this for real. How much are they?"

"£3.99 for a two-pack," Craig replied, grimly. "And the torch needs four."

"Shit," I said, working out the maths. "That's a lot of money just for lighting."

"Maybe you should just film it in the day?" Mittsy said.

"We can't," Craig snapped. "If we did, you'd see that the car wasn't really moving."

"Can't you just act and drive at the same time?"

"It won't be me, driving," I explained. "It'll be an actress, and I can't have anyone else on my insurance."

"Depends on your insurance," Pat commented. "Mine allows any driver."

"Bollocks," I replied.

"It aint bollocks," he said. "I've got it."

"Oh yeah?" I sniffed. "So, how does that work if you own a Ferrari?"

He shrugged his shoulders.

"I don't know," he repeated. "But I've got it."

"My uncle's got it too," Mittsy remarked. "It's business cover. It's for fleets."

"Yeah, that's it," Pat said.

"So-fucking-what?" Craig snapped. "Regardless of what stupid insurance you've got, this film has to be shot at night..."

"Why?" Mittsy asked.

"Because that's what it says in the script."

Everyone fell silent.

"Ok," I said, finally. "Shall we go back and have a look at what we've got?"

"I thought we were going to the pub?" Pat said.

I glanced at Craig, who sighed mournfully.

"Fine," he said. "We'll check the footage tomorrow..."

CHAPTER 3:
STEEL JUSTICE

The 'rushes' as Craig called them, were awful. Every shot was either too grainy and unclear, or too bright and washed out. The sound too, was horrible. Nothing could be heard above the humming of the engine.

"I think you should filter your lighting," Colin suggested, as he scrubbed through the feed on his PC. "If I was you, I'd tape some tracing paper over the bulb of the torch to diffuse the beam."

"Thanks for telling us," Craig huffed. "It would have saved us a journey."

"What about the sound?" I asked.

"Nothing you can do about that," Colin replied. "Unless you get yourself an external mic."

"How much are they?" I asked.

"Couple of hundred," he replied. "They sell them in Preston's."

I looked at Craig.

Neither of us had that kind of money.

"Failing that," Colin suggested, "You could just stick to filming things indoors."

"But our film is set inside a car!" Craig grunted.

"Make a different film then," his dad said.

Craig blew out his cheeks and stormed off.

I followed him into his bedroom, where I found him standing up against the far wall, facing it, with arms folded.

"Maybe we should take his advice?" I said, patting him gently on the shoulder.

"And scale down our vision?" he hissed. "What will we be left with? A story about two blokes in a park? Where's the fun in that?"

"I dunno," I replied, chewing the inside of my cheek. "But we need to start somewhere."

"Fine," he snorted. "What other ideas do we have?"

"I suppose we can have a go at *Steel Justice*?"

It was one of the ideas we'd rejected during our initial brainstorm, not because it was too hard to film, but because the story was a bit crap.

"Which one was that?" Craig scoffed.

"The one with the Android," I replied.

"Oh God," he groaned. "That one..."

"Yeah," I nodded. "But it's mostly set in the day, so should be easy to do."

"Ok," he huffed, placing his hands on his hips. "If you insist..."

* * *

Steel Justice was a modern-day adaptation of Pinocchio, replacing the title character with a Cyborg, and the Fairy Godmother with a mad scientist. The twist in our version of the story was that the protagonist only finds out that he's a robot at the end of the film, after being shot in the head repeatedly by the gangsters who murdered his father.

With a modest runtime of around eight minutes, it was an ambitious piece of storytelling.

Probably too ambitious.

Not that we knew any better.

In our eyes, it was nothing more than a super-simple project, involving a small number of indoor shoots that could be filmed during the day with our mates.

"Who should we cast as Steve?" Craig asked.

He was referring to the lead character.

"What about Baz?" I suggested.

Baz was a friend from school, who we sometimes hung out with. He was big and broad, and looked a little bit like a young Arnold Schwarzenegger.

"Perfect," Craig said. "What about the dad?"

"I dunno," I replied. "Maybe one of us could

do it?"

"Nah," he said. "We look too young. What about Allan? He's skinny and he's got long hair. If we tie it back and sprinkle it with flour, he'll pass for someone's dad."

"All right," I said. "What about the gangster?"

"Mittsy," he replied. "Because he looks rough."

With our casting sorted, we made a few calls and arranged a shoot for the following Saturday.

On the days leading up to it, I polished the script and dismantled an old PC motherboard for the 'Cyborg' effects.

"We can glue the bits to his face," I told Craig over the phone. "If we squirt ketchup around them, it'll look like the Terminator."

Looking back, I may have been overselling it a little, but Craig was completely sold.

"It's gonna look great," he said. "I can't wait."

When the weekend came around, I drove over to Craig's house, raring to go.

"We may have to change things round," he said, as he got in the car. "Allan's ill. He's got the flu."

"No worries," I replied, cheerily. "We can do his scenes next week."

We drove to first location, Baz's house, where we found him and Mittsy waiting for us outside. Both were holding cans of beer and already looked a little drunk.

"What's this?" Craig said, as he got out. "Drinking on set?"

"Dutch courage," Baz laughed.

He took a long swig from his tin then belched aggressively.

Mittsy started laughing.

"I hope you're going to be able to remember your lines," I said. "You have read the script I sent you?"

"Yeah, I had a glance," Mittsy chuckled. "How are you gonna do the robot effects?"

I held up the plastic bag containing the smashed-up motherboard and tomato ketchup.

"Prosthetics," I answered.

"Come on, then," Craig declared. "Let's make a start."

"Can I have a shit, first?" Baz said. "I've been holding it in all morning."

"Go on, then," Craig replied. "But make it quick, we need to save this light."

"It's 9am," Baz roared, as he headed inside.

Fifteen minutes later, he re-emerged looking several stone lighter. He was also holding a six-pack of Carling, which he offered to the group.

"Anyone want one?" he asked.

"Go on, then," Mittsy said, tossing away the one that he was holding.

"Dom?" Baz said.

"Sorry mate, I'm driving," I replied.

"Craig?"

He inhaled sharply.

"Just the one," he said. "I can't direct if I'm pissed."

Baz smiled then handed him a tin.

I then stood and watched as the three of them began glugging down their lagers as fast as they were physically able, wondering what kind of state they'd be in later...

* * *

We finally started shooting at 10:30, after Baz convinced his mom to loan us the use of her front room, which - somewhat bizarrely - we'd decided to use as a location for the Gangster's HQ.

Whilst writing the script, I'd pictured it being like the back room of a pub; all smoky and dimly lit, with greasy walls, and sticky laminate floors... Not the net-curtained charm of Marge's living room.

Still, we had to make them best of it, needs must and all that....

The first scene we needed to shoot involved a confrontation between Mittsy's gangster, *Leon*, and Baz's protagonist, *Steve*. On paper, it was a simple sequence, consisting of Baz bursting on Mittsy and demanding he tell him where his father was being held.

Baz had one line to say, something along the lines of, "Hey, fucker! Tell me where my dad is!"

It seemed straightforward enough...

How wrong we were.

After setting up the room, Craig put on his Directing hat and explained to the cast what he wanted from the scene.

"Passion!" he declared. "I want passion!"

His words made Baz giggle.

Or perhaps it was the booze?

By this point he'd had three cans.

Either way, the result was hilarious.

When Craig called 'Action', Baz stormed through the door theatrically, pointed a finger at Mittsy's face then loudly declared, "Hey motherfucker! Where's my dad, you motherfucking-fucking-fuck!"

Mittsy immediately corpsed, his body creasing with laughter.

I pissed myself too.

It was the funniest thing I'd seen in ages.

The only not laughing was Craig, who yelled, "Cut" straight away, then demanded to know what the hell was going on.

"Are you taking the piss?" he grunted, squaring up to Baz.

"Sorry mate, I forgot my line."

"It's, 'Hey, fucker - tell my where my dad is,'" I interjected.

"Oh," Baz said. "Can we try it again?"

He paced back to his mark, then gave Craig the thumbs up to start over.

"Action!"

As soon as Baz walked through the door, he started laughing and it set everyone off.

"For fuck's sake!" Craig declared. "What's so fucking funny? Has no one ever heard the word 'fuck' before?"

He looked to me for support, but I was too busy clutching my sides.

"Sorry, dude," I said. "I can't help it."

"Fucking amateurs!" Craig sniffed.

He put down the camera, went over to the table, then helped himself to another can.

"I thought you'd said you didn't want to get drunk," Mittsy chuckled.

"I think I'll need to, working with you," Craig replied.

"I'm having another one too, then," Baz said.

"Yeah," Mittsy added. "Grab one for me as well..."

* * *

We attempted the scene several more times before calling it a day. It just wasn't happening for us. Baz and Mittsy couldn't control themselves. And the more they drank, the worse it got.

In the end, Craig put away his camera then

joined them on the couch, drinking lager.

"Shall we watch something?" Baz suggested. "I got loads of videos."

He worked at the Stellavision in Cradley High Street. He could take home any film he wanted.

"What about Deathstalker II?" Mittsy said. "I've not watched that in years."

"Go on then," Craig replied.

"It's actually not a bad film," I said. "The characterisation is really good, and the final swordfight is brilliantly staged."

The three of them looked at me and laughed.

I hoped it had something to do with the alcohol...

CHAPTER 4:
CLAPPERBOARD

"**I** think we need to use people who are serious about helping us," I said to Craig one day in college. "I get the impression people aren't that interested in what we're doing."

"It's cos we're coming across as professional," he replied. "I mean, look at us. What are we? Two blokes and a camera. We use table-lamps for lighting, the internal mic on the camera... We haven't even got a fucking clapperboard, for God's sake."

"What's a clapperboard?" I asked.

"It's that blackboard thing they use to start the scene. When the cameras start rolling, the grip comes in, holds the clapperboard up to the lens, announces the scene and shot, then.... click! We're ready to roll."

"I think I know what you're talking about," I said.

"I know you know what I'm talking about," Craig replied. "With one of those babies, no one would ever fuck around on set. And it'd make editing really easy too, because it makes it easy to find the shot you want to use when you're editing."

"Have you done much editing yourself?" I asked.

Craig shook his head.

"Nah," he said. "I've never owned a clapperboard."

After class, we went to the McDonalds to talk strategy, ordering two-big macs, two large fries, and large milkshake. Each.

"Who sells clapperboard?" I asked.

"There's this shop I know in Quinton," Craig replied. "It's called *Masquerade*. They do props and shit for theatres. I'm sure they'll have one."

Without further ado, we jumped in the car...

* * *

The shop was located at the far end of the High Street, next to the KFC. A bold yellow sign hung from its frontage, with *Masquerade* emblazoned between a couple of domino masks.

"Kinky," I remarked, as we pulled onto the car park. "It looks like something out of *Eyes Wide*

Shut."

We got out then made our way to the door, which we found was locked.

"Please tell me it isn't closed," Craig sighed.

"No, it's defo open," I said, looking through the window. "There are people inside."

"So, why's the door bolted?"

Beside the door was a button. A sign beneath it said, 'Ring for Entry'.

"We need to ring the bell," I said.

"Go on, then."

I pressed the button. A shrill ringing sounded inside, and a middle-aged woman approached the door to let us in.

"Hello," she said. "Are you looking for a costume?"

"Sort of," Craig replied.

"We're after a clapperboard," I explained.

"Oh yes," the woman replied. "We do those, but we don't have any in stock. Come in and I'll place an order for you on the system."

"Sweet," Craig said.

She led us to the counter, where she pulled out the order book and pen.

"Could I have a name please?" she asked.

I gave her my name and she jotted it on the page.

"And do you a company name?"

A company name?

I looked at Craig.

He was thinking exactly the same thing.

What kind of production outfit were we if we didn't have a title?

"We'll get back to you on that," he said.

"It's still in the developmental stage," I lied.

After taking the rest of our details, the woman told us she'd give us she'd get in touch when it arrived. She then asked us if we'd like to have a look around the shop before we left.

"Sure," I said. "Why not?"

We spent the next hour browsing through the stock, marvelling at what was on offer. As well as costumes, the shop sold make-up and props. Craig was particularly impressed with a vial of theatrical blood that he'd found in the 'vampire' section. It came in a squeegee bottle and had a pointy neck, which allowed a tube to be connected to the tip.

"If we tape the tube under someone's chin," he said, "we can squeeze the bottle and it'll squirt out, like real blood."

"Cool," I said.

Sitting alongside the vials were various sets of teeth, including vampire fangs and dentures for zombies, werewolves and 'yokels'.

"We could use all this stuff for future projects," Craig grinned.

"Totally," I agreed.

We moved onto the make-up section, which featured a selection of face-paints and theatrical wigs. Some of them were awesome.

"We could use this if we ever do a film about

a werewolf," Craig said, holding up a dark-brown wig. "We could cut it up and glue the hair to the actor's face and body."

"And we could use this to darken the eye sockets," I added, pointing to a tube of black face paint.

"Wicked," he replied. "Let's note this down for later."

* * *

We left the shop on a high, inspired by what we'd seen. It was an Aladdin's Cave, a smorgasbord of opportunity; a real game changer in terms of what we could do going forward.

"So, what do you reckon to a name?" Craig asked, as we drove. "What shall we call ourselves?"

"I dunno," I replied. "But we need something that captures the essence of who we are and what we're about."

"It needs to be gothic," Craig said.

"Defo," I replied. "Something like *Hammer*."

Craig hummed, deep in thought, remaining quiet for most of the ride home.

When we eventually reached his house, he suddenly had a eureka moment, and with an excited gasp, he said a single word....

Shadowbright.

CHAPTER 5: BROTHERS IN BLOOD (I)

S everal weeks later, I received a call from the shop, telling me that the Clapperboard had arrived and was ready or collection. I immediately phoned Craig and told him.

"Let's get it now!" he said, excitedly.

I drove to his house, picked him up, then drove over to the shop, where the woman was waiting for us at the door.

"It came in this morning," she said with a smile. "I think you're going to like it."

She led us inside to the counter, where the Clapperboard was sitting proudly by the till.

It looked amazing.

So professional.

"How loud is the clapper?" Craig asked.

"Why don't you give it a try?" the woman replied.

She handed it over, and he clicked the stock. A loud crack echoed throughout the store.

"It's perfect," he grinned. "How much?"

"£29.95," she replied.

"Bargain!"

I handed over my debit card and the woman processed the purchase.

"Hope you have fun with it, boys," she said, as we left the store. "Come again if you need anything else."

"Don't worry," Craig shouted. "We will. We definitely will."

* * *

Back at his house, we laid the Clapperboard on his bed then stood for a moment, admiring it.

"This is final piece in the puzzle," Craig declared reverently. "Everyone will take us seriously now. We've got a camera, a name, and a Clapperboard."

"All we need is an idea," I said.

"I've been thinking about that," Craig said. "Why don't we do a martial arts film?"

"Like *Karate Kid*?"

"No," he said. "Something more like *Enter the Dragon*. We can get Knackers involved cos he's into that shit."

Knackers, or Knax, as he was often called,

was a kid we knew from school. He lived in Darby End with a mom and was a black belt in karate.

"Do you think he'd be up for it?" I asked.

"I'm sure he will be when he's see this," Craig replied.

We took the Clapperboard to Knackers' house and asked him if he'd be up for starring in our latest production.

"Yeah, man," he replied, without a moment's hesitation. "I'd love to be involved."

Craig looked at me a grinned.

"See," he said. "I told you it'd open doors for us."

"Great," I said. "I'll write a script."

I spent the rest of the night glued to my computer. By midnight, I'd penned Craig's martial arts masterpiece, a *Hard To Kill*-style revenge flick that I'd provisionally entitled *'Brothers in Blood'*.

It told the story of a Kung-Fu student named Scott, whose master, Chen, is murdered by an evil gangster named Rhodes. The plot follows Scott's quest for vengeance, culminating in a final battle with the villain and ten of his henchmen.

"This is amazing!" Craig declared, after he'd read the first and final draft. "It's got it all... Fighting, characters, dialogue. I can visualise it already."

"Thanks," I smiled.

He placed a hand on my shoulder.

"I want you to play Chen," he said.

"Me?" I said. "But I can't act."

"Neither can Knackers," he replied. "But this isn't about the acting... It's about the *action* - as long as we get the fight scenes right, we're laughing."

"All right," I said. "I'll give it a go. Who are we casting for Rhodes? Baz?"

Craig shook his head.

"Nah," he replied. "We need someone more professional. Is there anyone you know at college?"

"There's this bloke I know called Joss," I said. "He might be up for it."

"A bloke called Joss?" Chris said.

I nodded.

"What does he look like?"

"He's got blonde hair."

"Perfect," Craig declared. "Let's get him on board."

* * *

I approached Joss the next day, while he was eating his lunch in the college refectory.

"Hey, mate," I said. "How's it going? You fancy being in a film?"

"What, like acting?" he replied.

"Yeah," I replied. "It's a production we're working on called, *Brothers in Blood*. It's a martial arts film."

"Is Baz gonna be in it?"

"We might get him on board," I replied. "... As one of the henchmen."

"Who will I play?" he asked.

"The main baddie," I replied. "A gangster, named Rhodes."

Joss smiled.

"I can do that," he said.

"Great," I replied. I'll send you the script."

Later that day, I met up with Craig in Psychology and told him he good news.

"Fantastic," he said. "Let's get started!"

That night, I jotted down a shooting schedule and told everyone to meet up in the park on Saturday. Craig arranged for Pat and his other friend, Slater, to join us, to help us with the crewing.

"Slater can chalk up the clapperboard for each shot," he said. "Pat can do the lighting."

"But we're shooting in the day," I replied.

"I know," Craig said. "But we don't how long it's gonna take. We might be there all night."

I liked he meticulous approach. It showed he was thinking ahead and had everything covered. It inspired a lot of confidence in what we were doing. The only thing I was worried about was whether I'd be able to pull off a decent performance. It had been years since I'd done any acting. The last time I'd done it was in the school play when I was nine, playing a Shepherd... I didn't even have any lines! Now I was third on the rollcall...

All I could do was learn the script by heart and hope I didn't fuck things up...

* * *

On Saturday morning, I donned my Chen costume (which was nothing more than a black T-Shirt and joggers), then drew on a fake moustache with an eyeliner pen I'd picked up at Tesco's. To give myself a more 'oriental' appearance, I added a couple of points to my brows. Satisfied with my 'look', I'd grabbed a couple of scripts then headed to the park, where I found Craig and the rest of them standing around, looking bored.

When he saw me, Knackers came over and shook my hand.

"Hey dude," he said, warmly. "I'm so happy to part of this. Thanks so much for getting me involved."

"No worries," I said, with a smile. "Happy to have you."

"I can't wait to showcase my skills to the world. I've always wanted to be the next Jean Claude Van Damme."

Steady on, I thought... We're just two blokes with a camera.

"Shall we make a start then?" Craig yelled.

"Yeah," I replied, running over.

"We'll shoot the title montage first," Craig said, overriding the schedule. "We'll do it near the cliff, so it looks more epic. We'll start with a shot of you halfway up, doing some punches and kicks."

"Okay," I said.

When we got there, I began scrambling up the loose rocks and gravel that surrounded its base. About halfway up was a natural ledge, with a flat surface. I hauled myself onto it then stood up and turned around.

"Yeah, that looks ace!" I heard Craig shouting from down below. "Now do some *Kata*."

I gave him a nod then began punching the air in front of my face as if I was shadowboxing.

"Great," Craig said. "Now do some kicks too."

I raised my left leg and flicked it out at an imaginary opponent, making 'hoo-harr' noises with my mouth.

It must have looked hilarious, as everyone started laughing.

"Oh God," Pat groaned, covering his mouth. "He looks like Daniel LaRusso with arthritis!"

Shut up, you fat fuck, I thought to myself. *I'd like to see your fat ass do this...*

I continued with the huffing and puffing. After a good minute and a half Craig called 'cut' then told me swap places with Knax.

I slid down the slope on my arse and joined Craig behind the camera. Knackers then scrambled up to the ledge to do his version of the same take.

He soon proved to be consummate professional in front of the lens, holding his pose perfectly as he waited for Craig's cues. When 'action' was called, he performed what only be described as a masterclass of show-offery, thrashing the air with a blistering flurry of punches and roundhouse kicks.

He looked ace.

Much better than I did.

It made me wonder whether we should have cast him as Chen and me as Scott.

"Brilliant," Craig yelled, once Knackers had finished punching flies. "That looked great!"

Knackers smiled proudly.

"Thanks," he beamed.

As he made his way down from the perch, Craig turned to me and smiled.

"I've got a good feeling about this," he said. "Knackers is a fucking star!"

"I know," I said. "He really looks the part, doesn't he?"

Craig nodded.

"Ok," he said, "let's make a start on the training scene."

This was the opening shot of the film. A friendly fight between student and master. It was written to show the closeness of their friendship, and that they were two absolute badasses when it came to hand-to-hand combat.

"Right, Knackers," I said, as I squared up to him at the centre of the clearing. "How are we gonna do this?"

I'd asked him the night before if he would sort out some basic choreography for the day. It seemed apt, as he was the only one with any real martial arts skills.

"I want to you come at me like this," he said, acting out my part, "then throw a side kick into my ribs... I'll catch with my hand then flip you forward."

"What?" I said.

"It's ok," Knackers replied. "You won't get hurt. You'll land on the grass."

"All right," I said. "Let's give it a go."

"Are you both ready?" Craig asked.

We turned and gave him a nod.

"Ok," he said. "We're rolling..."

He held up his free hand. It was the signal for Slater to run into shot with the clapperboard, and he jogged over holding the stock.

"Brothers in Blood, Scene 1, Angle 1, Shot 1," he shouted, then clicked the shutter against the block.

As soon as he ran out of shot, Craig called 'action', and I raised my hands in a fighting pose. Following Knackers' instructions, I stepped forward and raised my leg to kick him in the belly... missing wildly.

Ever the professional, Knackers closed the gap between my foot and stomach then grabbed my calf with both his hands. With a mighty, "Huurrr," he pushed my foot away. Instinctively, I hopped backwards. I immediately knew I'd fucked up. I glanced over at Craig, expecting him to shout 'cut' but he gave me a thumbs up and urged me to carry on.

Not knowing quite what to do next, I flung myself forward, rolling onto the grass.

Pat and Slater started giggling.

It infuriated Craig, who called, 'Cut' then remonstrated them for ruining the shot.

"If you're gonna laugh," he rasped. "Do it over there where I can't hear you!"

Knackers helped me to my feet.

"What happened there?" he asked. "You were supposed to flip over when I pushed your foot."

"I know," I said. "I forgot."

I looked at Craig, who was faffing with the viewfinder.

"Do we need to go again, mate?" I said. "I did a roll instead of a flip."

"No, no," he replied. "We can work with it."

"But he didn't flip," Knackers explained.

"It doesn't matter," Craig said. "Just pick things up from where you landed on the floor. If it looks shit, we can fix it in post."

"You sure?" Knackers said.

"Yeah," Chris confirmed. "Piece of piss. Right, let's do the next bit...

* * *

Several hours later, we were still going at it. I'd hit the floor so many times that my costume was covered in grass stains, and my drawn-on beard was dissolving in sweat.

A small crowd of onlookers had also gathered nearby. Moms, Dads, kids, people walking their dogs... Pat did his best to keep them all at bay.

It felt weird performing in front of an audience. Especially one that were hear without invitation... I wondered what they were thinking while they were watching us. Did they believe they were rubbernecking on the set of a Hollywood movie? Or was it clear to them that we were just a bunch of stupid kids messing around in the park with a camera?

Either way, I was determined to remain professional, so ignored them as best I could.

Once we'd finished the 'fight', the next scene to shoot was a dialogue scene, which set up much of the plot. It involved several cheesy lines, which had been horribly plagiarised from Arnold Schwarzenegger movies.

Bizarrely, both of us read our parts using American accents. I don't know why we did this. It wasn't in the script. But once we'd started doing it, there was no going back.

After a good hour of freezing our bollocks

off sitting on the grass, Craig announced that we'd got all the footage we needed, and that we should spend the rest of the day getting random shots of us doing kicks and punches to pad out the titles.

I was glad to hear this, as it meant moving around.

Once we'd wrapped, everyone headed back to the cars.

"When's the next shoot?" Slater asked, mincing himself into the back seat.

"Tuesday," Craig replied. "It'll be round my house. We'll be shooting the scene where we introduce the villain."

"Cool," Slater replied. "Am I still on Clapperboard duty?"

"You're the key grip," Craig said. "It's your one and only job."

After dropping off Knackers, Pat, and Slater, Craig and I drove back to his house to start uploading the footage. His dad was waiting for us in his studio.

"Where've you been?" he asked. "You were supposed to have wrapped two hours ago."

"We had to do a few pick-ups," Craig replied, arrogantly.

He seemed to relish making his dad wait.

He ejected the tape from the camera then handed it to his dad, who popped into the VCR that was connected to his Amiga.

I sat and watched as the footage appeared

on-screen.

"Bloody Hell," Colin noted, as he scrolled through the tape. "How much did you film?"

"Coverage, dad," Craig grunted. "We needed to make sure we got everything."

"Yeah, but there's two hours of the stuff," he scoffed. "How long is this scene on paper?"

"About two minutes," I replied.

Colin blew out his cheeks.

"So, we're going to be here a while, then..."

He began digitising the tape. It was a long and drawn-out process, requiring each clip to be marked and saved before it could be filed.

"What's that bloke doing with the Clapperboard?" Colin asked, as he brought the first shot into the timeline.

"He's our Key Grip," Craig replied. "He's labelling the shots."

"Why?"

"So, we know which takes to use!" Craig snapped.

"So have you got a list then?" Colin said. "...Of the clips you want to use?"

I looked at Craig, who rolled his eyes.

He hadn't been noting the shots as we'd went along. It meant he'd be working from memory alone.

"Well?" his dad pressed.

"I know what clips I want," Craig said.

"Really?" Colin replied.

"Yeah," Craig said. "They're all up here."

He tapped his temple with finger.

Colin laughed.

"Good luck with that, Einstein... If I were you, I'd have just taped over the takes I didn't want."

"Shut up," Craig hissed.

* * *

It was way past ten by the time we'd finished.

Craig's mom had played a blinder, bringing us cups of tea all night. If she hadn't, we'd have all died from dehydration.

Once the final clip had been rendered, Colin sat back then played the footage.

The first thing I noticed was the sound. Whenever the footage changed angles, so did the audio. It was particularly jarring in the dialogue scene, as the background noise in each clip didn't match.

"Is there anything we can do about that?" I asked.

"You should have recorded a buzz track," Colin said.

"What's that?" I asked.

"It's when you record the background sound on a separate take, then overlay it onto your final cut."

"Is it easy to do?" I asked.

"You just film a tree for five minutes..." Craig

sighed.

I got the impression he'd been told to do this but had forgotten.

"...We might have to go back and do some pick-up shots at some point," he said to me. "Are you up for that?"

"Yeah, mate," I replied. "Of course."

Colin chuckled.

"You might wanna refilm some of the dialogue too," he said. "You broke the line of action."

Craig looked confused.

"What do you mean?" he said.

"There..." Colin said, pointing to the screen. "You go from Dom being on the right of the shot to Knackers being on the right in the next clip."

Craig squinted at the footage.

"What are trying to say?" he said.

"It's called the *Line of Action*," Colin replied. "It's an imaginary line between the two people who are talking that you're not supposed to cross. It's filmmaking 101."

Craig hummed.

He seemed upset but didn't want to show it.

"I think it looks fine the way it is," he said. "Leave it."

"Fair enough," Colin said. "It's your film..."

I could sense the tension between them, so made my excuses and left...

CHAPTER 6: BROTHERS IN BLOOD (II)

The next night, Craig phoned to tell that he'd added a soundtrack to the opening sequence, and I needed to see it right away.

He sounded excited, so I got in my car and drove round.

When I arrived, he dragged me upstairs to his bedroom, where he was playing the footage on his projector.

"You're gonna love this," he said.

I sat myself down while he rewound the tape.

When he pressed play, a thunderclap sounded, and the words 'Shadowbright Productions' appeared on-screen. The words were typed in a gothic font. It looked mightily impressive.

"Wow!" I said. "How did you do that?"

"On my dad's got titling software," he replied.

"It's really cool," I said. "It looks professional."

"So, it should," Craig replied. "Because we are."

He sat back as the image dissolved into the title sequence, which played out over an epic electronic soundtrack which reminded me of the theme from *Deathstalker II*.

"I composed this on my keyboard," he declared, proudly. "I had to time the chord changes to fit with the footage."

The score was excellent. It perfectly complimented the mood and tone of the images. It was catchy too. I couldn't get the tune out of my head.

"This is fantastic," I said, giving him a grin.

"I knew you'd like it," he replied.

"Like it? I love it!"

But I'd spoken too soon...

For as soon as the dialogue kicked in, things rapidly went downhill. It was like watching two different films. The montage looked like something you'd see at the cinema; the dialogue looked like something you'd see on *You've Been Framed*.

The sound was the worst.

None of the issues we'd spotted on the initial edit had been fixed, dialogue had been cut off mid-sentence, and the ambient noise was still incredibly jarring.

"Is there anything we can do about the hissing?" I asked.

Craig shook his head.

"Not without shooting the whole thing again," he replied.

"Oh..." I said, sadly.

"But don't worry too much about it. This is only the first scene. Once we get into the scene with Rhode, no one will remember it..."

* * *

On Tuesday night, I met Craig at his house to set things up while we waited for everyone to arrive.

The scene we were shooting featured the initial meeting between Scott, Chen, and the film's villain, Rhodes. There was no fighting in this scene, and because it was all filmed indoors (in Craig's living room), there would be less issues with the sound.

"I'll call cut if I hear a lorry driving past," he assured me, as he loaded a fresh tape into the camcorder. "It'll be annoying if you're halfway through saying something, but it'll be worth it in the end."

"Yeah," I agreed.

A few minutes later, Slater arrived at the front door.

He seemed happy.

"I've got some new chalk for the Clapperboard," he said, happily. "Thinner sticks, easier to write with."

"Great stuff," I said.

"You'll also need a pen and paper," Craig added. "So, you can log the takes we want to edit."

"No problemo," he replied, with a grin.

"Shall I put the kettle while we're waiting to start?" I asked.

"There's no time," Craig said. "If I were you, I'd start drawing on your bumfluff. We want to start shooting as soon as everyone's here."

* * *

Not long after, there was a knock at the door. I stepped out into the hall to see who it was and was surprised to find both Knackers and Joss waiting on the step.

"Nice beard," Joss remarked.

"Nice jacket," I replied.

He'd chosen to deck himself out in shiny leather coat. It fit the character... *If the character was into S&M.*

"How's it going?" Knackers asked. "What does the footage look like so far?"

"Excellent," Craig answered, coming out into the Hall "It's quality. All of it."

Knackers smiled broadly.

"Can I see it?"

"Not right now," Craig said. "We've too much to do tonight. We need to film as much as we can before my mom and dad get back."

"What if we finish early? Could I see it then?"

"Probably not," Craig replied.

It was clear he didn't want anyone to see it. Maybe he was more concerned with the initial dialogue scene than he'd let on...

"Have I got time to finish my beard?" I asked.

Craig looked at me, impatiently.

"Yes," he said. "But be quick."

"Can I have a beard too?" Joss asked.

His eyes were fixed on the eyeliner pen.

"But it's a brown pencil," I replied. "You're blonde."

"I think it'd look cool," Knackers said. "Contrast! And if you do it in the style of the Devil, it'll make you look evil."

"Okay," Craig agreed. "But don't faff around while you're drawing it on. We've only got two hours, remember?"

Joss nodded, then followed me to the mirror, where I quickly applied the finishing touches to my chin.

"You know, it makes you look so much older," he remarked, as I handed him the stick.

"Thanks," I replied, not quiet knowing how

to take it.

"I'm not feeling the eyebrows though," he said. "What's that all about?"

"I'm supposed to be Chinese," I replied. "I'm playing Chen."

"Chen's Chinese?" he said.

"Chinese-American," I clarified.

"Cool."

* * *

After applying our beards, we stepped into the Living Room, where Craig was busy blocking out the scene with Knackers.

"So, I'm gonna start with a shot of the door," he began. "When it opens, you and Dom come in. I'll then do a close-up of Joss, welcoming you both with an evil smile. We'll then cut to a wide of the three of you walking over to the table, where you'll sit down and start talking."

Excellent, I thought. Three shots. Nice and simple.

"...We'll also be doing several angles for each shot, so Slater, make sure you mark the different takes on the Clapperboard."

"Aye-aye, captain," Slater replied, giving him a salute.

"Right then," Craig said. "Let's make a start."

He went over to the table and picked up his camcorder, while Knackers and I backed out into the hall and closed the door.

"Rolling," Craig shouted.

We heard the patter of Slater's footsteps.

"Brothers in Blood, Scene 2, Shot 1, Angle 1..."

He clapped the clapper.

"Action!"

Knackers pushed open the door and I followed him inside. As I crossed the threshold, I accidentally looked into the lens.

"Sorry," I said. "Can we cut? I looked at the camera."

Craig grunted, rewound the tape, then asked us to return to our starting positions.

We went outside and closed the door.

""Brothers in Blood, Scene 2, Shot 2, Angle 1..."

Clap!

"Action!"

Knackers opened the door and stepped forward. As I followed him in, I accidentally kicked him in the back of the foot.

"Sorry, mate," I said, without thinking.

"What the fuck!" Craig yelled.

"I accidentally kicked him," I explained.

"You may have," Craig snapped, "But I didn't see it on camera."

"Sorry," I said. "Shall we go again?"

"Yes, obviously," Craig hissed.

We backed up into the hall.

"I'll get it right this time," I whispered to Knackers.

"Yeah, defo," he said, with a smile.

"Brothers in Blood, Scene 2, Shot 3, Angle 1..."

Clap!

"Action!"

Knackers pushed open the door.

I automatically looked at the lens.

"Fuck!"

"Sorry, Craig," I pled. "I don't know what's wrong with me."

"Me neither," he grunted. "There should be nothing easier than opening a door and walking into a room."

Slater started laughing, but Craig silenced him with a glare.

"We'll do this one more time," he said. "And this time we'll get it right, ok?"

I gave him a nod.

On the fourth attempt, I managed to get it right.

Knackers was pleased for me.

"See, mate," he said. "You *can* do it!"

"Ok," Craig said, "Let's do it again from a different angle."

He took a single sidestep to his right then lowered the camera to chest -height.

Knackers and I stepped back into the hall.

"Brothers in Blood, Scene 2, Shot 1, Angle 2..."

"Action!"

Once more, we stepped inside the room.

I didn't fuck up. Twice in a row! I was on a roll!

"Cut!" Craig called. "That's great. Let's do it again though, for safety. And we probably need a third angle too, for variation."

We continued the process for the next fifteen minutes. By the end of it, Craig had amassed at least 20 different shots of the same thing, from a multitude of different angles.

"Ok," he said finally, "I think we're good. Let's do the next bit."

* * *

The next section followed the same format, but as it involved a shot of Joss introducing himself and shaking our hands, the numbers of required shots trebled.

Craig seemed obsessed with capturing every element of the action several times over. He wanted close-ups, wide angles, shots with a Dutch tilt... Every possible variation that he could think of. He wanted lines of dialogue repeated over and over, said in different ways, said on-shot, off-shot, into the lens, away from it.

It was a nightmare.

By the time his parents came home, we'd only filmed half a page of script.

"How are things going?" Colin asked, as he came into the room.

"Well," Craig said.

"Are you nearly done?"

"Yeah," he lied. "But we'll need another fifteen minutes."

"Do you mind if I put a brew on?" his mom asked.

"Can it wait?" Craig replied. "We're in the middle of shooting dialogue."

"But we want to go to bed," she said.

"Jesus!" Craig exclaimed.

"It's ok," I said, playing the peacemaker. "We can film the rest some other time, can't we?"

I glanced at the cast and crew, who all nodded in agreement. It had been a tiring night. Everyone had had enough.

"I don't mind coming back next week, if you want?" Joss said.

"Next week?" Craig replied. "But that's a week away!"

"There's no time limit," Knackers said.

Craig glared at him.

"What about Friday?" I suggested, diplomatically.

"I can't do Friday," Joss said. "I'm going out."

"I can do Friday," Slater said, with a grin.

No surprise there...

"What's the point of you coming if we're missing an actor?" Craig sneered, bursting Slater's bubble.

"Maybe we could shoot a different scene?" I said.

"Which one?" Craig snorted. "They all

involve him."

He pointed at Joss as if he were an inanimate object.

"Oh yeah," I said, remembering my script. "Ok then, what if we pencil in next Tuesday then spend the rest of this week editing what we've got?"

"You can't edit half a scene!" Craig snapped. "It'll fuck up the continuity!"

"Yes, you can," Colin said. "You just need to remember where everyone was standing in the last shot."

"Sounds good to me," Knackers said.

"Me too," Joss agreed.

Craig let out an exasperated sigh.

"Ok," he said, defeated. "Let's pick things up next Tuesday.."

CHAPTER 7:
BITE (I)

A couple of nights later, I popped into Craig's to see how things were going with the edit, but instead of finding him in the studio with his dad, he was sitting on his bed watching Robocop.

"What's going on? I asked. "I thought you said you were busy editing?"

"There's no point," he replied. "Slater forgot to mark the takes."

"Oh," I said, sadly. "So does that mean we're done, then?"

"What do you think?" he snorted, his words dripping with sarcasm.

I sighed and sat down next to him.

"Do you think maybe we're overcomplicating things?" I said.

"What do you mean?" he asked.

"With all the shots and angles," I replied. "Maybe it'd help if we storyboarded it, so we'd know which shots we'd need beforehand?"

Craig hummed.

"I supposed it'd help a little," he said. "But if we did that, what's the use in having a clapperboard?"

He gestured toward the device, which was resting against the wall next to his camera.

"Maybe we don't really need it?" I said.

"Are you mad?" he spat. "We paid thirty quid for that!"

We?

"I'm willing the take the hit, dude," I replied. "...If it means getting something done."

"We'll never get *anything* done if we carry on working with amateurs," he growled.

"We will if we keep things simple," I replied. "Maybe we should change the way we write stuff?"

"How?" Craig replied.

"I don't know..." I said. "Maybe instead of starting with an idea and producing everything *around* it, we should start with what we've got, then produce an idea *from* it?"

"But that's backwards," Craig sniffed.

"I know," I said. "But it's the only way we'll get anything done. If we keep doing shoots over multiple days, we'll always run the risk of people not showing up."

"So, what you're saying is, strip everything

down?"

"Yeah," I replied. "Keep things as basic as possible... Maybe do a film with just two characters, with three or four scenes, max."

"Sounds pretty boring," Craig remarked.

"It doesn't have to be," I said.

He chuckled, unimpressed.

"Ok," I said, "Let's think it through... We have two characters..."

"They have to be blokes," Craig interjected. "We don't know any girls."

"Fine," I said. "Two Blokes... And they're in the park. What are they doing there?"

Craig stroked his chin.

"They're coming home from the pub," he answered.

"So why are they in the park?"

"Cos one of them stepped in some dogshit and needed to clean his shoes."

"Ok," I said, running with it. "So why did he step in dogshit? Was it accidental?"

Craig thought about for a second.

"No," he said finally. "He was tricked into doing it by his friend."

"why?" I asked.

"Because he wants to lead him onto the moors to kill him."

"The moors?" I said.

"Yeah," Craig replied. "It's not a park anymore."

"Ok," I said. "So, one of them's a murderer.

What's his motive?"

"Does he need one?"

"If we want a story, yeah."

"What if he's just a psychopath?"

"Even psychopaths need motives..."

"Ok," Craig said. "What if he's not a psychopath. What if he's a...."

"Vampire," we both said in unison.

Craig grinned broadly.

"You know what'd be even better," he said. "If the vampire is actually the other guy, and it's murderer who gets killed!"

"What a twist!" I said, excitedly.

"Yeah," he said. "Write it down, quick, so we don't forget."

He handed me a pen and paper and I began scribbling note on the page. Minutes later, I was penning the script. The concept was so simple and easy, it wrote itself. Ten minutes later, we were all done.

"Incredible," Craig said. "We're fucking geniuses!"

"I know," I agreed. "And all we'll need in terms of props is a set of vampire teeth and some blood."

"Are you thinking what I'm thinking?" he said.

I gave him a nod.

"Come on then," he said. "Let's head over Quinton..."

CHAPTER 8:
BITE (II)

An hour later, we were back at Craig's with set of glue-on fangs and a vial of theatrical blood. All we needed now were actors.

"I don't mind playing Bradley," I said.

"Cool," Craig replied. "Who's gonna play Todd?"

"Whoever we can get," I replied.

We made a few calls to the people we knew, asking them if they wanted to be in the film, which we would be shooting on Saturday.

Knackers was a no-no, as he was competing in a Karate Tournament.

Baz couldn't either. He was going clubbing with the Grebo squad.

"Shall we ask Slater?" I said.

Craig shook his head.

"I never want him on my set again," he barked. "He's the reason it all went tits up. Him and that bloody clapperboard!"

"Fair enough," I said. "What about Allan?"

"Allan?" Craig said.

"Parsons," I clarified. "He was my friend at school. He's always up for a laugh."

"What does he look like?"

"He's skinny," I replied. "And he's got a huge Adam's Apple."

"Oh yeah," Craig said. "He was the one who gobbed in Gareth's pop."

"That's him," I smiled.

I called him up and asked him if he fancied doing a bit of acting.

"Okily-dokily," he replied, in the style of Ned Flanders.

"Is that a yes then?"

"It certainly is."

I emailed him the script and told him to learn his lines. It wasn't a massive ask. The script was only two pages long.

After Craig came up with the title, *Bite*, we spent the rest of the day storyboarding each scene, drawing stick men in boxes and adding notes to explain the shots, using acronyms like, 'CU' for 'Close Up' or 'WA' for 'Wide Angle. It worked well for us, and we made a mental note to use the same process for future projects.

By the end of the night, we were all set and ready to go. To celebrate our achievements, we watched *Demon House* on Laserdisc.

I left his house brimming with confidence.

For the first time, I believed we were going to get something done.

"This was it," I told myself, driving back. "The start of something special..."

CHAPTER 9:
BITE (III)

On Saturday morning, I picked up Allan from his dad's house in Netherton, then drove around to Craig's. He was waiting on his doorstep when we arrived, holding his camera and a plastic bag containing the props.

There was no Clapperboard in sight.

"We ready to rock?" he said, as he got in the car.

"Hell yeah!" I replied, excitedly.

Ten minutes later, we arrived at the park. Because it was cold, the place was empty.

No onlookers.

Perfect.

"Right then," Craig declared, lifting the camera onto his shoulder. "Let's do this."

He began staging the scene. Learning his lessons from our previous films, he stuck to the plan.

"We'll do the first scene single continuous shot," he explained, following the instructions on the storyboard. "I want you both to walk in from over there, and then when you reach that clump of grass, you'll stop, and then you start saying the lines..."

We went over to where he was pointing. Craig then called 'Action', and we began walking down the path as directed. When we reached the clump of grass, Allan, looked down, sighed theatrically, then said the word, "Shit".

"Shit?" I replied.

"Dog Shit," Allan continued. "I just trod in some..."

"You can clean your shoes over there."

I pointed to the field behind him.

"The moors?" he responded. "But people get killed on the moors!"

"So, what, man?" I said. "Who gives a fuck! Come on, let's go!"

I took him by the shoulder then pushed him onto the grass.

"Come on man," I add-libbed, "This way... Come on!"

Craig tracked us with the camera as we disappeared out of sight.

"And cut!" he yelled excitedly. "Scene!"

We walked back and I asked him how it looked.

"Brilliant, mate," he said. "It'll be piece of

piss to edit too! Come on, let's do the next bit..."

We lugged the gear over to a copse of trees, where we'd planned to shoot the second scene.

Things went smoothly, and in less than ten minutes, we were all done.

"Right," Craig declared. "Just one more left to do...."

He led us over to the cliffs for the finale.

After telling us where to stand, he hoisted the camera onto his shoulder and looked through viewfinder.

"Hang on," he said, morosely. "Something's not right."

He put the camera down then reached into his pocket for the storyboards.

"No," he said, flicking the page. "There's a better way of doing this."

Oh fuck, I thought. *He's going off piste....*

I immediately began to worry.

We'd created those storyboards for a reason. They were there to keep us on track; to stop us deviating from the plan... The last thing we wanted was another million-shot, shit-show...

"What's going on?" I asked.

"These storyboards won't work," he replied. "I'll need to restage the scene."

"But we've already planned it out," I wailed. "We've drawn pictures and everything."

"Trust me," he replied. "I've got this."

Jesus Christ, I thought.

This is going to be a disaster... Like *Matter of Time*, or *Steel Justice*, or *Brothers in Blood*...

"Stand yourself over there," Craig said to me, pointing to the base of the cliffs.

"Do you really know what you're doing?" I asked.

"Yes. Trust me," he snapped.

I let out an exasperated sigh and did as he said.

"Ok," he grinned, "When I call 'Action', turn around then say your line into the lens..."

"All right," I grumbled.

I wasn't sure about this at all...

"Action!"

I turned on the spot then looked at the camera.

"Where the fuck are we, Todd?"

"Brilliant!" Craig grinned. "Best shot of the film!"

I saw Allan smiling in the background. He seemed to agree.

"Right then," Craig said. "Let's wrap this bastard up. Allan, you walk into shot from there then say your next line. Then I'll bounce between you until we reach the end. Got it? Good..."

* * *

After wrapping up, we dropped Allan home then went straight round Craig's to begin the edit. His dad was waiting for us in the studio. He was surprised we'd arrived so early.

"That was quick," he said. "Did you give up halfway through?"

"Winners never quit," Craig quipped, handing him the tape.

"There was no bullshitting around today," I said. "We were straight in, straight out, no messing."

"Well done," Colin replied. "That's how the pros do it."

Craig glanced at me and smiled.

I got the impression that Colin's praise was rare, and that it was something of an honour for Craig to receive it.

After popping the tape into the player, Colin then transferred the footage onto the PC. He then began scrubbing through the footage in the timeline.

"Ooh," he said. "I see you've been a bit more sensible this time in terms of your shots."

"We storyboarded each scene beforehand," I said.

"Every scene except the finale," Craig clarified. "That was all me."

I sat and watched as Colin started the edit.

"This actually works quite well," he remarked, flicking between the various cuts. "You've not broken the line of action once.... And your friend, Allan, isn't a bad little actor."

"He played the Joseph in the school play

once," I said.

"You can tell," Colin replied. "He's very confident."

Within an hour, all the clips had been trimmed. All we needed now was a soundtrack.

"What kind of music would you like?" Colin asked, handing Craig one of his copyright-free CDs.

"We need something gothic," he replied, scanning the track list. "...To give the ending a bit of resonance."

"Ahh, I've just the thing..." Colin said.

He took the disk then transferred one of the tracks into the music bar.

It was a recording of *O Fortuna* by *Carl Orff*.

It fit the action perfectly.

Craig was overjoyed with the result.

"Fuck me!" he declared. "This is a masterpiece!"

"It is!" I said, clapping my hands.

"It's not finished yet," Colin said. "We need to add titles and credits."

He opened a file on the PC desktop then dragged the *Shadowbright* Titler into the timeline.

"Do you want some music over this too?" he asked. "Or do you just want the thunderclap?"

"Just the thunderclap," we said together.

I looked at Craig and smiled.

We were on the same page.

Colin added the credits, exported the film

onto a videotape then handed it to Craig. We immediately went to his room to watch it on the projector.

"Bloody hell," Craig said, after watching it six times on the trot. "We're fucking awesome."

"We truly are," I agreed. "But now's not the time to rest on our laurels... We need to build on this and make something even better."

"Something more ambitious," Craig added.

"Yes," I replied. "But nothing too *out there*. We've got to remember what works and what doesn't."

"You mean stick to the process?"

I nodded.

"Why not, if it works," I said.

"Ok, then," he replied. "... Where do we go from Vampires?"

The answer was as obvious to him as it was to me...

CHAPTER 10:
HUNTED (I)

I t was late Summer by the time we got round to shooting our Werewolf movie, Hunted.

The originally title had been *Howl of the Lycanthrope*, but Craig thought it would be better for our brand if the names of all our films were single words.

This movie was a little more ambitious than the last. It featured three characters, instead of two, and two locations instead of just the one. It was also much longer than *Bite*, with an estimated runtime of twenty minutes.

The plot centred around a novelist named Richard Harris (!), who gets attacked by a werewolf on the moors. He's found the next day by a couple of farmers, Rob and John, who take him back to their house and nurse him back to health. For one reason or another, they're unable to contact a doctor or drive him into town, leaving them with no choice but to walk him across the moors to the hospital. Unfortunately, they do this during the night of a full moon, and Harris transforms into monster, devouring Rob. John manages to escape along the cliffs but is pursued by the werewolf, who ultimately falls to his death after being stabbed in the eye.

During the production phase, we were obsessed with making our creature look as convincing as possible. Craig was firmly against using any kind of mask, calling it a 'cheap gimmick that would make us look like amateurs'.

"It needs to look like Hammer's Wolfman," he said. "So, we'll do it with theatrical hair and make-up."

This meant a trip to Quinton. Along the way, we discussed casting.

"We should definitely get Allan back," Craig said. "He's reliable and doesn't corpse."

"We can't have him as the werewolf, though," I replied. "He's way too skinny."

"Yeah, I was thinking he could be one of the farmers," he said. "Whichever parts he plays; you take the other. I guessing you have no preference which?"

"No," I said. "They're pretty much the same character anyway."

I'd originally wanted the part of 'John' to be played by a woman. As Rob's wife, as it would have made more sense to the story, but I was forced to change it because we didn't know any girls.

"How about the werewolf?" I asked.

"It's gotta by Baz," Craig replied. "He's the only one big enough."

"Yeah," I agreed.

I'd earmarked him for the role from the start. He was big and broad and looked the part. I'd also deliberately limited the character's dialogue to two or three lines, to limit the number of times he'd ruin the shot through corpsing.

"Cool," Craig said. "We'll pop to his on the way back and ask him."

"Maybe we could test the make-up too?" I said.

"Yeah," he replied. "Why not?"

* * *

After purchasing a lock of dark brown hair, some glue to apply it, and some make up from the shop, we drove over to Baz's house, where we found him sunning himself in the back garden.

"Hey mate," Craig said. "Wanna be in another film?"

"Yeah," he replied. "What's it about?"

"A werewolf," I said. "And we want you to be the werewolf."

He laughed then howled like a wolf.

"Cool," he said. "I can do that."

"We'll have to do a make-up test first though," Craig replied.

"We can do it now if you're not busy," I said. "We've got all the stuff."

"Go on, then," he replied.

He got up out of his chair then led us upstairs to his bedroom, where we began blackening up his eyes with face paint.

After applying the shading, Craig opened the glue bottle while I began cutting strips from the theatrical hair. The woman in the shop had told us how to do it.

"Cut a little at a time," she'd said. "Then fan it out for coverage."

I cut off a strip and spread it out in the palm of my hand. Craig then dipped into the glue then mashed it onto Baz's cheek, threading it out with a little comb.

Baz looked at himself in the mirror.

"Ruurr," he growled.

Twenty minutes later, we'd covered his whole face. The result was much better than expected. From a distance, he looked very similar to the *Hammer* Monster, the only difference being that he didn't have the pointed ears.

"We should have probably bought some ear-tips while we were in there," Craig lamented.

"No worries," I said. "We'll pick them up during the week."

"When exactly are we shooting?" Baz asked.

"Next Saturday, if you're up for it?" Craig replied.

Baz smiled at himself in the glass.

"Yeah, defo," he replied.

* * *

When Saturday came, Allan turned up at mine wearing a red T-shirt, black joggers, and a pair of brilliant white trainers.

"What's with your costume?" I asked. "You're supposed to be a farmer, not a chav."

"Sorry," he replied. "I left all my tweed in Devon."

It was supposed to be a joke, but no one got it.

"Do you have something he can wear instead?" Craig asked me.

I glanced at Allan's skinny frame.

"Nothing that will fit," I said.

"Oh well," Craig sighed. "We'll just have to go with it."

"My Grandad's got an old coat he could wear," Baz said.

"Great, I said. "Where does he live?"

"Scotland."

Craig rolled his eyes.

"Come on," he snorted. "Let's make a start before someone says something clever..."

We'd divided the first shoot into two parts. The first involved a trip to the park, where we'd shoot the opening sequence and the discovery of Harris' body by Rob and John. The second part would be shot in my front bedroom, where we'd cover all the scenes of Harris being nursed back to health.

Without further ado, we jumped in the car and drove over to the park.

During the filming of *Bite*, we'd done a bit of scouting around and had identified a few locations where we could shoot the various scenes. The opening sequence would take place on the crest of the hill at the park's centre. We'd originally pictured ourselves shooting it in the early evening, with a huge full moon in the background. It would have been ace if we could have pulled it off, but we didn't have the lighting.

To solve the problem, Colin suggested we should film the sequence during the day then add a blue tint during the edit. He'd said the same technique had been used on *Clash of the Titans*.

"It'll look great," he'd said. "Just keep an eye on your exposure..."

"I always do," Craig had replied.

Even at the time, I wasn't entirely convinced.

After arriving at the park, we made our way to the hillock, where Craig explained what he wanted to see.

"This is the opening shot of the film," he began, "the part where you're attacked by the werewolf... So, I need a lot of energy in your performance, right."

Baz looked confused.

"Hang on," he said. "I thought *I* was the werewolf?"

"You are," Craig replied. "But I'm talking about the werewolf that bit you, originally. The one that turned *you*."

"So, who's gonna play that?" Allan asked.

"No one," I replied. "We're not going to see it. It's all gonna be off-shot."

"...So, you're gonna have to pretend it's there," Craig said to Baz. "You'll have to *act*. Can you do that?"

"I'll try," Baz said.

Craig instructed him to stand at the edge of the cliffs, then run into shot towards the camera.

"When you reach this rock," he said, pointing to a stone on the ground, "stop, then turn around, as if you're looking to see the thing that's chasing you."

"All right," Baz said.

"Remember," Craig said. "Lots of energy!"

Baz jogged over to his mark then shouted that he was ready.

"Cool," Craig said.

He lifted the camera and pressed record.

"Ok," he said. "Rolling.... And Action!"

Baz started running along the cliff line, stumbling over the ground, as if it were swarming with snakes. When he reached his mark, he gasped a couple of times then looked back as instructed.

"Cut!" Craig called. "Great job!"

Baz smiled.

He looked pleased with himself.

Probably because he hadn't corpsed.

Craig then stepped forward and pointed the camera at his face.

"Right," he said. "This is a close up... You're terrified of whatever it is that's chasing you, so I need you to show fear. You got it?"

Baz nodded.

"Yeah," he said. "Fear... with lots of energy."

"Lots," Craig echoed.

He fine-tuned the focus then pressed 'record'.

"Action!"

Baz repeated the motion of the turn then gurned horribly into the lens.

"Cut!" Craig yelled. "What the hell was that?"

"Fear," Baz replied. "...With energy."

"It looked more like you were taking an energetic shit," Craig said. "Let's do it again."

After several takes, he eventually nailed it. But only after Craig had told him to drop the 'energy' and concentrate only on the 'fear.

"Right," Craig said. "Last shot of the sequence... This is where the werewolf gets you."

"Ok," Baz said. "How are we going to do it?"

"I'm going to shoulder barge you to the

floor," I said.

"But if you so that, you'll be on camera," he chuckled.

"Not if I keep the lens pointed upwards," Craig explained.

He lifted camera from his shoulder, then cradled it under the crook of his elbow.

"From this angle, all we'll see is you flying backwards," he said. "We'll add a sound effect during the edit to suggest it's a monster."

"All right," Baz said. "Shall we practice it first though. I don't wanna hurt myself."

Craig glanced at his watch.

"Ok," he said. "But only once or twice."

I moved myself in front of Baz and he braced himself for impact.

"You ready?" I asked.

"Yeah," he said, "Go for it."

I came forward and rugby tackled him, wrapping my arms around his waist. Instead of falling back, he stood his ground, stopping me in my tracks.

"What are you doing?" I said. "You're supposed to fall back."

"Sorry," he said. "I didn't know how you were going to do it."

"Well now you do," I said. "Shall we go again?"

We repeated the process.

This time, instead of standing firm, he flung himself to the ground before I'd even made contact.

"He needs to actually hit you," Craig said. "Do it again."

The third attempt was a little better, but Craig complained that I was coming in too high and that my head was bobbing up into the shot.

"You need to go in lower," he said. "More around his waist."

I gave him a nod and tried it again.

"No," Craig complained. "Still too high."

"Maybe you should just grab my legs?" Baz suggested.

"Yeah, that might work," Craig said.

I stepped back then lunged at Baz's knees.

"Perfect!" Craig said. "Now let's do a take."

I moved to my starting position then waited for my cue. As soon Craig called 'Action, Baz started giggling.

"Fucking hell," Craig said. "What's up now?"

Baz covered his mouth with his hand.

"Sorry, mate... Couldn't help it."

We repeated the sequence once more, and he started laughing again. When it happened the next time, it became clear that the floodgates had opened, and that Baz would corpse every time the camera started rolling.

"Ok," Craig said, after the fifth unsuccessful take. "We'll pick up this shot later, after we've done the farmer stuff."

"No," Baz said. "I can do it. I won't laugh next time, honest."

Craig snorted.

It was clear he didn't believe him.

"Fine," he said. "We'll give it one last go."

"Thanks," Baz said. "I'll get it right now, I promise."

And to his credit, he did.

Craig was so pleased with the take that he even shook Baz's hand afterwards.

"Well done," he grinned. "That looked great. Brilliant acting!"

"Thanks," Baz replied, proudly. "See... I can do it."

Yeah, I thought... Well see about that when we get to the dialogue...

CHAPTER 11:
HUNTED (II)

After wrapping up at the park, we returned to my house to film the scenes in the farmhouse. On the way back, Craig spotted a house in the distance that could double for an exterior shot. He got a quick snap of it to save us having to do any location-scouting later.

I remember, at the time, we were worried that shooting the facade of the house without the owner's permission would be an infringement of copyright, but Craig gave us assurances that it would be ok.

"We're on public land," he said. "We can shoot anything we like."

We rocked up at mine, then went upstairs to the front bedroom. It was being used as a storeroom at the time but still housed my old sofa bed, which we covered with a blanket. Because we had no lighting, we had to shoot the scene with the curtains open, bathing everything in a weird blueish tint.

"It'll have to do..." Chris sighed, looking through the viewfinder. "If it ends up looking too cold, we can always warm it up in post."

"Why don't we shut the curtains and use the main light?" Allan suggested.

"Because it'll make everything look yellow," I explained.

I'd noticed this while watching at the rushes for *Brothers in Blood*. It was something that happened when you used standard bulbs.

"Can't you just *cool it down* in post?" Baz said.

It was good point.

The only problem was that it contradicted Craig's plan.

"We can warm it up, but we can't cool it down," he snorted. "It's all about the RGB levels and standardising the fields."

It was pure nonsense.

But it sounded good.

Good enough for Baz to shut his gob.

"Right," Craig said. "The first shot we'll do is of the two of you bringing him in and laying him on the bed."

"Cool," I said. "Shall we practice it first?"

I was mindful of what had happened earlier.

"Yeah," Craig said. "Let's do a run-through."

Allan and I each took one of Baz's arms then led him from the door to the bed. Soon enough we realised there was a problem. Because the room was so small, there was barely any gap between the side of the bed and the wall, the only way we could lay him down on the mattress was by sitting him down at the foot of the bed, then hauling him up to the pillow from the headrest. It made the staging very awkward, as we had to set him down first, then clamber over him to pull up.

I could see Craig's brain ticking over, desperate for solution.

In the end, he gave up on the shot completely.

"We'll have to film the sequence in two parts," he said. "I just set myself up over there."

He pointed to the door.

"But that's where we come in," Allan replied. "We'll be walking through you."

"Not if I squeeze myself into the corner," Craig replied.

"Let's give it a shot," I said. "See what happens..."

He manoeuvred himself over to the door then asked us to repeat the scene.

"Ok," he said, "Go."

We lugged Baz through the doorway into the room, doing our best not to bump into Craig or the camera, but Allan - somewhat inevitably -

stepped on his foot.

"Oww!" he yelled. "What did you do that for?"

"Sorry," Allan replied. "I couldn't see you."

"Maybe you should stand on the other side?" I suggested. "Back where you were before?"

Chris sighed.

"We've already established that we do that, it's gonna look weird when you pull him up the bed."

Baz sniffed.

"So why don't you just start the scene with me *on* the bed?" he said. "Do you really need to see me being brought in?"

It wasn't a bad idea.

"There's no reason we can't," I said.

I glanced at Chris.

He didn't seem happy.

I could understand why.

This wasn't his baby anymore. It was turning into a collaboration. Everyone was chipping in with good ideas and his inner auteur didn't like it.

"No," he said. "We'll stick with the plan. If it ends up looking shit, we'll fix it in post."

Baz started laughing.

"That's your answer for everything, isn't it?"

"Have you ever edited anything?" Craig sneered.

"No," Baz replied.

"Then you don't know shit, do you?"

"Ok, guys," I said, trying to calm things down. "We all need to listen to Craig. He's the director, he knows what he's doing. He's gonna make it look ace."

Baz smirked.

"...And once we're finished tonight," I added. "I'll take you all to the pub, and I'll buy you all a drink."

"All right," Baz said.

"Fine," Chris snorted. "Now let's get on with it."

* * *

Once we'd wrapped, I took everyone down to the Cradley Wetherspoons and brought the first round.

Despite all the tension on-set, Craig was pleased with the footage he'd captured, even going so far as to say as to say it was the best stuff he'd ever filmed.

"It's gonna look great when it's edited," he told me as handed him his pint. "We just gotta make sure we keep the standards high throughout, maintain the quality..."

"Yes," I agreed.

Consistency was the key. We'd learned that lesson from *Brothers in Blood*.

"What are we going to do about the nightmares?" Baz asked.

He was referring to a couple of dream sequences I'd inserted into the script to break up the scenes where his character was being nursed on the bed. I hadn't included too much detail, as I figured we could work it all out on the day.

"I've got a couple of ideas," Craig said.

"...Cos I've got this fake skull," Baz continued, talking over him. "I nicked it from college. I could paint it up, so it looks like there's blood on it and stuff."

"Why would we need a skull for?" Craig snapped.

"I dunno," Baz said. "But it'll look cool."

"Not without context," Craig said. "We can't just throw in shots of random stuff. We're telling a story, not making an art project."

"Maybe we *can* use it," I said.

"How?" Craig replied.

"I dunno," I said. "Maybe he sees a floating head in his dream?"

"That's random," Craig sniffed.

"So were the Nazi Zombies in American Werewolf," Baz remarked.

"It would be good have a skull," Allan commented.

"You're all fucking barmy," Craig snapped. "We're not using the skull, and that's that!"

CHAPTER 12: HUNTED (III)

After two hours of heated debate, Craig had finally relented on the skull, after Allan suggested we should set it on fire.

"I like the idea of it burning," Craig admitted.

I suspected it had something to do with the fact that after we had, it couldn't be used again.

"Yeah, but we need to do it safely," I remarked. "We don't want to all end up in A&E."

"We can do it on the barbeque," Baz said.

"Why would a skull be on a barbeque?" Craig replied.

"I dunno," Baz said. "Maybe he's cooking a burger or something and he turns away for a second... And when he looks back, it's turned into a skull?"

"A flaming skull!" Allan added.

"It could work," I said, looking to Craig.

He sighed, then nodded his head.

The next day, we rocked up at Baz's house. He'd already set up the barbeque in back garden and was spraying it with lighter fluid. When he saw us, he put down the bottle and picked up the skull, which he'd set down on one of the slabs.

"What do you think of this?" he said, holding it up. "I've plastered it with papier mache. It looks like rotting flesh, right?"

"It actually looks quite good," Craig said forcing a smile. "But will it burn?"

"I sprayed it with Lynx," Baz grinned. "A full bottle."

"You should have used your lighter fluid," I said.

"Oh yeah," he replied. "I've used that too."

Once we blocked out what we wanted to do, Woz lit up the barbeque and threw on a couple of frozen burgers from his fridge.

Craig had planned the sequence so that it consisted of five shots. The first was a wide angle of the garden, showing Baz's character standing over the barbeque. The second was a close-up of what he was cooking. The third was a medium shot of him reacting to a noise off-camera, (a 'howl' sound effect that we would add in the edit). The fourth was of him looking back, screaming in terror. The final shot was a reverse of the skull, burning on the grill.

It seemed simple. Straightforward. Just the

way we liked it.

But sadly, we'd not accounted for the fact that the skull had been so inundated with accelerant, that as soon as Baz placed it on the grill, it exploded in a ball of flame.

"Bloody hell," Baz cried, leaping away from the burning inferno. "I never expected it to go up like that!"

I glanced across the patio at Craig, who had set up shot behind Baz.

"Dude," I said. "Please tell me you got that on camera..."

He lowered the lens and smiled.

"I did," he said. "And it looked fucking great!"

* * *

Once we'd put out the fire, Craig told us he had an idea for the second dream sequence, and that we could film it straight away.

"We can having him sitting in that chair, asleep," he said, excitedly. "He the wakes up to see that his wounds have healed and thinks it was all a dream. But then, suddenly, his heart starts beating really loudly... It gets louder and louder until he has no other option but to pull it out with his bare hands."

Baz laughed.

"Someone's been watching *Temple of Doom*?" he chuckled.

"What are we going to use for the heart?" Allan asked.

"We'll buy one from the Butcher's," Craig replied.

"Not on a Sunday," I said. "They're all closed."

"They might sell them in Asda," Allan said.

"No, they don't," Baz scoffed. "I used to work there."

"So, we'll use something else," Craig said. "Something squishy. It'll be covered in blood anyway, so we won't be able to tell."

We went inside Baz's house and began looking around for something suitably mushy. After twenty minutes of searching, we paused for a cup of tea.

"We might have to go out a buy a heart after all," I said.

"Hang on," Baz replied.

He reached into the sink and picked out the used teabags, squashing them together in his hand.

"What about this," he said. "This could pass as a heart."

Craig took out the theatrical blood and poured it over his hand.

"Yeah," he said. "It could."

* * *

After completing the dream sequences, the

only scene left to shoot was the film's finale, which had to done over the park. We agreed to do it the following Saturday. During the week, we experimented a little more with the werewolf effects. Because we'd be applying them on-set, we had to be sure we knew what we were doing so could get him made-up as quickly as possible.

"We'll do the transformation with cutaways," Craig declared. "We'll make him up a bit, then cut to a reaction of Dom and Allan looking scared. We'll then add more make-up and repeat the process until he's fully wolf-a-tised."

"Cool," I said.

"I hope it's not too hot on the day," Baz grumbled. "It was itchy as fuck when we did the first test, and I don't want to be eaten by flies."

"You won't be eaten by flies," Craig said.

"How do you know?" Baz replied.

"Because flies don't eat people."

* * *

When Saturday came, and I picked up the guys for the final shoot. Much to Baz's consternation, it a scorching hot, and he started complaining as soon as he got into the car.

"I hope someone's brought some water," he grumbled. "As soon as we're done, I wanna wash all this shit off my face..."

"Still worried about the?" Craig laughed.

"I've good reason," Baz retorted. "I got stung by a wasp when I was a kid. It was a traumatic experience."

"What's what got to do with flies?" Allan asked.

"Flies, wasps, they're all the same," Baz said. "I don't like them, I never have."

We arrived at the park then made our way to the cliffs.

Once there, Craig gave us some direction and we started shooting the first sequence. It involved Baz waking up from his coma and asking us what was going on. He only had a few lines to say, most of them single sentences, but he struggled with them all, either forgetting what to say as soon as 'Action' was called, or corpsing as soon as he started to speak.

It was incredibly frustrating.

He had a particular problem with one line. It consisted of two words, "an animal." It was supposed to be phrased as a statement, but Baz kept phrasing it as a question.

"How many times, dude..." Craig told him. "You're not asking a question!"

"It's a statement mate," I explained. "When John says, 'You look like you were 'ad by an animal,' you say, 'An animal!' You got it?"

Baz nodded.

"Ok," Craig said. "Action!"

Baz took a breath.

"An animal?" he said.

"Cut!" Craig roared. "Wrong! Again."

He rolled the tape.

"An animal?" Baz said.

"No, dude," I laughed. "That's still a question."

Baz looked at me confused.

"How am I saying it?"

"An animal?" Craig said. "Remember, it's not a question."

Baz puffed out his cheeks.

"It doesn't sound like a question when I say it in my head..."

"Say it like it's a statement," I said. "Like you've suddenly realised what it was that attacked you, and that it was... an animal!"

"An animal?" he replied.

"An animal!" Craig and I said together.

"When he says, 'an animal', you say, 'an animal!" Allan explained.

"An animal!" Baz said.

"Finally!" Chris exclaimed. "Just like that."

He pressed record.

"Action!"

"An animal?"

"Fucking hell!"

* * *

After about half-an-hour, Baz finally managed to say the line in a half-decent way, and we moved onto the transformation sequence.

To save us some time, Craig decided to film the reaction shots of me and Allan separately, so we could both help with the make-up.

"We'll do you two dweebs, first," he said. "Stand over there and look scared."

We moved into position then waited for our cue.

"Action!"

At once we adopted terror-stricken expressions, holding up our hands to cover our eyes, ad-libbing phrases like, 'oh god no' through trembling lips.

Five seconds later, Craig called 'Cut'.

"Too much," he sighed. "Tone it down a bit."

We repeated the sequence without trembling so much.

"Cut!" Craig yelled. "What exactly are you looking at, Dom?"

"The werewolf?" I said.

"The werewolf's over there," he replied, pointing to a patch of grass on his left.

"Maybe I should lie on the floor to give them something to look at?" Baz suggested.

He got down on the grass and we trained our eyes upon him. Craig looked through the viewfinder.

"Ok," he said. "That's much better. Now it doesn't look like you're both frightened of trees...
"

We repeated the scene. Craig was happy. But Allan wasn't.

"Sorry, mate," he said. "I think we may need to do another take."

"Why?" Craig asked.

"He was doing an American accent," I said. "He said 'what the fuck is it, man?'... It wasn't very Yorkshire."

"Yorkshire?" Craig replied. "I thought he was doing Scouse?"

"No, it was definitely American," Baz said.

Craig sniffed.

"Sod it," he said. "We'll fix it in post..."

I stifled a chuckle. It seemed to be his answer for everything...

"So, are you gonna make me up, now?" Baz asked.

Craig nodded.

"We'll start with the eyes," he said.

I went over to the props bag and pulled out the black face paint.

"Oh shit," I gasped. "I've left the water in the car!"

"Jesus Christ," Baz exclaimed. "I'm gonna get eaten."

"You won't get eaten," Craig said.

"Maybe we could just use a bit of spit?" Allan suggested.

"Yeah, that'll work," I said.

"I'm not having your dirty spit on my face," Baz said.

"Use your own then," Craig replied.

I uncorked the tube and handed it to Baz,

who squeezed a measure of paint onto the back of his hand. He then hocked up some phlegm and spat it out on top, mixing the fluids together with the end of his finger.

"Now rub it into your eyes," Allan said.

"I know what to do," Baz hissed.

Gently, he began applying the paint onto his eyelids.

"Smooth out the edges more," I said. "We don't want it to look like mascara."

With an angry snort, he smeared the rest of the paint across his cheeks, nose and temples.

"I wish I could see what I was doing," Baz grumbled.

"You're doing, mate," Allan said.

"Yeah, you look beautiful..." Craig added. "So, are you ready for a take?"

Baz nodded then got to his feet.

"Right," Craig said. "When I say 'action', I want you to put your hands on your stomach, then crease over like you're a doing a big shit. Scream out in pain for a few seconds, then lift up your head and look directly into the lens."

Baz did as he was told, and Craig got the shot in a single take.

"Great," he said, "Now let's start adding the hair."

I got out the glue then began applying it to Baz's cheeks and arms.

"Not too much," Craig said. "We're doing this in stages, remember."

I cut off a small piece of theatrical hair, fanned it out in my palm, then mashed it into the glue.

"How's that?" I said.

"Great," Criag replied. "Let's do a take."

We continued the process until the transformation was complete. The result didn't look half as good as it had during the sessions but there was little we could do about it...

Once Craig had filmed the werewolf's final 'reveal', the next sequence involved the killing of my character, 'John'. I'd originally scripted it as a short chase sequence along the foot of the cliffs, ending with John tripping over a rock and being set upon by the creature.

On paper, it seemed relatively easy.

All we needed was a rock.

But we couldn't find one.

"Maybe he could just trip over his own feet?" Allan suggested.

"What, like a footballer?" Baz laughed.

Craig glared at me angrily.

"Did you know there'd be no rocks here?" he asked.

"I just assumed we'd find one," I replied.

I pointed up at the cliffs.

"Look," I said. "There's rocks everywhere."

"But none on the floor," Craig replied. "...Where we need them..."

"Why don't I just catch him?" Baz said. "Bring him down like a lion?"

Craig sighed.

"Fine," he said. "It's our option anyway..."

Allan and I returned to our marks then waited for Craig to tell us what to do.

"When we start," he began. "I want you, Baz, to come forward and make a lunge at Allan. When this happens, I want you, Dom, to push him out of the way and take the hit yourself."

"So, I'm sacrificing myself?" I said.

"Yeah," Craig said. "Your love for Rob runs deep."

Baz started chuckling.

"This isn't in the script," I said.

"Shh," Craig hissed. "We don't have time to faff."

He pointed the camera at us and started recording.

"Ok," he said. "Action!"

Baz growled then rushed toward Allan, who screamed like a girl and hoped backwards. I then stepped between them, offering myself to the beast. Baz then grabbed me by the shirt, and I fell to my knees, yelling 'no' at the top of my voice.

"Cut!" Craig called. "That'll do. Now pour on the claret."

Allan brought over the props bag while I lay down on the floor and buttoned my shirt. Baz then took out the vial of theatrical blood, flicked off the cap, then squirted it liberally over my chest.

"Jesus," Craig said. "Don't use all of it. We

need to save some for later."

"Don't worry," Baz grinned, "There's still a bit left."

I glanced down at my torso.

I was literally dripping with the stuff. He'd poured so much on that it was running down my sides.

It smelled horrible too. Sickly sweet, like warm cranberry juice.

"Ok," Craig said. "Now I want you to start eating him a little. Get your lips right down on him."

I couldn't help but notice his tone. He sounded like he was relishing this. Maybe it was his way of punishing me for not finding a rock?

On Craig's call, Baz leant over me and began sucking the 'blood' from my chest.

"Struggle a bit," Craig yelled. "You're still alive while he's eating you!"

I rolled back my eyes, stuck out my tongue, and made my body shiver.

Chris seemed happy with the result.

"Nice," he said, after getting the shot. "Very convincing."

Now that 'John' was dead, the only scene left to film was the final chase along the cliff top.

We hauled the gear to the top of the ridge then filmed a few shots of Allan running along it. Craig then reversed the angle to show Baz chasing after him. He seemed to be really enjoying his role. Though he had no more lines to say, he was giving it his all playing the monster, holding up his hands, growling, gurning into the camera... His enthusiasm seemed to be growing by the minute.

Unfortunately for him, his character was about to die.

Said death would occur via a pen in the eyeball, followed by a fall to his doom from the cliff. It seemed simple. But, to my discredit, I've not given it enough thought, and I soon discovered that no matter how much glue you use, pens don't just stick to people's eyes.

After fifteen minutes of faffing, we opted for a new approach.

"Can't we just have him being stabbed in the ear instead?" Baz suggested. "You can just stick it in my earhole."

"Fuck it," Craig said. "We're getting nowhere with the PVA..."

"But it'll look shit," I said.

"It's this or nothing," Craig sneered.

I handed Baz the biro and he pushed it into his ear.

"How does it look?" he asked.

Awful, I thought.

"It'll do," Craig sighed. "Now where are we doing this fall?"

We scouted the ridge for a section of cliff that lay above a buttress of rock. If we filmed from the other side, Baz could 'fall' onto it, giving the illusion that he was tumbling to his doom.

After finding a suitable spot, Craig explained what he wanted to see, then filmed Allan 'pushing' Baz over the edge. For some strange reason, Baz elected to add his own sound effect, vocalising a strange warble as he 'fell'. It sounded a little like "Scooby-Dooby-Doo", raising a chuckle from everyone, including Craig, who later said it was the 'funniest thing he'd heard since Knackers' lost his voice during *Brothers in Blood'*.

With the film now wrapped we headed back to the car.

"When do you think it'll all be edited?" Baz asked.

"Tomorrow at the latest," Craig replied. "I'll make a start on it as soon as we get back."

"Can I watch?" Baz asked.

"Sure," Craig replied. "Knock yourself out.."

CHAPTER 13:
HUNTED (IV)

After dropping off Allan and Craig, I took Baz home, where he changed into a set of clean clothes.

"Maybe me and you could do some stuff together in the future?" he suggested. "I've got plenty of ideas. All we need is a camera."

"I don't know anything about cameras," I replied. "That's Craig's job. I only do the writing."

"It can't be that hard," he said. "All you have to do is point and click."

"There's more to it than that," I said.

"Didn't look like it," Baz laughed. "Does he even know what he's doing?"

"Of course, he does," I replied. "His dad worked for the BBC."

"Yeah, but *he* didn't."

"Craig knows what he's doing," I said.

"Yeah, ok," he sniffed.

We got in the car then drove Craig's, where his mom welcomed inside. We went up the studio, where Craig and his dad were uploading the footage.

"How's it going?" I asked, as we made our way in and sat down on a couple of stools.

"Good," Craig said. "We've already finished the first scene."

"Let's have a look," Baz said.

Colin scrubbed the marker to the start of the timeline then clicked play.

The Shadowbright Titler appeared on the screen, followed by a shot of park that had been washed in a blue tint.

"This is the night-time effect," Craig said gleefully. "It's good, isn't it?"

"It looks great," I replied, as Baz appeared on-screen, running into shot.

"Wait until you hear the sound-effect in a bit..." Craig grinned.

The footage cut to Baz turning around, then falling back as he was 'attacked'. The action was accompanied by a blood-curdling roar, which really sold the shot.

"It's a Tiger growl in reverse," he said.

"That was my idea," Colin said proudly.

The image faded into a short title sequence, featuring a list of credits that had superimposed upon an image of the moon.

"What do you think of the music?" Craig

asked.

I recognised the tune. It was a swing cover of 'Blue Moon' by *The Marcels*.

"American Werewolf in London," Baz remarked.

"It's an homage," Craig sniffed.

We sat back and watched Colin continued the edit. Every now and then, Craig would chip to suggest a change.

"Add another frame there," he'd say, or "Use that shot first."

Their double act worked surprisingly well, and by the early evening, they'd edited more than half the movie. We stayed and watched until around ten, when Colin decided to call it a day.

"That's enough for tonight," he declared. "We'll pick the rest up tomorrow."

After dropping off Baz, I headed home and went to bed. I was so excited to see the final cut, I could hardly sleep, and woke up the next morning with a pounding headache.

After breakfast, I called Craig and asked him what time he wanted me round.

"Come over tonight, mate," he said. "I'm a bit busy at the mo."

As soon as I'd finished dinner, I drove over, and his mom let me in.

"I was wondering when you'd be round," she said, as I raced up the stairs. "They've been up there all day."

I felt a bit put out.

Craig knew that I liked to watch the editing.

If he'd been working on it all day, why had he told me he was busy?

At the top of the stairs, crossed the landed and knocked on the studio door. Craig opened it and shooed me inside.

"Good timing," he said. "We're nearly done."

I took a seat behind Colin, who welcomed me with a sultry nod.

"Would you like to see what it looks like?" he asked.

"Yeah, defo," I replied.

He scrubbed through the timeline to where we'd gotten to last night, then pressed play.

An image of Baz appeared on-screen. It was the transformation scene.

"You'll like this," Craig said, with a grin.

I watched scene play out, cutting between shots of Baz 'turning' and Allan and I screaming.

It looked ace.

The music was great too.

It sounded like the score from a real film.

"What's that tune?" I asked.

"It's from *The Wolfman*," Colin replied.

"The *Hammer Horror* version," Craig added. "We ripped the last ten minutes from the soundtrack."

"Cool," I said. "It fits perfectly."

Craig smiled smugly.

It had clearly been his idea.

The footage transitioned into the chase sequence across the ridgeline. The shots of Baz in his Werewolf garb were great, but the final battle was a little underwhelming. The cuts weren't as clean as they could have been, and it all felt a little rushed.

"We probably could have extended the fight a little more," I suggested.

"Nah," Craig said. "It's fine as it is."

When the credits started to roll, Colin rewound the footage and began transferring the edit onto VHS.

"You wanna watch it on the projector?" Craig asked.

I nodded and grinned.

* * *

Once the footage had been transferred, Colin handed Craig the tape and we rushed into his bedroom next door to watch it on the big screen.

It had me smiling from start to finish.

I loved everything about it.

After the third viewing, even the final battle seemed ok.

"We're legends, aren't we?" Craig said.

"Real filmmakers," I replied.

He smiled, proudly.

"What shall we do for our next project?" I asked.

"Well, we've done vampires, and werewolves," he said. "The next logical step is zombies."

I grinned.

Zombies were easy.

All you needed to create the effects were white face paint and theatrical blood.

"Sounds good," I replied. "We'll probably need a load of extras though. You can't have a zombie horde of two or three people."

"Yeah," Craig agreed. "Maybe something else then..."

* * *

Later that night, we got out our notepads and started jotting down some ideas.

The best of the bunch involved a man who sells his soul to a Banshee to get revenge on the gangster who killed his father, like a supernatural re-hash of *Steel Justice*, but featuring magic instead of cybernetics.

"We're doing it," Craig declared. "And we'll stick to one-word title format and call it, 'Banshee'."

"Cool," I said. "I'll start writing it tonight."

"We'll also need to run over Masquerade at some point too," he replied. "We'll need a mask and some make-up for the monster."

"Yeah," I replied. "I'm sure I saw an old woman's mask in there, last time we went..."

* * *

The next day, we drove to the shop but found that the mask we'd earmarked had already been sold.

"Someone bought it last week for a play," the woman told us. "But I can put one on order for you."

"How soon will we get it?" I asked.

"End of the month," she replied.

I looked at Craig.

I was starting University in a few weeks, living away at campus.

"I'll be gone by then," I said.

Craig sighed.

"What else have you got?" he asked.

We browsed around the shop for something we could use instead. There were loads of rubber masks on sale; ghouls, mummies, vampires, clowns... But sadly, nothing that could be converted into anything resembling an old hag.

"Maybe we could just do it with make-up?" I suggested.

Craig sniffed.

"With the greatest will in the world," he replied, "there's no way you could turn an 18-year-old bloke into an old woman... I mean, what are we going to do? Draw on the wrinkles?"

He had a point.

I was crap at drawing.

We needed the mask.

"Maybe we should just put the order in and wait for it to arrive?" Craig said.

"But how are we going to film it?" I said. "I'm gonna stuck on campus until Christmas."

"So, we'll just have to wait and film it then," he said.

"But Christmas is three months away," I replied.

"Yeah," he said, "...And that means we have three months to plan it all out."

CHAPTER 14:
THE BANSHEE (I)

In December, I returned from university then met up with Craig to discuss the project. The mask had arrived while I was way, and he opened the front door wearing it.

"What do you think?" he said.

My first reaction was to laugh.

It was way too big for his tiny head and the forehead piece was sagging down over his eyebrows.

"You look like that bloke from *Robocop*," I said. "The one who gets covered in acid and melts..."

He removed the mask and blew out his cheeks.

"We'll need to use someone with a big head then," he said.

"Baz," we said together.

We went upstairs and he showed me a copy of the script I'd sent him, which he'd annotated with notes.

"I've marked all the shots next to the lines," he said. "Can you read my writing?"

I looked at his infantile scrawls on the page.

"It doesn't matter," I said. "As long as *you* can read it, we're fine."

He grinned.

"I've been thinking about locations, too," he said. "Maybe we do the 'Old Man' sequence over Clent. There's an old stone circle at the top of the hill. It'll be perfect."

He was referring to one of the scenes that happened early in the story, where the main protagonist meets an old hermit in the wilderness, who gives him a magic mirror to summon the Banshee.

I pictured the place he was talking about.

It was perfect.

"Great," I said. "What about the casting? Have you thought about who's gonna to play the other parts?"

There were four main characters in the film. The main protagonist, John, the old hermit, the gangster, Conrad, and the titular Banshee.

"Yeah," he replied. "I was thinking Baz for the Banshee and the old man, Mittsy for the Gangster, and you for John."

"Me?" I said.

"Yeah," Craig grinned. "You were great in

Hunted. You'll be great in this, too."

I gave him a grin.

"Ok," I said. "When are we going to do it?"

"Next Saturday," he said.

"That's Christmas Eve," I replied.

"Yeah," he said. "So, we know for a fact that everyone will be available. Plus, it'll be really quiet out, so we won't be disturbed while we're filming."

I nodded.

It made a lot of sense.

"Cool," I said. "Let's make some calls?"

* * *

We spent the rest of afternoon on the phone to Baz and Mittsy, explaining the project and what we wanted them to do.

Both seemed excited about it, particularly Baz, who said that he would ask his sister to make him a costume for his role as the Hermit.

"She's doing a course on needlework," he said. "I'm sure she'll agree to help us."

"Excellent," I said. "Has she got all the materials?"

"Yeah," Baz said. "I've got this old sack I pinched from the market. She can use that."

"An old sack?" Craig sniffed.

"Yeah," Baz said. "I found it behind one of the stalls. I always knew it'd come in handy..."

When I hung up the phone, Craig started

sniggering.

"Bloody ridiculous," he said. "He's supposed to be a hermit, not a bloody tramp..."

"What's the difference?" I said. "And you never know, it might look good. His sister's always been pretty creative."

"She's like a female version of him," Craig snorted. "Down to the eyebrows..."

I laughed out loud.

He wasn't being mean. He was just letting out his annoyance. Baz, once again, was stepping on his creative shoes.

"At the end of day, he's just an actor," Craig told me, later. "Why does he always try to run things?"

"It's his nature," I replied. "He's an artist."

"But this is our project, not his."

I suspected Craig feared him a little. Not for what he could bring to the table, but for what he could take from it. He'd always been a popular with the kind of people we were looking to impress - the hippies, the musicians, the creative types... They loved him. He was one of them. It would be easy for him to share our work with them, exaggerate his involvement, pass it off his own...

"If we're not careful, he'll steal all our glory," Craig said. "I can see it happening. He'll get his hands on one of our tapes, show it to the Grebo-crew then say he did all the work..."

I couldn't disagree.

It was just the kind of thing Baz would do.

"Maybe should just cut him from the project then?" I suggested.

"Nah," Craig replied. "We need him for the mask. He's the only bloke we know with a big enough head..."

CHAPTER 15: THE BANSHEE (II)

On Christmas Eve, we rocked up at Clent Hills Nature Reserve for the first shoot, figuring it would be better to get the outdoor scenes filmed first.

It was a really cold day, and the ground was covered in a layer of ice and frost. It was windy too. Very windy. Especially at the summit, where we were filming.

By the time we got to the stone circle, I was shivering like a leaf.

Baz was already there, waiting for us. He was dressed in his sackcloth robe, its hood pulled down over his eyes.

"What do you think?" he said, giving us a twirl as he approached.

"I-it l-l-l-looks w-w-wicked..." I replied.

"It's all right, I suppose" Craig said. "Dunno about the writing though. What's that all about?"

He pointed to one of the arms, where the words, 'Jersey Royals' had been stencilled in black ink.

"Don't worry," Baz laughed. "You won't see it on camera."

"I hope not," Craig sneered.

He turned to me.

"You ready to get things going?"

I gave him a nod.

I was so cold, I couldn't speak.

"Are you gonna be ok with your lines?" Baz asked. "You look a bit out of it."

"I-I-I'll b-b-be f-f-fine," I replied.

I was wearing nothing but a thin shirt, trousers and tie.

"Ok, I want you to walk in from there," Craig said, pointing down the slope. "Then we you reach the circle, stop then start looking around."

I nodded then made my way down the bank.

"Ready?" Craig called. "Action!"

I began walking up the slope to my mark. Every part of my body was shaking from the cold. When I reached the stones, Craig called 'Cut'.

"Ok," he said. "Now for the reveal of the hermit. Baz, I want you hide behind that stone, then when I call 'action', come out then stand in front of Dom."

Baz suddenly started laughing.

"What's up with you?" Craig said.

"Look," Baz chuckled.

He pointed to my head.

Craig turned and looked at me, then grinned.

"W-w-what's g-going on?" I said.

"Your forehead," Baz giggled. "It's covered in ice."

I touched the skin above my eyebrows. It felt cold and slick.

"W-what the f-f-fuck!" I said, as a thin sheet of ice dropped down my face.

"You're turning blue," Craig said. "You feeling ok?"

I shook my head.

I wasn't.

I really wasn't.

"Maybe we should film this part some other time?" Baz said.

I nodded in agreement.

"Fine," Craig huffed. "Let's head back..."

* * *

Later that night, I phoned Craig to tell him I was ok. After coming home, I'd spent most of the day wrapped in a blanket by the fire, drinking hot cups of tea.

"I'm ok now," I said.

"Good," he replied. "For a while there, I thought you might have died."

"Me too," I laughed.

I'd probably been close to it.

"I reckon we should pick up those scenes in the New Year, when it gets a bit warmer," he said. "We should just focus on the indoor stuff for now."

"Sounds good," I replied.

"Cool," he said. "Are you good for Boxing day?"

"I am," I replied, "But I think Baz might be working."

"Shit. What about the day after?"

"Sorry mate," I replied. "I'm going then to Wales to see my aunt."

"When are you back?"

"Thursday," I said. "Is that any good?"

He hissed down the phone.

"I've got family stuff then," he said.

"Maybe we should put the project on hold?" I suggested. "... Pick things up and start again in Easter?"

"Easter!" he scoffed. "That's months' away."

I didn't know what to say.

"Fuck it!" he said loudly. "You obviously haven't got time for this anymore."

"Craig..." I said.

But he'd already hung up.

I called him back, but he didn't answer.

He was clearly frustrated. He wanted nothing more than to make movies with his partner-in-crime.

But I'd let him down.

I suddenly felt guilty for telling him 'No'. I wanted to cancel my plans, call him up, then tell him that it had all been a joke and that we were good to go...

But I couldn't.

And even if I could, it wouldn't have mattered... For as soon as the Spring term started, I'd be back in the halls, away from all the action.

I let out an anguished sigh.

Going to University had ruined everything!

Why had I chosen to do this stupid degree?

Because you want to make your parents proud, my inner voice answered.

"Fuck off, conscience," I yelled.

"Is everything ok, Dom?" my brother shouted from his room.

"No," I hissed. "My life is fucking ruined..."

CHAPTER 16: RECONCILIATION

After finishing University, I started working in a catalogue shop at the local shopping centre. It was a terrible job with long hours, little pay, and zero hope of progression.

The year before, Craig had married my cousin, Della, and the two of them had bought a house around the corner from his mom's.

I hadn't seen much of him since *Banshee*. I didn't know whether he was still into filmmaking or had lost all interest.

During the second year of my course, I'd lent my copy of *Bite* and *Hunted* to one of my classmates, and she'd shown it to her flatmates. They'd then loaned it to their neighbours in Selly

Oak and it had been passed down the street from house-to-house. I had no idea where it ended up.

Within days, I had random people coming up to me in the Arts block, asking if I was that guy in the film with the 'werewolf'. It was exactly the kind of celebrity Craig had craved.

At the time, I'd wanted to phone him up and tell him about it but I'd struggled to make the call.

In the March of 2002, I got told off at work, so I quit my job in a petulant outburst. When word got through to Della, she asked Craig to speak to his sister, who worked as a Practice Manager in a local surgery. She'd been looking for someone to do some clerking and Della thought I'd be a perfect fit.

Craig called me up, explained the role, then told me his sister was going to get me in for an interview the following week.

It was great to speak to him again. Even if it had nothing to do with the films.

After landing the job, Craig invited me around to see how I was getting on. I turned up with a bottle of vodka and we got drunk and talked about the good old days.

Several hours later, Craig went upstairs and brought down a videotape.

"Is that what I think it is?" I asked.

"It sure is, bud," he replied.

Lo and behold, it was the original copy of *Bite* and *Hunted*.

It had been ages since I'd last seen our films, and when he put them on, I found myself laughing from start from finish.

"Bloody hell, we had a lot of fun, didn't we?" I chuckled, hiccupping into my glass.

"We sure did," Craig replied.

"Shame we stopped doing it," I said.

"Yeah," he nodded. "Maybe we could start it all up again?"

I smiled from ear-to-ear.

"I'd love to," I said.

I glanced at Della, who was sitting beside him on the couch. She looked pleased with herself.

"I'm glad you two are back together," she said, as if we were a couple of gay lovers. "You need each other in your lives."

"Come here, you," I slurred, drunkenly.

She leant forward and I gave her a hug.

"Best cousin ever!"

She gave me a grin then returned to Craig's side.

"So," Craig said. "What are we gonna do?"

CHAPTER 17: MAN ON THE EDGE

During our time apart, our tastes in film had broadened from horror to comedy, and comedy-horror. Both of us had also developed a particular fondness for the TV show, League of Gentlemen, loving its fusion of black comedy and gothic imagery.

We also loved the fact that the entire cast was played by three actors. It mirrored the ways we'd previously worked, giving us an insight into what we could achieve with our limited resources.

Women, for example.

We'd never used one in a film.

But after watching League of Gentlemen, it didn't matter. Any one of us could put on a wig and wear a dress. It wasn't gay. It was practical. And it opened a whole new world of possibilities.

We kept our comeback project as simple as possible, adopting our former strategy of starting with what we had then working our way backwards.

"So, we have two blokes," I said. "Where are they?"

"On the edge of a cliff," Craig replied.

"And what are they doing there?"

"One's about to jump off," he replied.

"Why?"

"Because he wants to kill himself."

"Why?"

"Because he hates his life."

"Ok," I said. "So, why is the other guy there?"

"He's trying to stop him...."

"Nah, too obvious."

"Ok... He's pissed off at him."

"Pissed off, why?"

"Because he stole his seat..."

We burst out laughing and jotted it down. Two hours later, we'd written *Man on the Edge*, an expletive-filled comedy about a man who is driven to suicide by an egregious jobsworth.

"So, who are we gonna get to play the parts?" I asked.

Craig laughed.

"I want to play the arsehole," he said.

"In that case," I replied. "I'll be the bloke with the Deathwish."

"Cool," Craig said. "And we'll get Della to film it... It'll give her something to do."

* * *

The next day, we visited *Masquerade* and bought a selection of cheap wigs and props. It didn't matter which ones we got. We figured we'd find a use for everything as we went along.

Later that evening, we drove to the park with Della, then climbed to top the cliff, to shoot the scene.

It was hilarious.

We laughed from start to finish.

I'd never had so much fun.

We knew from the off that we were making a pile of crap, but that wasn't the point. We'd rediscovered of love of the process; the brainstorming, the writing, the acting....

Even the editing was a blast.

"This is funny," Colin said, when he cut it in the studio.

Neither of us could disagree. The whole thing was a chaotic shamble of irreverent mirth. The over-liberal use of swearing made it even funnier. Every other word was 'fuck' or 'fucking' or 'motherfucker'. We even used the 'c' word several times... For no good reason.

The terrible direction and photography took it to another level. Because we'd all taken turns holding the camera, the clips were incredibly disjointed; dodgy angles, out-of-focus close-ups, and images that were either too dark or washed out. In one shot, towards the end, we had to the cheat the angle, so cut from a close-up of Craig's face to a wide angle of myself, which clearly showed him lying on the floor, ducking beneath the lens.

It was a beautiful mess of a production, a total shit show.

But it was brilliant.

Many years later, I uploaded it to YouTube. It still makes me laugh when watch it today...

CHAPTER 18: MRS CRUMPTON

One of the wigs we'd bought from Masquerade was long and grey. The label on the packaging read, 'Elderly Woman'. We wanted to make use of it somehow, so we invented the character of 'Mrs. Crumpton', a demented old crone, with a terribly memory.

After an hour-or-so of brainstorming, we came up with a plot involving a physicist who solves the riddle of life. After writing the equation on a whiteboard he leaves the room to inform the President, but on his way out, he bumps into his cleaner, Mrs. Crumpton, who is carrying a bottle of Mr Sheen and a dust cloth.

Before she enters the room, he tells her not to wipe the equation off the board, stressing that it is the most 'important work in the history of mankind.'

As soon as he leaves, Mrs Crumpton goes into the room, forgets what he's just said, then proceeds to clean the board. When the Physicist returns and sees what she's done, he starts slagging her off, calling her every name under the sun. She gets upset and starts crying, to which he remarks, "For God sakes, mom... I'm glad I don't pay you."

"This is fucking hilarious," Craig said, after we'd thrashed out the first draft.

"I know," I giggled.

It was probably the funniest thing we'd ever written.

"Where are we going to film it?"

"We can do it at mine," I said. "I've got a whiteboard in my bedroom."

"Cool," he replied. "I'm guessing you wanna play Mrs. C?"

I nodded.

"And you can be the scientist."

We looked through the other wigs and found a long brown one, labelled 'Hippy'. It seemed appropriate for a science-nerd.

"You'll need glasses and a beard too," I said. "To complete the effect."

Craig smiled.

"I've always wanted to see what I'd look like with a bush," he laughed.

I handed him my specs.

"Here," I said. "Try these."

He put them on, and his pupils

immediately gravitated towards his nose.

"Shit," he said. "These are strong."

"I know," I replied.

My eyesight was fucked. Always had been.

"Do we need another trip to Masquerade for hair?" he asked.

"No," I said. "We've still got loads from *Hunted*. I kept it, just in case."

Craig smiled.

"Then what's stopping us from filming it right now?"

"A dress," I said.

* * *

The next day after work, I popped into a charity shop and asked the woman inside if she had old women's dress that would fit me.

"To fit you?" she giggled.

"Yeah," I replied. "I'm in a film... I'm playing an old woman."

"Yes," she chuckled. "Of course, you are..."

"It's ok," her colleague - another old bat - remarked. "We understand."

She looked at her mate and winked.

"I'm not a transvestite," I said. "I'm doing some acting."

"Whatever you say, dear..." the first woman said.

She got up from her chair, then led me to clothes rack near the window that contained a multitude of vintage dresses.

"Most of these will be small," she said. "But you might find one or two that fit. Shall I leave you to it?"

"I don't understand the sizes" I said.

She looked me up and down.

"I'd say you were a 16-18... Best you make a note of that for the future."

"I'm not a transvestite," I repeated.

"No, love," she said, with a smile. "You're whatever you want to be."

Once she'd returned to the counter, I began shifting through the smocks, pulling out any that were size 16 or over. The best of the bunch was a dark brown one, covered in yellow splodges. It was huge, with a hem that hung below the knee. It looked like the kind of thing Mrs. Crumpton would wear, so I took it to the counter.

The woman looked at me and smiled.

"Nice choice," she said.

"Very you," the other woman added.

"How much is it?" I said.

"Ten pounds," the firs women replied.

"Ten quid!" I exclaimed. "But it's a knackered old rag."

"We can't do anything about the price, love," the second woman said. "At the end of the day, we're still a business."

"Fine," I said, handing over the cash.

She put the dress into a bag and handed me

a receipt.

"See you again soon," she chuckled, as I made my way out.

* * *

I drove over to Craig's, picked him up, then we headed over to his dad's house to grab the camera. While we were there, I showed him what I'd bought.

"That's ace," he said, as I held up in front of me. "Have you tried it on?"

"Not yet..." I replied. "I'm a scared I might break it... I've got a feeling it might be a bit too small across the chest."

"Well, there's only one way to find out," he said.

I took off my jumper then pulled the thing over my head. Surprisingly, it was quite snug.

"You look good," Craig laughed. "Very sexy."

"Crone-Chic," I chuckled.

Just then, his bedroom door opened and in came his mom with two cups of tea.

"Oh, sorry," she said. "I didn't realise you were..."

Her words faded to nothing, and she stood staring at me, opened mouthed.

"It's for a film," Craig explained. "Dom's playing an old woman."

"Oh," she sighed, relieved. "I thought it might be something else."

"I'm not a transvestite," I said.

I felt like I'd said this phrase a lot lately.

"No, no, of course not," she replied.

She left the cup on Craig's bedside table then left the room.

He turned to me a grinned.

"She thinks you're gay..."

* * *

After getting back into my normal clothes, Craig grabbed his dad's camera, and we drove back to mine. where we went straight upstairs to my room and pulled out the bed to create some space in front of the whiteboard.

Craig then donned his wig, and I helped him apply the beard, using the same 'cut and fan' technique we'd used on *Hunted*. To our surprise, it matched the colour of his hair perfectly. To complete the look, he put on the suit-jacket I'd worn for my interview at the surgery.

He stood in front of the mirror and smiled.

"I look fucking ace with a beard!" he beamed.

"Shame you'll never be able to grow one..." I laughed.

He'd never been able to. The best he'd ever managed was a thin line of bumfluff.

"Come on," he said. "Put on your dress, so we can film this shit."

Once I'd donned my frock, he switched on

the camera, pressed record, then asked me to shoot him as he wrote a random equation on the whiteboard with a marker pen. Once he'd spattered it with random numbers and symbols, we started filming the dialogue.

Because it was just the two of us, we had to hand each other the camera between takes, cheating a little by moving from to the side, so neither of us were looking down the lens.

As imperfect as it was, the result was quite good, and Colin complimented our work during the edit.

"You, know, this isn't too bad at all," he said. "You can hardly tell that you filmed it yourselves. "

"That's because we're so talented," Craig quipped.

I started giggling like a little girl.

"I hear you've got some music for the credits?" Colin said.

"Yes," I replied.

At the end of the shoot, Craig and I had filmed me singing a theme-song I'd written for the character.

Its lyrics went...

> *Simple things are way too demanding,*
> *She's got problems understanding,*
> *Mrs. Crumpton has got no brain....*

...And I'd sung it live, playing the music on

my keyboard.

"It's quite catchy that," Colin remarked, as he played the click on the screen. "And you're not a bad singer, are you, Dom?"

"Thanks," I said.

"You need to work on your keyboard skills though," Craig sneered.

He'd only said it because he was a Grade 5.

When Colin had finished the edit, he transferred the film onto tape, and we took it round Craig's house, where we watched it on his new 60-inch TV. Della watched it too. She laughed her ass off.

As soon as the credits started playing, he asked what we should do next.

"I dunno," I replied. "But I'm sure we'll think of something...."

CHAPTER 19:
THE MAGICAL
ENTRANCE

A few days later, I was pulling weeds in my back garden when my dog, Shandy, spied a cat, and began chasing it. It ran across the lawn before disappearing behind a row of conifers that had been planted near the fence. My dog followed it into the treeline, yapping furiously.

"Shandy," I called. "Leave it alone. Come here!"

There was no response.

I suddenly heard him scratching one of the fence panels.

Dropping my tools, I went over and pushed myself through the branches to get to him.

I suddenly had an idea for a film.

Leaving the dog to his own devices, I ran inside the house, picked up the phone and called Craig.

"Dude," I said. "I've just had an idea for a story."

"Go on," he replied.

"It's like *Chronicles of Narnia*," I gushed. "But instead of a wardrobe, it's a bush."

Later that night, we met up at his house, where I explained what I had in mind.

"So, there's this guy who owns a dog," I began. "...He lets it outside to have a piss, but it disappears through the trees and doesn't come back. When he goes into the trees to find him he steps through a portal into a magical world."

"What's this world calls?" Craig asked.

"The Land of Harri-Bo-Dairy-Dumpling," I replied.

Della started laughing.

"Harri-Bo-Dairy-Dumpling?" she tittered.

"Yes," I said. "And there he meets a Dwarf, named Fairy-Mackerel-Man, who speaks in riddles."

"I guess that'll be me then," Craig grumbled.

I gave him a nod.

* * *

That night, I jumped on my PC and wrote the script. I was so inspired by the story; it took me less than an hour.

Once I'd finished, I emailed it to Craig, who read it straight away.

Two minutes later, he called me on the phone.

"Fuck me," he said. "This is completely nuts!"

"Yeah," I agreed. "But in a good way, right?"

He started chuckling.

"Yeah, I suppose," he replied. "So where are we going to film *Narnia*?"

The answer was obvious.

* * *

The next evening, we made our way through the park to the cliffs.

"Here, again," Craig noted, as we stopped near a copse of trees to shoot the core dialogue.

He was fully kitted out in his Dwarf costume, which consisted of a cloak made from a crocheted blanket and a pair of slippers that had been tied around his knees. Della had darkened his eyes with face paint and glued a fake moustache to his upper lip. To complete the effect, he wore a short brown wig, crowned by a helmet, made from an upside-down wicker basket.

I'd never seen anything so ridiculous.

"Let's try and get this done quick," Craig said. "I'd hate to be seen like this in public..."

"Too late," I laughed, as a man passed by

walking his dog.

He handed Della the camera and we made a start. I kept the script close at hand, because neither of us had bothered to learn our lines. We decided it would be easier this time to film of dialogue in blocks, rather than cutting back and forth.

It worked well, and within twenty minutes, we'd finished.

"Thank fuck for that," Craig said, once we'd wrapped. He pulled off his wig and deposited it in the props bag. "That thing's itchy as fuck!"

We made our way back to the car, jumped in, then went around his dads for the edit.

A few hours later, it was all done and dusted.

"You're banging these out," Colin remarked, as he handed Craig the finished tape. "If you keep going like this, you'll have 50 of these by the end of the year."

"That's the plan," he replied, giving me a sly wink.

CHAPTER 20:
BOUNTY FOR
BREAKFAST
& SUCKER

C ome the weekend, we were ready shoot something else.

I'd hit peak form with my writing and was churning out short scripts ten-to-the-dozen. Among them was *Bounty for Breakfast*, a sketch about salesman who tricks a punter into buying Life Insurance by feeding him a poisoned Bounty.

It was simple shoot.

No costumes were required, and in terms of location, all we needed was a doorstep.

"Let's do it at mine," I said, volunteering my house. "I've got a porch. And if we keep it closed during the shoot, we'll have good sound."

"Sounds like a plan," Craig said.

I drove down and we picked up the camera and came back. We then got into our costumes. Craig - the 'punter' - wore a dressing gown, while I put on my suit.

We then spent the next ten minutes or so, shooting the thing at the door.

It was easy.

A piece of piss.

From start to end, it had taken less than an hour.

We were flying.

And loving every minute.

We'd wrapped so fast, that we had enough time to do another one, so I suggested we film, *Sucker*, which told the story of a dodgy IT call handler, who takes the piss out of his customers.

For this one, all we needed - props-wise - was company logo, which we quickly knocked - up on PowerPoint. After printing it off, we blue-tacked it to the wall next to my brother's PC.

"Perfect," I said. "Now all we need is a phone."

I went downstairs, unplugged the housephone and brought it up.

"What if someone calls your house?" Craig asked.

"It's ok," I replied. "No one ever does."

I printed a copy of the script and handed it to Craig.

"So, I'm the call handler, right?" he said with a grin.

I nodded.

The role was right up his street. I'd even written the part with him in mind.

"Shall we do your parts first?" I asked.

"Might as well while we're here," he replied. "Then we can go downstairs and film your bit."

He quickly drew on a pencil-thin beard with the eyeliner pen.

"Does this make me look more evil?" he asked.

"Yeah," I nodded. "But we're missing something."

I popped into my bedroom and grabbed a black cap.

"Here," I said.

I handed it over and he put it on.

"Perfect," I said. "Now you look like a proper IT dickhead."

"Great," he replied.

I picked up the camera then aimed the lens at his face. Straight away, I knew something wasn't right.

"What's wrong?" he asked.

"It's too dark," I said. "It's probably got something to do with these stupid spotlights."

They were right above him, pointing down over the peak of his cap. The only part of his face I could see where the whites of his eyes.

"Maybe we can twist them round a bit?" he

suggested.

He pulled out his chair, and I climbed onto the seat and started messing with the bulbs. Sadly, none of them would turn more than 90 degrees.

"Fuck," I said. "We're gonna need to move the desk."

It wasn't something I wanted to do.

It was heavy as fuck.

But he needed to be *in* the light, not *under* it.

"Hang on," he said. "Can't we use this instead?"

I looked down and saw him pointing toward an old desk lamp beside the screen.

"Do you think it'll be bright enough?" I asked.

"There's only one way to find out."

He plugged it on, flicked the switch, then angled the bulb towards his face.

I looked through the viewfinder of the camera.

"Fuck me!" I said. "This is ace!"

The upward angle of the light shrouded his face with a sinister glow. It looked creepy.

"Show me," he said.

I handed him the camera and we swapped positions.

"Bloody hell!" he exclaimed. "This is amazing! We should do this for every shot!"

"Yeah," I agreed. "Defo!"

* * *

We started shooting.

Craig was in his element from the off, chewing the scenery with devious relish. He delivered one of his lines so well, that it became part of our movie making folklore. Five words that we'd quote to each to other forevermore.

"What you trying to say?"

On paper, you wouldn't think it was funny. But the way Craig said it was hilarious.

It still makes me piss myself today.

When he first said it, I burst out laughing, turned off the camera, then said it myself several times, imitating his mid-Atlantic tone and falsetto inflection. Then he said it again. It cracked me up. The tape wasn't even rolling.

After about ten minutes of giggling, we finally composed ourselves and finished the scene.

I then grabbed one of the wigs and we went downstairs to film things from the perspective of the customer. Donning my headwear, I sat at the dinner table in the back room, then read my lines into the same phone we'd used upstairs.

After twenty minutes, we'd shot the lot, and we drove over to Craig's dad's to do the edit.

"Why don't you do this one yourself?" Colin suggested, when we arrived. "You've seen how the software works. Why don't you give it a go?"

Craig's eyes lit up.

It was the moment he'd been waiting for.

After the footage had been imported he started cutting the clips. Several hours later, both films were edited.

"Bloody hell, that was easy," Craig said, once we were done. "Maybe we should edit everything ourselves from now on?"

"Makes sense," I said.

He ran off two tapes and handed me one.

"Maybe it's time we started putting together a master copy?" he said. "...Of all the films we've done so far."

"That'd be brilliant," I replied.

He inserted a new tape into the recorder then started transferring the footage from *Bite*, *Hunted*, *Man on the Edge*, *Mrs Crumpton*, and other two we'd shot today. In total, the runtime was 37 minutes.

"That's the length of a TV programme," I remarked.

"Yeah," Craig said. "But if we keep adding to it, it'll soon be the length of a movie."

"Wow," I cooed.

"We've just gotta keep doing what we're doing," he said. "At this rate, it won't take long."

It was impossible to disagree...

CHAPTER 21:
JOHN STALLION
VS PADDY
O'NEILL

For our next project, we decided to do something a little different. Like many boys of our generation, we'd both grown up 1980's action films, and John Stallion vs Paddy O'Neill was our homage to the genre.

It featured a wisecracking, hard-as-nails cop, named John Stallion, who goes to battle with his arch nemesis: a generic Irishman-with-a-Cockney-accent, named Paddy O'Neill.

The plot had no backstory.

But we didn't need one. It was clearly a parody.

The film consisted of one scene: the final

battle between the two leads, kicking off with Stallion bursting into the villain's lair to save the life of Paddy's hostage.

When Stallion asks him to surrender, O'Neill refuses, then slits the victim's throat and makes a run for it. The cop chases after him, cornering him on the balcony, where the two men engage in hand-to-hand combat. After a long and protracted fight, Stallion gains the advantage and puts a bullet in the bad guy's head. He makes a bad pun, and the film ends abruptly.

It was perhaps the easiest script I'd ever written.

And the shortest...

It consisted of no more than ten or eleven lines, and the action sequences were written in the form of notes, as we figured we could choreograph everything on-set.

"I've got to play Stallion," Craig said, after we'd done a quick readthrough.

It wasn't a request, but I didn't mind.

I wanted to play Paddy in any case.

He was much more interesting.

"We need someone for the girl," I said.

"Della can do it," Craig replied.

"She'll need to film it," I said. "We can't both be fighting and shooting it."

"Who then?"

Maybe I can ask Glen?"

I was referring to my brother. He was 15 but had the features of a ten-year-old girl. All he needed was a wig.

"Do you think he'd be up for it?" Craig asked.

I nodded.

"Glen loves our films," I said. "He's watched them all."

Craig smiled.

"Cool," he said. "Casting sorted. So, what are we going to use for the gun?"

"No worries," I replied. "Already sorted."

I had old toy cowboy gun from when I was a kid. It was silver, and for some strange reason, it was big enough to fit into the hand of an adult.

"It can't look shit," Craig said. "I can't be John Stallion if I'm holding a gun that's bright green."

I laughed.

"It looks real enough," I replied. "...As long as we don't do any close-ups!"

* * *

The next night, I drove to Craig and Della's to pick them up.

He seemed excited about his role.

"I can't wait for this," he said. "I've been practising my voice all day."

"You're doing a voice?" I replied.

"Yeah, obviously," Craig said. "John Stallion can't sound like he's from Dudley..."

"Let's hear it then...."

"Ok," he said. "Give me something to say."

I tried to remember from the script, but nothing came to mind.

"Just say anything," I said.

"Like what?" he replied.

"I dunno," I said. "Say, 'Hi my name in John Stallion'."

He grinned then said the words aloud.

"Haay, my neem is Johhn Staalliooon."

"What the fuck was that?" I said.

"Arnold Schwarzenegger," he replied.

I shook my head.

It sounded more like John Jones from Swansea...

* * *

When we got to my house, Glen was waiting for us at the door. He'd taken the liberty of raiding the props bag and was sporting the same wig that Craig had worn for his role as the Physicist, in *Mrs. Crumpton*.

"Who's that chick?" Craig laughed as we got out of the car.

"Do I need to wear a dress or something?" Glen asked, as we came inside. "I don't look very girly in these jeans..."

"You'll pass," Della laughed.

"It's ok, bro," I said. "We'll mostly be focusing on your girly face, so it won't matter."

We gathered in the front room, where Craig began setting up the camera.

"Shall we use the same lighting we used for *Sucker*?" I asked.

"Yeah, defo," Craig replied. "I loved that."

I raced upstairs, grabbed the desk lamp, then brought it down and plugged it into one of the wall sockets.

"Do I have any lines?" Glen asked, as Craig stood by the mirror drawing on a moustache.

"No," I replied. "But you may have to scream when he cuts your throat."

"I can scream," he replied, happily.

"Cool," I replied. "I'll go and get a knife."

I went to the kitchen, looking for a suitable blade. Before she'd died, my mom had bought a set of Shoguns, which were sheaved in a block, near the microwave. They looked ace, perfect weapons for a character as evil as Paddy. I was loathe to use them however, as I didn't want to accidentally cut my brother's throat for real.

In the end, I opted for a butterknife. It had a fair-sized blade but was completely blunt. I tested it on the back of my hand.

Not even a scratch...

After returning to the living room, I got into costume - a balaclava and Parker Jacket - and completed the look with a pair of shades.

I looked ridiculous.

But, then again, that was point.

Without further ado, we started shooting.

It was hilarious from the get-go. Because the script was written in note form most of the dialogue was ad-libbed, with Craig and I blurting out anything that came into our heads, often punctuated with unnecessary swear words, Fs, Bs, Cs... Anything we could think of that was tropey or controversial. A lot of the time, we were repeating the last things we said. Before long, things descended into a slanging match of insults...

"Fuck you, Stallion," I said.

"No, fuck you," he replied.

"No, fuck you, you fucker."

"Fuck you, you fucking-fuck," etc....

Glen was pissing himself throughout. So was Della. She was creasing so much I was surprised she could hold the camera straight.

After half-an-hour or so of junk dialogue, Criag decided to move things on by going off-script by shooting the hostage.

No one expected it.

But by this point, no one cared.

He pulled the trigger, adding a bit of fake recoil to sell it. Della then cut to Glen, who pretended to be shot. To cement the fact that I was the bad guy, I drew the blade over his throat as his body crumpled to the ground at my feet.

"What's wrong with you, Stallion?" I spat. "See what you made me do!"

I started corpsing.

I couldn't help it.

But only after Della had got the shot.

"Finally," Craig said. "Now we get to the

fight like men...."

After a brief chase sequence through the house, we started shooting the final fight, which would take place on the balcony, which overlooked my garden.

"Nowhere to go, Paddy," Craig said.

It was perhaps the only time he'd stuck to the script.

I turned around then gurned into the lens.

Della reversed the shot and Craig lifted his gun.

"You don't need the gun, John," I said.

It was a direct quote from the Schwarzenegger movie, *Commando*. It was one of my favourite Arnie lines, along with the classics, "See you at the party, Richter," and "Stick around."

Craig theatrical tossed away his gun then I lunged at him with the point of the butterknife. He grabbed me by the wrist.

"Now what?" I said.

"Maybe I could twist your arm around?" Craig replied.

"Where?" I said.

"Up your back... Then maybe I could push you into the railings."

He told Della where to point with the camera then she pressed record.

Craig the twisted my arm round then shoved me to the left. When my chest connected with the rail, I draped myself over it, clutching my sides as if he'd broken all my ribs.

"Ok," I said. "What now?"

Craig hummed.

It quickly became apparent that we should have blocked things out beforehand.

"Maybe I could turn around," I said. "And you come at you with a double-axe handle?"

"A double-what?"

It was a wrestling move from WWE. It involved palming your hands above your head then bringing it down on your opponent, as if you were holding an axe.

I demonstrated what I meant.

"All right," he replied. "Maybe when you go to hit me, I can duck out of the way."

We blocked it out.

It seemed to work.

"Ok," I said. "Let's do it."

Della pressed record and we acted it out.

"Do we need to speed it up a bit?" I asked.

I was conscious of how slow we were doing the moves.

"Nah," Craig replied. "We can always speed it up in post."

We blocked out the next sequence, which involved Paddy aiming a kick at John Stallion's torso. I didn't want to kick him for real, so we had to cheat the shot.

"Stand behind me," Craig said to Della. "If you shoot over my shoulder, you'll see the kick, but not where it lands."

She did as he said, and we performed the move.

"How did it look?" Craig asked.

"All right, I think," Della replied.

"Cool," I said. "Now what?"

"Maybe this is where we should wrap things up?" Craig said. "I'll fall over next to my gun, then if you come at me with the knife, I'll pick it up and shoot you in the chest."

We practiced it a couple of times, but it didn't feel right.

"Why doesn't this work?" I asked.

"Dunno," he replied, shaking his head. "But I'm sure we can fix it in the edit."

Della started filming and we performed the routine.

To confirm the fact that Paddy had been killed, Craig suggested we should film an extra shot of the walking over to Paddy's body, where he would shoot him in the head another three times.

"This'll work," he said, with a grin.

He was thinking of his last line.

It was, "Hey Paddy... You're a real headache."

I couldn't agree more.

"Yeah," I said. "Let's do it!

* * *

After wrapping the shoot, we headed down to Colin studio to start the edit. Della and Glen joined us. They both seemed to enjoy watching the process.

My brother loved it when we added the sound effects. Most were imported from Colin's copyright free CDs, but there were also a few we had to create on our own, like the neck slice, which we achieved by dribbling water into a cup.

When we were done, Craig transferred the footage onto the 'master' tape and then we all went round his to watch it on his telly.

It was great night.

In addition to watching our new film, we also watched the older ones.

All of them.

In a row.

Twice.

"That's another fives the runtime," Craig declared, proudly. "Now we've nearly got an hour's worth of film."

"How long's the tape?" I asked.

"240 minutes," he replied.

I smiled.

"Plenty of room for a few more then!"

"Defo," he replied. "So, what's next?"

CHAPTER 22:
CITY BOY

Craig and I had always liked horror films featuring inbreds... Stuff like The Hills Have Eyes, Texas Chainsaw Massacre, and Wrong Turn... so we decided to do our own take on the subgenre.

I quickly wrote a script, entitled *City Boy*, about a young couple who are attacked by a cannibal in the forest.

"I'm playing the Inbred," Craig announced, before he'd even read the script.

"We'll also need someone to play the girl," I said. "Do you think Della would be up for it?"

"Does she have any lines?" he asked.

"No," I replied. "She dies at the start."

"How?"

"Eaten," I said. "But it all happens off-camera, while her husbands is having a shit."

"Cool," he said. "I'll get her to do it."

* * *

The next evening, we drove up the park, then made our way to the cliffs.

"Bloody hell," Craig laughed. "This is like our second home..."

"Yeah," I agreed.

It sure felt like it.

I took out the script then explained to Della where she needed to stand and what she needed to do.

"Craig will be filming us from over there," I said, pointing to a copse of trees. "All you need to do is walk alongside me into shot."

She didn't look happy.

"Just walk?" she said.

"Yeah," I replied. "Using your feet. Is that ok?"

She hummed.

I got the impression she was a little camera shy, and that Craig must have had to twist her arm to get her involved.

He called 'Action' and we started strolling up to our mark.

"Cut!" he said.

He moved in to do a close-up.

"Action!"

I looked at Della, then said my line...

"Excuse me, dear. I need to take a shit."

She didn't react as I walked off-shot. Normally, it would be grounds for a retake, but Craig decided to run with it as her non-plussed expression was hilarious.

I positioned myself by the trees, dropped my trousers, then began gurning into the lens.

"Oh God, Oh God!" I yelled, as if I was passing a house-brick.

"Cut!" Craig said. "That's fucking ace. Now pull up your kecks, look at the turd, then smirk at it, as if it was no big deal."

I laughed.

It was classic Craig.

He had a knack for comedy.

I carried out his instruction, then walked back to where my 'wife' was standing.

"Marsha!" I called. "Where are you?"

To this day, I've no idea why I used the name, 'Marsha'. It just seemed appropriate...

Craig then filmed me as I turned my head from side-to-side, chewing the scenery with my over-the-top facial expressions.

"Fantastic," he grinned. "Now let's see what you're looking at."

I quickly placed Della's umbrella by the treeline, then he reversed the shot to show my point of view.

"Ok," he said. "React to seeing the umbrella."

He called 'Action' and I cut my eyes and hummed. It was possibly the worst 'noticing' acting that had ever been committed to screen.

Not that Craig cared.

"Great," he said. "Now for a close up on the brolly."

He went over to the treeline, pointed the lens at the umbrella, then panned up as I walked into shot and said, "Oh, I see... You're hiding, are you? You want me to come and find you..."

Craig tittered then zoomed in for a close-up.

"Action!"

"...Ok, then," I continued. "Daddy's on the case, baby. Daddy's on the case..."

He stopped the tape and started chuckling.

"That was great," he laughed. "You sounded like a real pervert."

I grinned.

It was exactly what I was going for.

"So how did it feel?" he asked, as I moved myself into position for the next take.

"How did what feel?" I replied, confused.

"Saying that about your cousin?"

I suddenly felt sick.

Thank God it was only acting...

* * *

Before I'd left the house, I'd filled up the props bag with things we could use in the shoot. Amongst them was one of Shandy's bones. It was shin of a sheep, which my dad had bought from the market.

I took it out of the bag and placed it on the ground near the stump of a tree. Craig then filmed me as I stepped into the clearing and picked it up.

"Oh God, no!" I exclaimed, holding it up to my face. "Marsha!"

I then sniffed it.

"Oh no!" I yelled. "It *is* you!"

I was proud of this gag. It was one of my best.

I knew I'd pulled it off well when I heard Della giggling out of shot.

"Marsha!" I yelled at the top of my voice. "Maaarrrrshhhhaaaa!"

"Fantastic," Craig said. "Now for my bit."

"Della," I called, "Grab the make-up!"

* * *

Ten minutes later, we'd transformed Craig into an Inbred monstrosity, complete with tusks. We darkened his eyes, put a wig on his head, and had drawn on some horrendous facial hair, which made him look two-parts werewolf. In terms of clothing, he wore a tatty old cap and same Parker we'd used for Paddy's character in the previous film.

He looked great.

Proper Inbred.

"Do you reckon I should do a southern accent?" he said.

"What, like Bristolian?" I laughed.

"No," he chuckled. "Southern American.... Like I live in the Bayou."

I started chuckling.

It was a great idea. Madcap! Thus far, I'd delivered all my lines in RP!

"That'd be great," I said.

"Eeeet shoo wuuud, Sh-itty Bo-oy!" he replied.

Della nearly pissed herself.

I picked up the camera while he hid himself behind a tree.

"Action!" I yelled.

He stepped out, parting the branches to reveal his ghoulish face.

"She ca-an't hear yoo, Sh-itty Ma-an," he growled.

I handed him the camera, to shoot my reaction.

"What have you done to wife?" I gasped.

He passed it back.

"I cooked her up, Sh-itty Boy," he said, rubbing his tummy. "Real gooood. She was a maarty faaan, chicken!"

It was my turn to piss myself.

He was brilliant.

He'd nailed it.

His performance was even better than Baz's werewolf in *Hunted*.

"Bloody hell," I said, after cutting the shot. "That was the best acting I've ever seen."

He responded with a coy smirk.

* * *

After shooting all the dialogue, it was time for the chase sequence. One of our favourite horror films was *Evil Dead 2*, so was decided to emulate the sequence where Ash was being chased through the woods, shooting from the perspective of the Redneck.

The rushes looked great.

Sam Raimi would have been proud.

The final shot of the sequence involved my character emerging from the treeline, at the foot of the cliffs. With nowhere left to run, he holds his head in despair, as the Inbred emerges behind him.

This is where it all went horribly wrong.

After the excitement of the chase, the script called for a sudden shift of tone, from action back to comedy. The result was incredibly jarring, especially when the two characters started about kebabs...

"I think we've let ourselves down a bit in that last scene," Chris admitted later, while we were editing.

"Sorry, mate," I replied. "It's my fault. I shouldn't have rushed the writing so much."

"Don't worry about it," he said. "It's still funny as fuck."

"Yeah," I agreed, "But it's a bit of step

backwards, filmmaking-wise...."

He rolled his eyes.

He couldn't understand why I was beating myself up about it.

"Relax," he said. "We'll get it right next time..."

CHAPTER 23:
THE BASTARD
SON

The script for The Bastard Son was nothing more than League of Gentleman fan fiction. Reverting to the format of a single scene sketch, it told the story of a conservative father's failed attempts to engage with his wayward son.

At the time of writing, the context was quite topical. According to the Mainstream Media, Britain was being terrorised by 'Hoodies' - gangs of feral kids who smoked drugs, stole cars, and attacked pensioners in the street - and *The Bastard Son* was my half-baked attempt at social commentary.

Craig wanted to play the part of the 'father', Nigel, which meant I would have to play the 'son',

Christopher. The contrast between the two roles was huge. Nigel was old school and traditional. He spoke with 1950's BBC accent, wore tweed, and saw the world through rose tinted lenses. Christopher was modern and cynical. He talked like a chav, swore profusely, had long hair and wore a cap.

The plot centred around Nigel's suggestion that they should go on holiday together, spend some time away, which would give them an opportunity to bond as father and son. When he discusses the plan with Christopher, his suggestion is met with a tirade of abuse.

I was quite happy with the first draft. It was much better than my previous stuff.

"This is quite deep," Craig said, after I'd emailed it over. "You've worked hard on this."

"Thanks," I replied.

It was my way of making up for the *City Boy* shitshow.

"Where are we going to film it?" he asked.

"We can do it round mine," I said. "We'll use Glen's room."

* * *

The next night, I picked up Craig and Della, then brought them back to mine, where we donned out costumes ready for the shoot.

"Are you sure your bro's cool with this?" Craig asked, before we began.

"Yeah," I replied. "I asked him last night."

I hadn't.

I'd totally forgot.

Not that it made any difference. He was out with his friends.

We started filming.

Once again, Craig nailed his character from the off, delivering the kind of polished performance that you'd expect to see on TV. I did my best to match his efforts but the gulf in class was obvious. He was much the better actor.

"You're blood great at acting," I gushed between takes. "How do you do it?"

"Natural talent," he replied.

"I wish I had some," I groaned.

"Don't be daft," he said. "You're doing ace."

"I feel like I'm letting you down," I said. "You're a different league to me."

He shook his head.

"You worry too much," he said.

We finished the scene then went to his dad's to do the editing. It didn't take long. Half an hour at the most.

He added it to the master.

"Another one done," Craig grinned.

"Yeah," I replied.

He could sense the consternation in my tone.

"What's up?" he asked.

"I'm worried about my acting," I sighed. "I can't do it."

"Yes you can," he laughed.

He scrubbed through the master and played a snippet from *Mrs. Crumpton.*

"See," he said, pointing at the screen. "You played her really well."

"Are you saying I should always cast myself as a woman?"

He gave me a grin.

"If the shoe fits..." he said.

CHAPTER 24:
OH, SHUT UP
CHARLIE!

Taking Craig's advice, I spent the next week penning a script involving a female character, who would be played by myself.

Drawing inspiration from *Bo Selecta!'s* Mel B, I created a hideous beast of a woman, named Rhonda. She was northern, foul mouthed, straight-talking, and very masculine.

It was a role I felt I could confidently play.

The film's plot centred around Rhonda's relationship with her husband, Charlie, a fat lazy slob, who spends his days watching football and drinking beer. One day, she comes home with her new boyfriend, an Eastern European immigrant named Savo, and throws Charlie out.

Because it felt like a soap-opera, I decided to finish the scene on a cliff-hanger.

Craig loved it the idea.

"If only we could pinch the drums from Eastenders," he said.

"Yeah," I laughed.

"So, I guess you're playing Rhonda then?" he said.

I gave him a nod.

"I've been practising the voice all week."

"Ok, let's hear it..."

I read a couple of the lines in my worst Yorkshire accent.

"Perfect," he said. "Sounds ace."

I smiled.

"I grew up watching *Sharpe*," I replied.

"So, who are we going to get to play Charlie?" he asked.

I looked at him, confused.

"I'd pencilled that role for you," I said.

"Nah," he replied, shaking his head. "I want to be Savo. He's got all the best lines."

He held up the script and began reading from the page.

"I iz... 'Ow do you say, needing zi sheet right now...."

I pissed myself.

"Bloody hell," I said. "You sound just like Borat!"

"Borat?" he replied.

"Yeah," I said. "From *Ali G*!"

He shook his head. He'd never watched it.

"Ok," I laughed. "So, who are you thinking?"

"I'm not sure," he replied. "Mittsy maybe?"

"Nah, I said. "He can't act."

"Allan, then?"

"He's moved to Liverpool," I said.

He scratched his chin, deep in thought. The obvious choice was Baz, but he was loathe to say it. The two of them had hardly spoke since *Banshee.*

"I suppose we could ask him?" I said.

"Yeah," Craig sighed. "I suppose we'll have to..."

"Are you sure?" I asked. "You're not worried he'll step on your shoes again?"

Craig chuckled defiantly.

"No chance of that," he said. "We're solid, me and you..."

He was right.

Our bond was strong.

We were close friends. We'd worked on ten films together. We'd even gotten to the point where each of us knew what the other was thinking. Even before we'd thought it, sometimes...

"... And if he does start taking over," he continued, "we'll tell him where to go..."

* * *

The following Saturday, we all met at mine

for the shoot.

Baz seemed excited to be involved again.

"I'm glad you invited me," he said, as he put on one of my dad's shirts to look the part. "You know much I love the 'old' acting."

"What do you think of the script?" I asked.

"I like it," he replied. "I've not remembered any of my lines though."

"It's ok," Craig said. "Della will prompt you at the start of each take."

I went upstairs, put on my wig, then squeezed into my new dress, which I'd bought from the charity shop during the week.

The women who worked there recognised me as soon as I'd stepped inside.

"Oooh," one said. "It's you again!"

"See, Shirley," her colleague shouted, "I told you he'd be back."

This time round, I'd played up their bigotry.

"Yes," I declared. "It's me, the transvestite. I've come for another dress. Something short and tight, to show off my figure."

It'd shut them up, good and proper.

I came downstairs and revealed myself to group.

"Bloody hell!" Baz laughed. "You don't half look sexy!"

"Yeah," Craig replied. "...Not sure about your legs though."

I looked down at my hairy knees.

"Do you think I should have a shave?" I said.

"Nah," Craig replied. "It'll ruin the effect..."

* * *

After setting up the scene in my dad's living room, Craig handed Della the camera then instructed her film a wide shot of Baz, sitting on the couch.

"I'll need a beer," he said. "It says in the script he's drinking."

I went to the garage and got him a can of Fosters, and he opened it up and began glugging it down.

"Not so fast," I said. "You need to be lucid."

"I'll be fine," he laughed. "I drink ten of these a night."

It probably wasn't an exaggeration.

"Ok," Craig said. "Let's do this."

He stood behind Della, looking over her shoulder into the viewfinder.

"There," he said. "That's the shot!"

She pressed record and filmed a few seconds of Baz supping his lager.

"Cut!" Craig called.

He shunted her to the left.

"Now film the door to watch us come in."

I followed him into the hall and shut the door. For some reason I started having flashback of the of the scene I'd done with Knackers for *Brothers in Blood*.

We stood in silence, waiting for 'Action'.

But it never came.

Craig opened the door.

"Everything ok?" he asked.

Della nodded.

"Yeah, I'm filming," she said.

"You need to call, 'Action'," he replied.

He stepped back then closed the door.

"Action," Della squeaked.

It was barely audible.

"Was that 'action'?" I said.

Craig shook his head.

Della squeaked again. Again, it was barely audible.

After waiting a couple of seconds, Baz boomed 'Action' at the top of his voice, immediately corpsing into a fit of laughter.

Oh god, I thought.

It was happening again...

"Hey," Craig yelled, "Stop fucking around. We'll start again. Della, speak up."

We stepped outside and shut the door.

This time, Della shouted 'Action' loudly. I breathed a sigh of relief, then opened the door and said my first line.

* * *

Things progressed smoothly, only stopping the once, when my dad returned home with the shopping.

I was shocked by his reaction to what

I was wearing. In my head, I'd pictured him looking disappointed, shaking his head, before disowning me in front of my mates... But instead, he was completely non-plussed.

"Dad," I said, as he carried his bags of shopping into the kitchen. "I'm wearing a dress."

"Yes, I know," he replied. "Very nice."

It drew a fit of giggles from Baz and Craig.

"He thinks you're gay," Baz laughed.

"I've heard that one before," I replied.

* * *

After we'd wrapped, I drove everyone home. We talked about the shoot on the way.

"I've really loved it, today, guys," Baz said, happily. "I can't wait to do the next one."

"Me neither," Craig said. "You did well."

It seemed the hatchet had been well and truly buried.

I was happy with Baz being back in the fold. Though I'd previously shared Craig's concerns that he was a bit of a control freak, I loved what he brought to the table. He'd always been a funny guy. Comedy suited him. Some of his mannerisms were hilarious, and his timing was always spot on. Audiences warmed to him too. When the tape of *Hunted* was circulating around the University, people often commented on the guy playing the werewolf.

And why wouldn't they.

He was a natural lead.

* * *

I mentioned it to Craig during the edit.

"You're right," he agreed. "He's definitely got the X-Factor."

"How do you feel about that?" I asked.

"It doesn't bother me," he shrugged. "I prefer playing the antagonists, anyway... They're much juicier roles."

He then quoted one his lines from *City Boy*.

Straight away, I got what he meant.

As I watched him arrange the clips in the timeline, I wondered what it would mean for me? If Baz would play the face and Craig, the heel, going forward, what would I do? Would I be pushed to the side? Consigned to writing, and nothing else?

It hoped not.

I liked acting.

Even though I was bad at it.

CHAPTER 25: FRUITY ALLEGATIONS

After a few days of anguished contemplation, I decided that if I had no future in front of the camera, I'd make myself more useful behind it.

Without further ado, I went to Waterstones and looked for books on filmmaking. Two titles immediately stood out: *The Guerrilla Filmmakers' Handbook*, which gave advice on how to make films on a microbudget, and *Shot-by-Shot*, which focused on directing.

I purchased both.

As soon as I got home, I started reading *Shot-By-Shot*. After finishing the first chapter, which was about common filmmaking mistakes, I knew I'd made the right choice. I couldn't help but chuckle to myself when it talked about *breaking the line*, remembering what had happened on *Brothers in Blood*.

The more I read, the more it resonated.

We'd made so many mistakes...

I put on the tape of our films, then re-watched them with a critical eye. I jotted down each error I spotted on a notepad. After watching all eleven, I'd listed over 300 mistakes.

I shook my head in despair.

How could we have been so careless?

The reason was obvious.

We'd not known any better.

I cursed the fact I'd not bought this book sooner. It would have saved us so much time and hassle.

I always knew our films looked crappy.

But now I knew why...

It was a Eureka moment.

* * *

The subsequent chapters outlined photographic techniques, like shot composition and framing. I learned the correct dimensions for extreme close-ups, close-ups, medium close-ups, two-shots, wides, reverse angles, tracking shots, POVs; how to use the rule of thirds to frame a subject, how to maintain continuity by using over-the-shoulder shots, how it's ok to lose someone's forehead but not their chin...

Once I'd digested it all, I phoned Craig and asked him if I could shoot and direct the next project. After telling him about the book and what I had learned, he agreed.

"Go for it," he said. "Make me look sexy."

"I'll try my best," I replied.

I looked through some of the scripts I'd written during my 'golden' age. I'd filed them all away in a folder, which I'd indexed by date. I'd printed them all and stored them there for posterity... Even the ones that were impossible to film.

Among them was a script called, *Fruity Allegations*, which told the story of woman who was being investigated by the council, after a complaint had been made by one of her neighbours that she was using her house as a brothel.

It was a funny script, but we'd never shot it because we needed a girl to play the part of Mrs. Slaithwaite.

Normally, this would have been the end of it, but since Craig had brought back Baz, and was thus now open to the prospect of casting other people, I decided to push the boat out and look for an actress.

The only girl that came to mind was Mary, a girl I knew from college who'd done a couple of terms at drama school. She lived locally too, just around the corner.

After obtaining her number from a mutual

friend, I gave her a call and asked her if she fancied being in a film.

"Bloody hell, yeah!" she replied. "I'd love to. I bloody love acting, I do. It's something I've always been into... I bloody love it... It's great."

"Ok," I said. "We're gonna be filming something next week. Can I send you the script?"

"Yeah, yeah, yeah," she replied. "I'll do anything, me. Anything at all. What shall I wear? I've got all sorts of clothes; old ones, new ones, vintage, modern... Shoes too, I've got the lot. What kind of look do you want to go for?"

"Just normal house wear," I said. "You'll be playing a woman who's been accused of running a brothel."

"A madam?"

She laughed hysterically down the phone.

"That sounds great!" she continued. "What kind of accent do you want? Is she well-to-do, or a bit of a scrubber? I can do either, or both if you want... I'm good at accents, me..."

I found it little hard to keep up with what she was saying. She talked so fast, hardly pausing for breath.

"You can interpret the role however you like," I said.

I didn't really mean it.

I'd written the character in a particular way. The accent, mannerisms, etc., were all clearly discernible from the text.

"Great!" she said. "I love doing characters.

I'll see you next week then!"

"See ya," I replied.

"Ta-rar, ta-rar, ta-rar...."

I hung up the phone feeling incredibly tired.

As lovely as she was, she was hard work.

I wondered what I'd let myself in for...

* * *

The following week, I picked up Craig for the shoot.

"Where's Marie?" he asked, as he got in the car.

"I thought I'd get you first," I replied.

"Why?" he asked. "I thought you said lived around the corner from you?"

"She does," I replied. *...But I want to give you a heads-up before you meet her.*

Craig read my thoughts.

"So, what's wrong with her?" he asked. "Is she weird?"

"No," I said. "Just a bit... Fretty."

"Fretty?"

"Yeah," I said. "She talks as if she's on Speed."

He scoffed.

"So, she talks fast, then?"

"Really fast," I said.

He shook his head.

"I don't get you sometimes," he said. "You worry about everything..."

* * *

We arrived at Mary's house, and I beeped the horn. Her front door opened, and she raced out to the car, clutching a couple of carrier bags.

"All right Dom," she said, excitedly, as she got into the back seat. "I couldn't decide what to wear so I just brought everything. Could you have a look at it when we stop, to see what's best?"

"Hi Mary," Craig said. "I'm Craig."

"Oh, hi Craig," she said. "Thanks so much for letting me do this! I've always been into acting, me... I went to drama school too. I only did one term, but I loved it. I've always wanted to be an actress. It's the one thing in the world I've always wanted to be. I hear you're an actor too... Have long have you been into it? Years, like me, or is it just a recent thing?"

I glanced at Craig, who gave me a knowing smile.

* * *

When we got back to mine, Mary emptied her bags onto the sofa and began sifting through the items.

"What do you think of this?" she said, holding up a black and white frock.

Craig shook his head.

"Too mumsy," he said. "You're a madam, not

a granny."

She started laughing.

"Oh yeah," she giggled, "I get what you're saying!"

She put the dress into the bag, then grabbed another item from the pile.

"What about this then?"

She held up a dirty brown dressing gown.

"Yeah, that'll do," Craig said.

I got the impression he didn't really care.

"What about underneath?" Mary replied. "I've got a couple of nighties in here..."

She turned to the pile.

"Anything white or cream," I said. "We'll need a bit of contrast."

I looked at Craig.

"For the colour balance..." I bullshitted.

He shrugged his shoulders.

"Whatever floats your boat..."

* * *

An hour later, we were ready to start.

While Craig and Mary had been getting into their costumes, I'd been playing around the camcorder, to familiarise myself with the functions and settings. I'd learned a lot from the book and wanted to put it into practice.

"Ok," Craig said, once they were ready to go. "What are we doing?"

He was his way of telling me that I was in

charge, and that it was time for me to step up to the plate.

I suddenly felt incredibly nervous.

"R-right," I stuttered, trying my best to sound confident. "We'll shoot everything chronologically, starting with the scene at the door."

"Cool," Craig said.

He gave me a nod, then led us into the hall, where he opened the front door and stepped outside.

"Where do you want me?" Mary said.

"Just here, while I set up the shot," I said, pointing to the floor at my feet.

She moved to her mark, and I pointed the lens over her shoulder at Craig. Once I was happy with the framing, I told Mary to step back then walk into shot after Craig rang the bell.

"Cool," she said, moving back.

"You all right mate?" Craig asked.

He could tell I was shitting myself.

I gave him an anxious nod and he stepped backwards into the porch then closed the door.

"Ok, rolling..." I said, pressing record. "...Action!"

The bell rang.

Mary walked into shot then opened the door.

Craig said his first line.

"Cut!" I said.

I'd got it.

A wave of relief rolled over me.

"How did it look, mate?" Craig asked.

"Good," I said, grinning like a cat. "Really good."

He gave me a smile.

"Cool," he said. "Now do it 99 more times, and we'll have ourselves a film..."

* * *

99 shots later, we finally wrapped.

The shoot had taken longer than usual, but it didn't matter. We'd got all the shots we needed, and they all looked nice.

Craig's acting had once again been excellent. He'd played his part well. Mary had been good too. She also been incredibly professional throughout.

After dropping her off, I asked Craig what he'd thought of her.

"She's a bit 'stage school' for my liking," he said. "But I thought she did a good job. I'd definitely work with her again."

"Me too," I said. "And I totally get your point about the stage school thing."

It had been quite noticeable. She'd clearly been trained to project her voice when reading her lines, as if she were performing on stage.

"Maybe next time we could ask her to tone it down a bit?" I said.

Craig chuckled.

"I don't think that'll be possible," he laughed.

* * *

The following night, we started the edit. I was really excited to see how the footage would look after it had been transferred, and I watched with glee as each of the thumbnails appeared in the timeline.

"This looks ace," Craig said, as he started cutting the clips. "You've done a good job on this. It looks professional."

"Thanks," I said.

I was happy that he liked it.

I was also happy because it kept me in a job.

"It'll be even better once we sort out the lighting," I said.

"No one ever notices that..." Craig sniffed. "As long as people can see what's going on and aren't being distracted by random shit, they don't care..."

Yeah, but I do...

A few hours later, Craig transferred the finished film onto the master tape, and we went round his to watch it on his big telly.

The difference in quality to our previous films was stark. Though we'd still had problems with lighting and sound, there was a marked improvement in the look and feel.

"I can imagine seeing this being on telly,"

Craig said. "It's as least as good as anything you see on ITV."

We'd often taken the piss out of ITV shows like *The Grimleys* or *Men Behaving Badly*. We hated the way cast members shouted out their lines like everyone was deaf, or how the editors would add a laughter track, even when the jokes weren't funny. We also disliked their lack of edge when it came to comedy. Everything they put out was so safe and innocent, as if they were desperate not to offend.

It was one of the reasons we loved *League of Gentlemen*. It was modern and fresh, and the writers focused on what was funny, rather than what would draw the fewest complaints.

When the credits started rolling, Craig asked me what we were doing next.

"I dunno," I replied. "I've still got a few old scripts knocking around..."

"What about *Deadly Deceit*?" he said. "I'm sure we could give that a go now?"

It was an idea we'd explored during one of our early brainstorming sessions. The plot centred around a murderous Gasman, who uses his position to get into the homes of his victims. We'd mothballed it because the lead role was female, and we didn't know any girls.

"I'll dig it out," I said.

"Cool," he replied. "Give Mary a call, too. Ask her if she's up for it..."

CHAPTER 26:
DEADLY DECEIT

When I got home, I looked inside my folder for the script. To my horror, it wasn't there.

Where had it got to?

I pawed through all the papers several times but still I couldn't find it.

Had I binned it by accident?

Rather than tell Craig the bad news, I jumped on my computer and re-wrote it from memory.

Later that night, I'd completed the first draft.

To my relief, it was much better than the original. Before I'd even started, I knew Craig would want to play the role of killer, so with him in mind I expanded his part to include a monologue where he describes his motive.

"I'm an artist," it went. "But no one likes traditional stuff anymore. These days, you need to shock.... And nothing will shock more, my dear, than the sight of your pretty-little head, spinning around in a washing machine!"

I pictured him saying it, chewing over the line with a gleeful malice. In many ways, he was a writer's dream. Talented, versatile, professional... He could play part and hardly ever messed up his lines.

Writing for Mary was much tougher. I didn't know what she was capable of, so I kept her part pretty much the same.

We'd pencilled in the shoot for the following weekend, so I emailed her the script and asked if she'd be interested. Sadly, she unavailable.

"Sorry, I'm going to the zoo with Dave," she wrote back. "But I'll be free in a couple of weeks..."

It wasn't the response I expected.

To be honest, it slightly annoyed me.

I'd gone out of way to cast her in *Fruity Allegations*. Now she was ditching me for a stupid Elephant.

I started composing a reply, telling her that she didn't cancel her plans, her part would be recast...

But I never sent it.

I just went ahead and recast her anyway.

During my time at University, I'd befriended a girl on my course named Becky.

After watching the tape of *Bite* and *Hunted* (before it AWOL in Selly Oak), she'd asked me if she could be in the next one. At the time, I'd told her I wasn't doing films anymore...

But things were different now.

I got out my phone, called her up and asked if she was free on the weekend.

"Why?" she replied, lazily.

For some reason, she always sounded tired...

"Wanna be in a film?" I asked.

"A film?" she replied. "What, like *Bite* and *Hunted*?"

I was impressed that she'd remembered their titles.

"Not quite," I said. "We've moved on a bit from then."

"Oh...." she groaned.

For some strange reason she sounded disappointed.

"Don't worry," I said. "It'll still be a laugh. How do you fancy playing a girl who gets her head chopped off by a serial killer?"

She started giggling down the phone.

"You know, Dom," she replied. "I've waited all my life for someone to ask me that..."

* * *

After securing Becky's services, I called Craig to give him a sit-rep.

"Mary can't do it," I said, "But don't worry, I've got someone else."

"Who?"

"Her name's Becky," I replied. "I went to Uni with her."

"What does she look like?"

"Slim, blonde, tiny ass," I began.

"Does she look like a hag?"

"No," I replied. "Just a little bit sleepy."

"Can she act?"

"No idea, mate," I replied. "But she's willing to give it a try."

I heard him sighing on the other end of the line.

"I hope she's decent, mate," he said. "I'd fed up of with working with amateurs."

I couldn't help but grin.

He was turning into a real thespian.

"I'll do some work with her during the week," I replied. "I'll take the script round to her and help her with her lines."

"I'll come with," he said. "I'd like to meet her beforehand, so I know what I'm working with."

"Cool," I said. "You free on Thursday?"

* * *

On Thursday evening, I printed three copies of the script, picked up Craig, then drove over to Selly Oak, parking as near as I could to Becky's bedsit.

Craig wasn't impressed with the locale.

"It's fucking horrible around here," he remarked, as we walked down Dawlish Road. "Proper dingy!"

"Student living," I remarked.

"I'm glad I was never a student..." he scoffed.

It was a lie. I'm sure he'd have loved it.

We rocked up at her door then rang the bell. Her housemate, Jay, answered.

"Hi guys," he said. "Come inside."

He held open the door and beckoned us in.

"Becky told me the two of you are filmmakers," he said, as we made our way down the hall to the living room.

"That's right," Craig answered.

"What a coincidence," he replied. "I'm an actor."

"You're an actor?" I said, as we sat ourselves down on the couch. "How come you never mentioned it before?"

"It never came up," he replied.

He shouted up the stairs to Becky.

"Becky, you're friends are here."

"Coming," she replied.

Jay looked at us and smiled.

"She's just doing her face..."

He took a seat opposite us.

"So, what kind of acting have you done?" Craig asked. "Stage work?"

"A little," Jay replied, smugly. "But I've also

done some film. I had a speaking role in *Heartbeat* last year. It was only line, but the experience alone was priceless."

"Have you seen *Bite* and *Hunted*?" Craig said.

"Yes," Jay replied. "Very humorous, both of them."

Craig smiled.

He'd always been a sucker for praise.

"Maybe we can give you a role in this?" he replied, nudging me in the ribs.

"I suppose I can write you in," I said. "I'll have to create a new character though."

"That'd be great," Jay replied. "And you're filming on Saturday, right?"

I nodded.

"Whereabouts?"

Before I could respond, Becky staggered down the stairs. She was wearing a dressing gown and looked half asleep.

"Hi," she said, weakly. "Sorry, I was just having a nap."

"Yeah, looks like it," Craig chuckled.

He'd never known subtlety.

Her lips parted into an upside-down grin. She wasn't frowning, it was just the way she smiled.

"I'm anaemic," she said. "I've got low iron."

"Are you narcoleptic, too?" Craig laughed.

Becky giggled.

She appeared oblivious to his insults.

"Do either you want a coffee?" Jay asked.

"She does," Craig grinned.

Becky laughed out loud. She was loving it.

"Yes please," I said. "Two sugars for me."

"And six for her," Craig said.

Becky clutched her sides. She was laughing so hard, it looked like she was dying.

"Oh god," she tittered... "I can't breathe."

She stood with her hand against the wall, trying to compose herself.

Craig gave me a nudge.

"I like her," he whispered. "She gets me..."

* * *

After Jay had brought us our drinks, Becky sat down and began flicking through the script.

"Is this it?" she said.

"Yeah," I said.

"But it's only nine pages..."

"It's a short film," Jay explained, sipping his latte.

"It generally works out to be around 60 second a page," Craig explained, "so with the titles and credits, it'll be about ten minutes long."

Becky hummed and nodded.

"Shall we do a read-through?" I said.

"Ok," she replied, nervously.

"We open we a shot of a regular house on a street," I began, reading from the page. "A man dressed in overalls approaches the front door. He rings the bell, and a few seconds later, a woman answers..."

I waited for Becky to read her line.

"Becky?" Craig said. "That's you."

"Oh sorry," she laughed. "You want me to read it out?"

"That's the idea," he replied. "It'd be a pretty crap read-through otherwise..."

She giggled, then read her line.

"Hello," she said, plainly. "

"Hello," Craig replied, sliding into character. "I'm Allan Parsons."

I'd decided to give the serial killer Allan's name for a laugh, an in-joke that only we would understand.

"She gives him a pensive look," I continued. "She's unaware of who he is..."

"...I'm from the Gas Board," Craig said.

Becky scrunched up her face.

"How come she doesn't know who he is?" she said. "Isn't he wearing. uniform?"

"He's in overalls," I said.

"Yeah, but don't they usually have a logo on them? Like *British Gas?*"

"He doesn't work for *British Gas*," I said. "He's a serial killer. He's just posing as a Gasman to get inside the house."

"So why would I let him in?" she asked.

"Because he says he's from the Gas Board..." Craig replied.

"So, I'm not expecting him?" Becky said.

"No," he said. "Like Dom said, he's really a

serial killer. He doesn't actually work for *British Gas*."

"...Or any other company," I added.

Becky hummed.

"But if I'm not expecting him, why would I let him in? Wouldn't I just tell him he's got the wrong house?"

I shook my head in despair.

"Gas men don't book ahead to check people's meters," I explained. "They just turn up."

"Dom's right," Jay remarked. "They don't give you in advanced warning. We had one come round here last week."

"Really?" Becky said. "Was I in at the time?"

"Yeah," Jay replied. "But you were asleep."

"Oh," Becky said. "Sorry... It just doesn't seem right to me that a Gasman would turn up announced..."

"Ok," I said. "It may not seem right for you, but it does to your character..."

Becky laughed.

"So, my character's stupid then?"

"Yes," Craig replied. "Very."

"Oh, okay..."

I immediately felt queasy. Was she going to be like this for every line in the script? I'd come here to a do a read-through, not be ripped apart.

"Shall we carry on?" I asked.

Becky nodded, then picked up from where we'd left off. Thankfully, there were no further comments.

When we were finished, I asked her what she thought.

"Yeah," she said. "I like it. It sounds like it's gonna be a lot of fun. Do I need to learn all the lines for Saturday?"

"Yes," I replied. "But wait until I send you the revised script tomorrow night. I'm adding a scene a start between you and Jay."

Becky turned to her housemate and smiled.

"So, you're gonna be in it too?" she said.

"Yes," Jay replied. "The guys have kindly agreed to accommodate me."

"We just don't know how, just yet," Craig said. "But we'll think of something."

He gave me a nudge.

"Yeah," I said. "He'll probably play your husband or boyfriend or something... We'll figure something out."

"Great," Becky said. "And where are we filming it?"

"At my house, in Rowley," I replied. "Are you ok to get there for 10am on Saturday?"

"Oh," she said. "There might be a problem with that..."

"Why?" I asked.

"My car's off the road... It failed its MOT."

"What about you?" Craig said to Jay. "Do you have a car?"

"Sadly, not," he replied.

Shit, I thought.

"No worries," I sighed. "I'll pick you up in

the morning then drop you off afterwards... But you'll both need to be ready for 9am."

"I don't get up until 9:30," Becky gasped.

"Why doesn't that surprise me?" Craig snorted.

"Guys," Jay said, leaning forward. "This may sound a little crazy but, err, why don't we just film it here?"

"Huh?" I responded.

"...I mean, this is a house isn't it? We've got a hall, a living room, a kitchen, a washing machine... Pretty much everything you need."

"What do you think?" Craig said to me.

"Yeah," I said. "But I'll need to see the kitchen, first."

"Sure," Becky said. "It's this way."

She led me into the kitchen, which was attached to the rear of the house. The room was long, narrow and dark. All the utensils and appliances were old and knackered, including the washing machine, which stood beside the sink.

"What do you think?" she asked.

It was perfect.

It was better than perfect.

"Yeah," I said. "This'll work."

"Great," she replied. "No early start!"

* * *

On the way home, Craig and I discussed

how we would shoehorn in a role for Jay.

"I think him being her husband is way too obvious," Craig said. "He needs to be something else, like her brother or cousin..."

"If that's the case," I replied. "Then why would he be at her house?"

"People see their families, Dom," he scoffed. "It's not beyond the pale."

"Yeah," I said. "But he can't just be there randomly. There's got to be a reason... Otherwise, it's just contrived."

"Fine," Craig said. "It's her birthday, and he's brought her a card. Then he leaves, just as I arrive."

"Ok," I said. "So, why's that important to the story?"

Craig shrugged his shoulders.

"He needs to be there for a reason," I said. "Something that links his visit to the wider the plot... Maybe to explain why she's all alone?"

"I've got it," Craig said. "He's coming round to console her."

"Why?" I asked.

Craig's eyes lit up.

"Because her husband just divorced her. He left her for someone else, and she's all cut up about it."

I hummed.

"Or maybe it's the other way round?" I said. "Maybe *she's* the one who divorced him?"

"Ahh," Craig replied. "I see where you're

going.... She's all like, 'hey girlfriend, I don't need a man', and her brother's like, 'yes you do, you're a woman...''

"Mmm..." I said. "Isn't that a bit sexist?"

"Yeah," he replied. "So?"

I thought about it for a moment. In terms of the narrative, it made a lot of sense. It would create a natural conflict between Becky and Jay's characters; a conflict that could lead to an argument, which would see him storming out of the house at the end of the first scene. On a deeper level, it would also explain why her character chooses to let a stranger into her house. If she thinks she's independent and untouchable, it naturally followed that she was the kind of person who would take unnecessary risks.

"Ok," I said. "I can work with that."

* * *

On Saturday morning, I picked up Craig and we drove over to Selly Oak for the shoot.

Jay answered the door. He seemed bright and bushy-tailed; ready to go.

But Becky was nowhere to be seen.

"Where's Sleeping Beauty?" Craig asked.

"She's still in the process of waking up," Jay replied.

"Why am I not surprised?" he sniffed.

Jay led us inside then made us drinks

while we waited for Becky to emerge from her protracted slumber. Ten minutes later she came downstairs, looking like she'd woke up on the wrong side of the bed.

"Hi guys," she said sleepily. "Is there any chance I could have a coffee before we start? I'm so tired."

"Yeah," Craig said, looking her up and down. "Maybe even two."

She responded with a giggle.

Why did she find him so funny?

This time, he wasn't even joking.

After drinking our drinks, we made a start. The shoot went well, running smoothly from start to finish. Becky's acting skills weren't the best, but they were fair enough to support another virtuoso performance from Craig, whose skilled were praised by Jay.

"Are you sure you've not had any training?" I overheard him ask.

"None at all," Craig replied. "It's all natural."

I couldn't help but smile.

How many times had I heard him say that?

* * *

After wrapping up, we drove back to Cradley to work on the edit. I was less nervous about this time. I was still riding high from the success of *Fruity Allegations*.

When we arrived at Colin's house, we

found him working in his studio on a Lenticular photograph.

"Sorry boys," he said, as we walked in. "But the studio's out of bounds."

"But we've got footage that needs editing," Craig replied.

"You'll have to wait until I'm finished. I'm busy."

"How long you gonna be? Craig asked.

"A few days," came the reply.

The colour drained from Craig's face.

"A few days!?" he exclaimed. "But we need to edit now."

Colin shook his head.

"The world doesn't revolve around you, son," he said. "If you're that desperate, maybe you should buy your own PC?"

Craig huffed.

"I've just bought a house," he rasped. "I'm up to my eyeballs in debt."

Colin ignored him.

"It's ok, mate," I said. "We'll figure something out."

We left the room and went back to the car.

"Bloody Lenticular photographs!" Craig fumed. "What's the point of them!"

I didn't know what to say.

I didn't even know what a Lenticular Photograph was.

"I wish we had our own bloody studio," he snorted. "Then we wouldn't have to put up with this kind of crap..."

He seemed genuinely upset.

"Maybe we can?" I said.

He turned and looked at me.

"What do you mean?"

"I've got some money," I said. "A couple of grand."

"How have you managed to save that?" he asked.

"I don't have a mortgage for one," I replied. "And because I still live at home, I don't pay rent. And because I spend all my time making films, I don't go out."

Chris laughed.

"Well, it looks like we're back in business!"

"Yeah," I replied. "The only thing is, I've got no idea what to buy..."

CHAPTER 27:
ONCE YOU
GO MAC...

T he next day, we paid a visit to PC World, to buy a computer. Not knowing where to start, I asked one of the sales assistants for advice.

"Excuse me," I said. "I'm looking to buy a PC. Can you help me?"

The man shook his head.

"I'm SDAs, mate. Bryan's the compo guy."

He pointed to a bloke who was standing at the other end of the store.

"Thanks," I said.

We walked over to him.

"Are you Bryan?" I asked.

The man nodded.

"We want to buy a PC," Craig said. "Your

mate told us we need to speak to you."

He gestured towards the SDA guy.

"Jit?" he scoffed. "*He's* not my mate..."

I don't care, I thought. *Just sell me a bloody PC...*

"Listen, we're in a rush," Craig said. "Can you help us or not?"

"Yeah, I suppose," he sighed, scratching his chin lazily "... What do you need it for?"

"Filmmaking," I replied. "We're filmmakers."

"Video, then?" the man said. "You'll probably be wanting a Mac, then, not a PC..."

"What's the difference?" I said.

The man blew out his cheeks.

"They're like chalk and cheese, mate," the man replied. "...And to be honest, I don't know much about them. Phil might, though. He's got one. He's always banging on about how good they are..."

"Who's Phil?" I asked.

"The Mac Guy," Bryan replied. "But he's not here now. His shift starts at 1pm."

I glanced at my watch.

It was 12:30.

"Maccy Dees?" Craig suggested.

I gave him a nod.

"We'll be back later," I said.

* * *

We popped over the road to the drive-thru McDonalds, where Craig ordered two big macs, large fries, and a strawberry milkshake. I ordered a Happy Meal... Without the toy.

"It's like being back at college," Craig beamed, as we carried our food to the table.

"Yeah," I replied.

"So, do you reckon that 'Phil' guy will be helpful?" he asked, munching into his first burger.

"I hope so," I replied. "I've never used a Mac before."

"Me neither," Craig said. "But they look nice..."

After finishing our food, we returned to the store, asked to see Phil, and we were directed to the Mac counter, at the other end of the shop, where several iMacs were on display. Each of them was white. They all looked very futuristic.

Pottering amongst them was a bald, stocky man, who looked like he's just been released from prison.

"Hi, are you Phil?" I asked him.

"I am," he replied. "Are you the bloke who's looking to buy a Mac?"

"I was told it was good for filmmaking," I said.

He smiled broadly, revealing a set of golden crowns.

"You've come to the right place."

He gestured towards the computers.

"Any one of these little babies will sort you out."

He led us over to one of the counters. Upon it stood one of the machines. Its design was bizarre. I'd never seen anything like it.

Its base was egg-shaped and white, and attached to its paper-thin screen with what appeared to be a silver stork.

"This is the new iMac," he said proudly. "Best home computer that money can buy."

"Where's the CD player?" Craig asked.

The man pushed the Eject button on its pure-white keyboard. Something whirred then a CD tray emerged from a hidden slot in the base.

"Cool!" Craig said.

He seemed impressed.

"How does it work for filmmaking?" I asked.

"Easy," the man said.

He dragged the mouse to the bottom of the screen then clicked an icon that looked like a video camera.

"iMovie," he said. "Best editing software in the world."

The program loaded, showing a split screen with a grey background. The left-hand panel contained thumbnails of video clips. The right was blank. Beneath it was a timeline and a scrub-bar.

"I've made a little demo for the customers," he said. "Watch this."

He dragged the cursor onto one of the clips, then dragged it onto the timeline. The clip appeared in the right-hand panel. He then repeated the process with three more clips.

It all looked incredibly easy.

"Looks simple," I said.

"Yeah," he replied, "It is."

He clicked the 'play' button beneath the right-hand panel, and the clips began to play one after the other.

"How do you cut the clips?" Craig asked.

"Like this," the man replied.

He selected one of the clips and it appeared in the right-hand panel. He then hovered the mouse beneath the square, then started dragging it to the left. A yellow bar appeared, bookended by two square blocks.

"That's the part of the clip I want to keep," he said, pointing to the yellow bar. "To get rid of the chaff, all I need to do is this..."

He moved the mouse to the Menu Bar, clicked Edit, then selected the option 'TRIM CLIP'.

At once, the two sections either side of the blocks disappeared.

"There you go," he said. "Easy as that."

"Fuck me," Craig said. "We've been doing things the hard way..."

"How do you import footage?" I asked.

He turned the base unit around and pointed to a port at the back.

"Firewire," he said. "You connect it directly

to your camcorder and it transfers the files."

"Does it take SVHS?" Craig said.

The man sniffed.

"Analogue?" he scoffed. "Why would you need that in this day and age? No, this is all digital."

I glanced at Craig, who pursed his lips.

"So, we're gonna need a digital camcorder then?" I said.

"Yeah, if you want to use a Mac," Phil replied.

I sighed.

"I'm guessing you sell them too?"

"Yeah, we do," he grinned.

"What kind of price am I looking at, for the lot?"

"Well, it's £1500 for the iMac, £450-ish, for the camcorder, and another £30 for the cable, so all-in-all, around two grand."

My heart skipped a beat.

"Two grand?" I said.

The man nodded.

"Filmmaking isn't a cheap mate..."

I glanced at Craig, who responded with a shrug.

"All right," I said to Phil. "We'll have a look at the cameras, then come back for the Mac."

"Lovely jubbly," he said. "See you shortly."

We went over to the camcorder section and started talking to one of the assistants.

"We're looking to buy a camera," I said.

"...Something around the £450 price mark," Craig added.

"Yeah," I sniffed. "What's best?"

The man pointed to one of the shelves, casually.

"All the low-end shit's there," he said. "If you want good a picture, go for Sony; if you want good sound, go Panasonic. You won't get both for less than a grand..."

He turned around and walked away.

I got the impression he didn't give a fuck.

"Come on," Craig said. "Let's see what they've got."

After twenty minutes of hard browsing, we decided to go with a Panasonic. It was tiny, a fraction of the size of Craig's camera. It also had a screen that could be flipped out, meaning you didn't need to look through the viewfinder.

I began playing with one of the demo models that were sitting above the boxes.

"What do you think of it?" Craig asked.

"Fantastic," I said. "It's so light... "

We grabbed one that was in a box then took it back to Phil, who was waiting for us with the computer and Firewire cable.

"You've found one then?" he said.

"Yeah," I replied. "A Panasonic."

"Nice," he replied. "You'll need some DV Tapes for that, too. They sell them by the till."

"Bloody hell," I sighed, glancing at Craig. "Now I'm as skint as you..."

CHAPTER 28:
WHAT THE FUCK
ARE YOU DOING
IN THE SUN?

After spending my life's savings, we went back to mine and cleared a space on the bedroom desk. Chris then started playing with the video camera while I opened the box containing the Mac.

"Fuck me, this thing's heavy," I said, as I lugged it onto the countertop.

"Yeah," I know," he replied. "I weighed a ton when I was carrying it to the car..."

Inside was an instruction sheet, containing a series of images showing you what to do. There were no written instructions.

"Look at this," I said. "No manual."

"How very post-modern," he replied.

I assembled all the pieces accordingly, then turned it on. Seconds later, the base unit emitted a warm tone, and a series of questions appeared on -screen, asking me who I was, where I lived, and what language I spoke. It also asked me for my home internet details, which I skipped because it was 2003 and broadband had yet to be invented.

After filling in my answers, the desktop appeared.

"Here we go," I said to Craig.

I glanced to my right and saw him pointing the camera at my face.

"What are you doing?" I asked.

"Documenting the moment," he chuckled. "This is a momentous day in the history of Shadowbright. We finally have all the tools we need to make our own shit."

It was true.

We were free now.

Free to film, edit, and produced anything we wanted without having to rely on Colin.

"Shall we try importing some footage?" I said.

Craig stopped the tape, then handed over the camera.

"We'll that cable thing," I said.

He reached into the bag, handed it over, and I connected it to the base unit. The movie making software then launched automatically, and a message appeared on-screen

DO YOU WANT TO IMPORT YOUR VIDEO?

"I think that's a 'yes'," Craig said.

I clicked the button, and the footage he'd just shot began to transfer.

"Fuck me," I said. "Is this for real?"

Craig chuckled.

"I know," he said. "It's almost too easy, isn't it?"

A minute later, all the clips were transferred, each one appearing as a thumbnail in the left-hand side of the screen.

"Ok," I said. "Let's start the edit..."

I dragged the clips into the timeline then began cropping them down using the yellow bar.

The whole process took less than thirty seconds.

"Jesus," I exclaimed. "It's so fast."

"It is," Craig agreed. "And it changes everything."

I couldn't disagree.

It felt as if we'd stepped into a whole new era.

* * *

We spent the next hour experimenting with the software, adding titles, credits, etc., but we were most impressed by the FX options that could be applied to the clips, such as 'reverse footage' and 'slow-motion'.

"This is so cool," Craig said. "Imagine if we had this sort of stuff for *Bite* and *Hunted*?"

"I know," I said. "It would have been ace..."

"Why don't we film something now?" he said. "Something short to properly test it out?"

"Yeah," I replied. "Why not?"

We came up with an idea for a sketch then went downstairs to film it. The plot was simple and straightforward, telling the story of a man who goes ape shit after finding out his wife is moonlighting as a Page 3 girl.

I started things off with a wide-angle of Craig on the chair, holding a copy of *The Sun*. When he turned the page, I cut to a reverse angle of the page. I then cut to a close-up of his face to show his reaction.

"My wife!" he rasped. "She told me she had the flu!"

We then cut to a shot of Craig in the hall, on the phone.

"It's me, bitch," he began. "I wanna speak to my whore of a wife.... Put her on now, motherfucker!"

All the dialogue was ad-libbed.

As you can probably tell...

"Linda," he growled. "You told me you had the flu! What the fuck are you doing in *The Sun*?"

I crash-zoomed into a close-up.

"I had big plans for you, bitch," he continued. "But not anymore, you vile, egregious cunt..."

This was where the film should have ended, but Craig decided to add a surprise twist.

Without warning, he gurned into the lens.

"Wrong number?" he said. "Oh... Sorry mom."

I pissed myself laughing.

"Fuck me, dude," I said, pausing the tape. "Where did that come from?"

"I dunno," he laughed. "It just popped in my head."

* * *

Without further ado, we ran upstairs and began transferring the clips. Ten minutes later, the whole thing was edited.

I was really pleased with how it looked. The digital image was much sharper than the SVHS we'd used on previous projects. The sound too, was much crisper, less hissy.

"Let's add some music," Craig said.

I handed him my little electronic keyboard and he spent a couple of minutes composing a ditty for the intro.

"Ok," he said. "I'm done. Let's record it."

Just above the clips pane was a microphone icon, which allowed you to add a voiceover track.

I clicked it and Craig began playing his tune.

When he'd finished, I clicked 'stop' and a sound file appeared in the timeline.

I then dragged the clip to the start of the

scrub bar and pressed play.

"Ha-ha," I laughed. "It fits perfectly!"

Craig smiled proudly.

"Add it to the end too," he said.

I copied the clip then pasted it onto the credits.

"There," I said. "All done!"

I glanced at my watch. It had only been an hour since I'd taken the Mac out of its box.

"Craig," I said. "Can you believe simple this is?"

"I know," he replied. "It's unreal."

"It's a shame we can't add it to the master," I sighed.

"Why do we need tapes," he chuckled, "when we can burn DVDs?"

* * *

Included in the iMac was a program called iDVD, which allowed users to burn their films onto blank DVDs. It also allowed you to create menus and title pages.

Craig loved it.

"Bloody hell," he said. "This is great. We can put all our films onto a single disk!"

"Yeah," I agreed. "And if we save the image, it'll be easy to create copies too... No waiting around for the tapes."

This had been the thing I'd found most annoying about transferring things in analogue.

A tape could only be copied from another tape, and could only be copied in real time, meaning that if your footage was 30 minutes long, it would take 30 minutes to copy.

Burning a DVD took less than ten minutes, regardless of the content.

"We should a rip a still of the Shadowbright Titles," Craig suggested. "...Use it as the background for the menu screen."

It seemed a great idea.

The only problem was that I didn't know how.

"There's no *Print Screen* button," I said, scanning my eyes over the keyboard.

"There must be," Craig replied. "What's the point of all this fancy-looking shit, when you can't take a basic screenshot?"

"Maybe we should use 'Help'?" I said.

Craig scoffed.

"Since when has 'Help' been helpful?"

He had a point. Back in 2003, the *Help* function wasn't what it is today. Searches typically returned unrelated user manuals, which were nothing more than paragraphs of confusing technobabble.

"I suppose we could give it a try?" I said.

I clicked on the 'Help' button, then typed, "How do I do a screenshot?"

Surprisingly, the answer came up straight away.

Even more surprisingly, it was written in

English - not *Geek Speak* - and contained a step-by-step guide.

"Fuck me!" I said. "It's given us the answer!"

"Bollocks, has it!" Craig snorted.

"Here, look..."

I pointed to the screen.

"Well bugger me sideways," he exclaimed. "These Macs are good, aren't they?"

"Yeah," I said. "Much better than PCs."

Craig laughed.

"You sound like you're in love?" he said.

Yes, I thought.

I probably was...

CHAPTER 29: DAMN YOU FRED

After faffing around on iDVD for an hour, we decided to do another film. We put our heads together and came up with sketch about a shady character named Fred, who had been called into the office to explain his inappropriate behaviour in the workplace.

"I'm playing Fred," he said. "I've always wanted to be a degenerate."

"Are you sure you're not one already?" I laughed.

We raided the props bag for wigs.

"Fred needs to be old," Craig said, holding up the one I'd used for Mrs. Crumpton. "This'll be perfect."

He removed the hairclips, fanned out the strands, then put it on. He looked like a dirty old man.

"You'll need a beard, too," I said. "...And a dirty jacket and hat."

I looked inside my wardrobe while he drew on his beard.

"Here you go," I said. "Try these."

I handed him an old jacket and flat cap.

Craig put them on and chuckled.

"Bloody hell," he said, looking at himself in the mirror. "I look like a complete perv!"

"That's the idea," I replied.

"So, what are *you* going to wear?"

"I'll use my work suit," I said.

"Cool," he replied. "And what are we going to use for the office?"

I glanced around the room.

"Let's do it here," I said. "We'll take the pictures off the walls and shoot it like *Sucker*, but without the wide angles..."

"Cool...."

* * *

After setting up the room, we started filming.

The first shot showed Fred coming in and taking a seat at his manager's desk.

"You wanted to see me, Sir?" Craig sneered, licking his teeth as he sat himself down.

"Yes, Fred," I replied in a posh voice. "It's about all these complaints I've received from our female members of staff."

We passed the camera between us, filming each other as we said the lines.

The story finished with a classic Chris twist. After the manager fires Fred for his various perverted acts - all listed in graphic detail - he gets up, makes to leave, then tells his boss that he 'isn't bothered,' as he 'doesn't even work here.'

It cracked me up.

He really knew how to make me laugh.

After taking off our wigs, we transferred the footage onto the Mac. During the edit, I came across a function I'd not noticed before: *Extract Audio.*

I wondered what it was, so I clicked the button.

The soundtrack of the videoclip appeared in the audio bar below the timeline.

"What's that for?" Craig asked.

"No idea," I said.

Two minutes later, we discovered its purpose by accident. When I trimmed the clip, I noticed that the video was cropped but the sound file wasn't.

"Weird," Craig said. "Looks like the audio is spilling over into the next clip..."

"Holy shit!" I said. "This is fucking awesome!"

He gave me a curious look.

"Watch," I said.

I cut the first clip in half, scrubbed the

cursor back, then clicked play. As the clips transitioned, the dialogue from the first clip continued to play over the second... Giving the illusion that we were using two cameras.

"Holy shit!" Craig said. "You've overlayed the sound!"

"I know," I said, proudly.

It was an historic moment.

Until now, we'd always wondered how TV shows had perfect sound from multiple angles. We'd assumed the technique had been done using multiple cameras and an independently recorded soundtrack.

But here we were, doing it ourselves... With a £400 camera and a Home Computer.

"Fuck me," Chris said. "This is immense. We'll never have problems with dialogue again."

It was true.

No more jarring audio.

"I fucking love this Mac," I said aloud.

"I fucking love it too," Craig replied.

CHAPTER 30:
SUCKER 2

We were on a roll. Now we had the freedom to film anything we wanted whenever we wanted, we wanted to film as much as we could in as short a time as possible.

The only issue we had was that we were running out of ideas. I still had a few scripts lying around, but none of them involved just two characters.

After sitting down and scratching our heads, we decided to shoot a sequel to one of previous films, *Sucker*.

It turned out less a sequel and more of a remake. Craig and I reprised our characters, then pretty much reshot it take-by-take, modifying the script to change the 'sucker's' reason for calling... Instead of it being an IT Helpdesk, he was calling a GP surgery to book an appointment. Once again, the call handler proved obstructive, doing everything he could to be as unhelpful as possible. From the audience's perspective, it appeared as if the caller had simply dialled the wrong number, but at the end of the film, we learn that the call handler is in fact the doctor, and that he is suckering one of his own patients.

To better sell this, we decided to incorporate the character of Rhonda, from, *Oh Shut Up, Charlie,* who would play the part of the Doctor's receptionist.

It worked a treat.

At the end of the shoot, we rushed upstairs for the edit, thrashing it all out in the space of half an hour. To finish it off, I added the *Guns'N'Roses* song, *Anything Goes* to the opening titles and end credits. It seemed a fitting track given Craig's character's propensity for breaking the rules.

When done, we added it to the DVD Project and burned off a disk. As usual, we then drove over Craig's to view it on the big screen.

"Bloody hell," Craig said. "It's so much better than the original..."

I couldn't disagree.

"The image quality is so much better," I replied. "And the sound is great."

It was.

It really was.

No hiss, no buzz.

Just pure, clean audio.

"I really like the fact we've included Rhonda in his," Craig said. "It's like something they'd do on *League of Gentlemen*."

I nodded my head.

It was exactly what they would do.

"We should do this again," I said. "It'd be good to mix and match our characters."

Craig smiled.

"Yeah," he said. "As if they all exist in the same universe..."

"The Shadowbright-verse," I said.

He nodded his head.

"It could be massive, this," he said. "I can see this taking off... If it does, need to buy our own studios, with sets for each skit."

I gave him a grin.

"We should buy Cavendish House," I said.

It was a derelict office building in Dudley. It stood next to Cousins and had been unoccupied for years.

"Yeah," he replied. "And it's the right colour too."

"Nearly," I said. "It's dark brown, but I'm sure we could paint it black to match our logo."

I could see him dreaming. He wanted it to happen.

"How much do you reckon they're selling it for?" he said.

"No idea," I replied. "But I'm sure it's cheap. It's pretty much a squat right now..."

"We'd better start saving, then..." he said, giving me a wink.

CHAPTER 31:
MY LAST FIVER

I'd never felt so excited about the future. Craig and I were making plans. Serious plans. Probably on a scale that was far beyond what we could achieve.

But it didn't matter.

The world was our oyster.

And we were loving every minute.

The only thing holding us back was a lack of exposure.

"We need to get our stuff out there," I said to Craig, one evening. "It's no good making all these films if no one gets to see them."

"Yeah," he said. "But how are we going to do that?"

I hadn't got a clue.

Back in 2003, there was no *YouTube*, no Broadband, and no *Facebook*. In terms of social media, the only side that existed was *Friends Reunited*, but no one was on it because everyone was on dial-up.

"We need to get our stuff on the circuit," I said.

The 'circuit' was the Festival scene. I'd read about it in the *Guerrilla Filmmaker's Handbook*.

"...We need to enter our stuff in competitions."

"What competitions?" Craig asked. "Do you know any?"

"Not off the top of my head," I replied. "But I'm sure we can find some."

We jumped on the internet, opened Yahoo, then searched for 'filmmaking competitions'.

The query returned a list of events, topped by the Edinburgh Film Festival.

"I've heard of that on," Craig said.

"Yeah, me too," I replied. "It's the biggest one in the country."

I clicked on the link and read the submission criteria. They didn't accept DV format, only 35mm.

"I think this is only open to pros," I said.

"Oh well," Craig replied. "Their loss..."

I returned to the menu then scrolled down the list. Something caught my eye near the bottom.

It was the word 'Dudley'.

"Shit," Craig said. "That one's local."

I clicked on the link.

Lo and behold, it was an event that was being held in our local cinema. By a strange quirk of fate, it was taking place in a fortnight.

"What's the crack?" Craig asked.

"It's a competition," I replied.

I quickly read the entry requirements.

"Ok," I said. "So, we'll need to turn up on the Saturday morning to register, where we'll be given a title and a line of dialogue. We'll then need to produce a film no longer than five minutes, which we'll need to submit the following Monday."

Craig laughed.

"Make a film from start-to-finish in 48 hours!" he scoffed. "Piece of piss."

At the bottom of the page were the details of a screening event, which would be taking place the following weekend.

"Every film that it submitted will be screened," I said, reading the words aloud. "...Regardless of where they finish."

"Why should that worry us," Craig sneered. "...We're obviously the favourites?"

It wasn't bravado.

It was confidence. After all, we were flying high, our films getting better with each production.

"Shall we give it a go?" I said.

"Do bears shit on the Pope?" he replied.

* * *

On the day of the competition, I picked up Craig at 8am, then drove over to the Odeon to submit our registration. To our surprise, there was a long queue waiting at the door.

"Bloody hell," Craig said, when he saw it. "I never realised so many people were into this shit."

"I know," I replied. "I thought we were the only ones..."

"Obviously not," he huffed.

He sounded annoyed.

We joined the queue, where we eyed up our competition. Most looked like students, fresh out of Uni. At 23, we were probably the oldest people there.

"I can't these hippy bastards," Craig whispered. "They remind me of Baz's mates."

I chuckled.

"They're probably all Arts students," I said. "I wouldn't worry about them though... They're probably illiterate..."

I wasn't being glib. I was speaking from experience. During my studies, I'd hung around with several people who were doing Arts courses and their writing skills were awful. I remembered, once, having to explain to one of them how to use a semi-colon... *And he was doing an English Degree!*

I glanced down at my watch.

It was nearly 9am.

"The doors will be open soon," I said.

"Thank God," Craig replied. "The sooner we get out of this queue, the better..."

* * *

A few minutes later, a young man appeared behind the glass door and started letting everyone in.

"Ok, all," he said, in a plummy voice. "Could you make your way to the desk, where we'll take your entrance fee and assign you your titles..."

"Gay," Craig said.

"Yep," I agreed.

It was strictly an observation, not a judgement.

We shuffled down the line, eventually reached the front, where we were greeted by a young girl with bright green hair.

"Hi guys," she said. "What's the name of your team?"

"Shadowbright Productions," Craig said proudly.

"Good name," she replied.

She made a note of it on the pad.

"Is that one word, or two?"

"One," Craig sniffed. If it was two, you'd say *Shadow-Bright*, wouldn't you?"

She chuckled to herself, wrote it on her pad, then handed us an envelope.

"This contains the title and line of dialogue

you'll need to include in your film," she said.

"Why can't we just make what we want?" Craig asked.

"Because we need proof that it's only taken you 48 hours."

"Oh," he replied.

We stepped out of the queue, and into the foyer, where we opened the envelope to see what was inside. It contained a piece of paper. On it was written, "Title: My Last Fiver.... Line of Dialogue: That's the Biggest One I've ever Seen."

"Fuck," Craig said. "Are they having a laugh? How are we going to link that dialogue with that title?"

"That's the challenge," I said. "Come on... Let's go to Maccy Dee's and have a think..."

* * *

After placing our usual order, we took a seat by the window and started brainstorming. A few of the other teams were in there too, clearly doing the same thing.

"My Last Fiver..." I said, keeping my voice low so that none of them could hear us. "It sounds like a comedy. A story about a bloke who spends his last five quid on something...?"

"But what?" Craig said.

"I dunno," I replied. "What costs a fiver?"

Craig looked at his food.

"A double-big Mac?" he laughed.

"Yeah," I said. "But it hardly a gripping plot..."

"True," Craig hummed.

He scratched his chin, deep in thought.

"Why does it have to be five pounds?" he said. "Why can't it be something else?"

"What?" I laughed. "Like five dollars?

"No," he replied. "Something more 'out there'... Something you wouldn't expect."

For some strange reason, *Judge Dredd* came to mind.

"What about five Credits?" I said.

"Credits?" Craig replied.

"Yeah," I said. "Like in 2000 AD..."

His lips parted into a smile.

"Yeah, I like that," he said. "Futuristic!"

"Woah," I replied. "Let's not go overboard... We're working on a zero-budget, remember..."

"It doesn't have to be the far future," he explained. "Maybe just ten-or twenty-years' forward..."

"Ok," I said. "So, what would you buy in 2010 for five credits?"

He sucked on his straw, then appeared to have a brainwave.

"Sex," he declared.

"Sex?" I replied. "For Five Credits?"

"Yeah," he said. "Free market Globalism has driven down the price... But on the flip side, all electronic... In order to shag, you need to buy a sex device... One that you plug into your nuts."

I immediately started thinking of *Demolition Man*, the VR sex-scene between Sly Stallone and Sandra Bollocks.

"Yes!" I laughed. "And it'll fits perfectly with the line of dialogue too!"

We high-fived each other across the table.

"Fuck me, dude," I said. "You're a fucking genius!"

* * *

We spent the next hour thrashing out a plot which involved a man who uses his 'Last Fiver' to buy a *Pleasureatron 3000*, a device that allows him to have sex online. Things go horribly wrong, however, when he catches a CSV (a Cyber-Sexual Virus), which causes his face to melt.

To establish that we were in the future, we started with an advert for the *Pleasureatron 3000*, which explained to the premise to the audience. We loved the idea of doing this, as it paid homage to our favourite Director, Paul Verhoeven.

"I want to do the advert," Craig said.

"Cool," I replied. "So, who's going to be the lead?"

"It's gonna have to be Baz, isn't it?"

After visiting Asda to buy some props, we went back to mine and gave him a call.

"Hey, dude," I said. "Wanna be in a film?"

"Yeah, sure," he said. "What's it about?"

"It's a Sci-Fi movie," I explained. "...It's set in a future where physical sex is banned, and all shagging has to be done online."

He started chuckling down the phone.

"Brilliant," he said. "When do you need me?"

"Right now," I said. "We've only got 48 hours to make it."

"No pressure, then," he laughed.

"Oh, and we may also need a girl who's willing to go down to her bra and pants. Do you know anyone?"

The line went quiet.

"Yeah, maybe," he said finally. "I'll give her a call."

* * *

After creating the *Pleasureatron* from Paper Bowls and Tin Foil we drove round Baz's to pick him up.

"Who's this girl, then?" I asked, as he got in the car.

"Her name's Kathy," he replied. "I know her from JBs."

JBs was rock club in Dudley. He went there every weekend with the Grebo gang.

"Cool," Craig replied. "What does she look like?"

"Short and blonde," Baz replied.

"She's not a heifer, is she?"

"Nah," Baz replied. "She's slim...."

"And she's ok with getting her norks out?" I asked.

"Yeah," Baz replied, with a grin. "She's well up for it."

We drove over to her bedsit, which was just off the ring road in Stourbridge. After parking up, we knocked on her door and she welcomed us inside.

"Hi Baz," she said, wrapping her arms around his neck and kissing him on the cheek.

"Hey Kathy," he replied.

He looked at me and winked.

"These are the Directors," he said. "Craig and Dom."

We said hello, and she led us into the lounge, which was filthy and smelled of weed.

"Sorry about the mess," she said in a plummy middle-class accent. "I've not been up long, so haven't had chance to clean."

It was clearly a lie.

The place hadn't been cleaned in months.

"So, this film then," she said. "What exactly do you want me to do?"

I glanced at Baz.

He clearly hadn't told her.

"It's set in the future," Craig said. "Where the only cyber-sex is allowed."

"Cool," she giggled. "And who do I play?"

"A virtual hooker," I said. "Someone the main character watches on-screen the screen while he's wanking himself off..."

"...With a sex-machine," Craig added.

She gave us a curious look.

"Ok," she said.

"Did Baz tell you we need to see your bra?" Craig asked.

She looked at Baz then laughed.

"No," she said. "But I'm than fine with that. I'll even go topless if you want? I've no qualms about performing nude."

"Thanks," Craig said. "We'll keep that in mind."

"So, how are we doing this?" she asked.

I explained that she needed to lie on floor, making sex-noises into the lens.

"Lots of 'oohs' and 'arrrs'," Craig said. "The filthier it sounds, the better..."

"You'll also need to work in a line of dialogue," I said, remembering the rules.

"What will I need to say?"

"That's the biggest one I've ever seen," I replied.

She laughed out loud.

I suspected she was high on something.

"Ok," she said. "Let's do it..."

* * *

She led us up a set of creaky stairs to her bedroom on the first floor. It was even filthier than the living room, the carpet littered with unwashed clothes and cigarette butts; the tops of her cabinets cluttered with junk.

This time, she made no apologies for the mess.

"In terms of bras, what would you prefer?" she asked, opening one of the drawers.

"Any will be fine," Craig replied, nervously.

"Great," she said. "In that case, I'll wear my favourite."

She rooted through the drawer and pulled out a hideous cream number, with matching knickers.

"I like this one, because it's padded," she said.

I glanced at Craig, who was clearly thinking, *'Yeah... because you're flat-chested...'*

"Great," I said. "Put it on."

Kathy smiled, then pulled off her shrift. She was totally naked underneath. Completely starkers. *Gash out and everything!*

Instinctively, I turned away. Craig turned too.

But Baz didn't.

He stood there watching her, with a big grin.

I'd never seen anything so brazen.

A few seconds later, she told us she was ready.

"Ok," she said, "I'm all done. Where do you want me?"

"On the bed," Craig replied.

She skipped across the floor then flopped

herself down on the mattress.

"I'll need to shoot from above," I said. "Is that ok?"

"Yeah, sure," she replied.

I slipped off my shoes, climbed onto the bed, then stood with my feet either side of her hips.

"Ok," Craig said. "When I call 'Action', start moaning."

She nodded, giggling.

I set the focus and pressed record.

"Rolling," I said.

"Action!"

Kathy immediately went full-on whore, moaning with pleasure as she stroked her breasts with the tips of her fingers.

It was pure filth.

Exactly what we wanted to see.

"Ok," Craig said. "Cut!"

"Was that ok?" she asked.

"Yeah," I replied. "But can you do it again, saying the line?"

"Yeah, course..."

I zoomed into her face and clicked record.

"Action!"

"Uuuh, Uuuh," she groaned. "That's the biggest one I've ever seen!"

I glanced at Craig and gave him the thumbs-up.

"Cut!" he said. "Cool, all sorted."

"Is that it?" she asked.

"Yeah," I replied, stepping off the bed. "We're all done."

"Are you sure you don't want a topless version?" Kathy asked. "I don't mind being nude."

It was the second time she'd mentioned it.

"Nah," Craig said. "We're good.""

"But I really don't mind," she insisted.

I looked at Craig, who shook his head.

"I'll shoot it," Baz said.

He strode over and snatched the camera from my hands.

"Do you just press record?" he asked.

"Y-yeah," I replied.

"Cool."

He climbed onto the bed, and she removed her bra and pants.

I glanced at Craig, who blew out his cheeks.

"Let's wait outside," he said.

He headed for the door, and I followed him out.

"What was all that about?" I said.

Craig blew out his cheeks.

"God knows," he replied. "But if the two of them end up fucking, I won't be happy. We've got loads more to shoot today..."

He was right.

Kathy's sequence amounted to around ten seconds of the total footage. We still had four scenes to shoot in three different locations...

* * *

Twenty minutes later, Baz came out with a big smile on his face. Kathy was standing behind him, looking slight dishevelled. It was obvious what they'd been up to...

"I hope you've not used all the tape," I said, sarcastically. "We've only get 45 minutes on each cassette."

"Nah," he replied. "We spent most of the time shagging..."

Craig shook his head dismissively.

"Amateurs..." he groaned.

We left the house then headed back to mine to film the 'advert'. After Craig had put on my work suit and slicked back his hair, we made our way to the park. Working off the handwritten script we'd written in McDonalds, he delivered another virtuoso performance as a futuristic corporate shill.

"After the 2009 Sexual Ban Charter," he began, "...Physical sex in all forms, is now illegal. Mortality rates from STDs have fallen, but at what cost to our freedom?"

I stopped the tape, moved to his left, then called 'Action'.

He turned his head to camera, dramatically.

"Sexually frustrated?" he continued. "There is an answer."

"Cut!" I said. "Great."

I moved back to the original position, then zoomed in to a medium close-up.

"Sex need not be a thing of the past," he continued. "Call 7248-PLEASURE."

He then smiled at the lens, wickedly.

"We're here to *relieve* you..."

"Cut," I yelled. "Fantastic!"

He'd done it all in a single take.

Legend.

I glanced at Baz, who replied with an impressive nod.

"Nice," he said.

Craig responded with a boastful smile.

He was clearly showing off.

"Right," I said. "Back to mine for the next bit..."

* * *

We returned to the house to shoot the scene where Baz's character 'caught' the CSD. We used my Mac as a prop, wrapping tinfoil around its screen to make it look more futuristic.

In truth it looked ridiculous.

But not as ridiculous as the *Pleasureatron 3000...* Which we made from a SCART lead and a toilet roll.

When Baz saw it, he laughed out loud.

"What the fuck is that?" he roared.

"The *Pleasureatron 3000*," Craig replied.

"It looks shit," Baz replied.

"It's supposed to," I said. "We're going for future-kitsch."

"Future-kitsch?" he exclaimed. "Future shite, more like..."

"You'll need to wear this too," Craig said.

He handed him a silver paper bowl.

"What do I do with this?" Baz chuckled. "Wank into it?"

"No," I said. "That goes on your head."

"Before or after?" he laughed.

"Stop faffing around," I said, glancing at my watch. "We're running out of time..."

We gave him some basic instructions, I got into position with the camera.

"So, do you want me to actually put my cock inside it?" Baz asked.

"No," Craig sneered. "This is a family show... Just hold it over your pants..."

Baz looked confused.

"So, how's that gonna work?"

"Have you ever used a condom?" I asked.

Baz laughed.

It was a sign he probably hadn't....

"Come on," Craig said. "Let's get on with it..."

He gave me the nod to press record, then called 'Action'. As directed, Baz then dropped his kecks and held the toilet roll over his package.

"Ok, shake it a little," Craig said. "Make it look like it's vibrating."

Baz chuckled then started wobbling it over his junk.

"Are you sure this looks ok?" he laughed.

"Yeah," I said. "It'll be fine once we add

sound effects..."

* * *

After finishing the sequence, it was time to move on to the CSV scene, which involved smothering Baz's face in PVA, then getting him to it off with his fingers. In our heads, we thought it'd look cool, like his skin was melting in his hands. But when we came to film it, it just looked like glue.

"Is there any way we could make it bloodier?" I said. "Maybe paint his face red before we add the PVA?"

Baz shook his head.

"It won't work," he replied. "The glue won't stick if my cheeks are wet."

Craig snorted.

"I suppose we'll have to go with what we've got," he said.

He was watching the clock.

He needed to get back by 9pm.

"Ok," I said. "Let's wrap things up..."

The final scene to shoot was outdoors. It featured Baz's character staggering around in a daze as his body succumbed to the CSV.

For a change, we decided not to film it in the park, but on an area of wasteland near the quarry. I'd scouted the location previously and thought it would be good to use if we ever needed a post-apocalyptic environment.

We parked up in a street nearby, then made our way to the location. Luckily for us, there was no one around, so we quickly shot what we needed to shoot then fucked off back to the car.

* * *

After picking up the last couple of shots, we began the edit.

Baz seemed intrigued by the iMac's capabilities, cooing, like Craig had, over the different filters and effects.

"Bloody Hell," he said. "This is good, isn't it?"

"It's brilliant, mate," I replied. "You can do anything on this."

I could see the cogs turning in his mind.

He was thinking of ideas for future films.

"This shit's the future," Craig remarked. "No more faffing around with SVHS..."

After cutting the together, we started to record the narration.

Baz slipped back into character effortlessly, delivering a faultless rendition of his lines. I added the sound clips to the audio bar, moved the scrub bar to the start of the timeline, then played it back.

"You've got a good voice," Craig remarked, as he watched the footage unfold.

"Yeah," Baz replied. "I've been told that."

He'd been singing and writing songs since

he was 15. He fancied himself as a bit of a crooner.

"What are we going to do for music?" he asked. "the advert needs a background track."

"Yeah," Craig agreed. "What have we've got?"

The movie-making program came with a multitude of built-in jingles, which were copyright free. I played a few to test them out.

"Nah," Baz said. "That's no good...It needs to be more futuristic,"

Craig suggested trying the 'electronic' section, so I scrolled down the list and found a sample entitled, *Future Dreams*.

"What about this?" I said, clicking play.

"It's perfect," Craig said. "Add it to the timeline."

"Hang on," Baz said. "Let's see what else there is."

I played a few more samples.

Some were good, some weren't.

"I like the original one," Craig said. "It fits the style and tone."

Baz rubbed his chin.

"I dunno," he said. "The second-from-bottom is better, in my opinion."

"Which one, guys?" I said.

"Go with the mine," Craig said.

"Are you sure?" Baz said. "Don't you think it's a bit full-on?"

"No," Craig replied. "It's perfect."

Baz looked at me.

"What do you think, Tom?"

I didn't want to get involved, so gave him an indefinite answer.

"I think both work..." I said. "In different ways."

"Go with mine then," Craig said.

Baz blew out his cheeks, defeated.

I dragged the first tune into the timeline, then played the footage.

"See," Craig said. "You can't get better than that!"

"Yeah," Baz grumbled.

* * *

With the film now finished, we were ready to transfer it onto a disk, so I opened up iDVD and dragged in the video file.

"We need a still for the background," I said. "Shall we screenshot one of the scenes from the film?"

"Yeah," Craig said. "One from the finale, when he's lying in the ditch."

Baz scoffed.

"Why that?"

"It'll intrigue the audience," Craig argued. "They'll wonder how he ended up there?"

"If you want to intrigue people," Baz replied, "Wouldn't you be better using a clip from the wanking scene?"

"No," Craig snorted.

"Why not?" Baz said.

"Because it's crude," Craig rasped. "This story is all about how men are undone by their base desires..."

"Oh," Baz laughed. "I thought it was about cyber pervs..."

"It's about both," I said, trying to keep the peace.

I restored the iMovie window.

"Maybe we could add a clip of the last scene to the very start of the movie," I said, "...As a pre-title teaser?"

Before either of them could respond, I copied a section of the final shot and pasted it into the timeline.

"Here," I said. "Like this..."

I pressed play to show them what I meant.

After a few seconds, Craig nodded his head.

"Powerful," he said.

"Yeah," Baz added. "Not bad."

"But I still don't want the wanking scene on the DVD," Craig added. "It makes us look childish."

Baz shook his head.

"Isn't it supposed to be a comedy?"

"It's a satire," Craig replied. "There's a difference."

"Whatever," Baz said. "It's your film, do want you like."

I took a still from the end shot then added it

to the DVD background.

"There," I said. "All done... Now all we'll need to do is burn the bugger off..."

CHAPTER 32: COMPETITION

The following Saturday, we arrived at the cinema for the screening. After parking up, we made our way into the foyer, which was packed with the other entrants.

"Bloody hell," I said. "There's a good turnout."

Craig glanced around the room, scornfully eyeing up the competition.

"There's no way we're gonna be beaten by these morons," he said.

There wasn't a trace of irony in his voice.

Baz laughed through his nose.

"You don't like people much, do you?" he said.

Craig didn't answer.

"Hello everyone!" someone called.

We turned our heads towards the voice and

saw that it was the organiser of the event.

"Gay," Baz commented.

Deja vu...

"Thanks for coming today and submitting your films," the man continued, "We're about to start, so if you could all make your way through to screen 4..."

We followed the crowd into the theatre then grabbed some seats near the front. Once everyone had made themselves comfortable, the organiser made his way to the front.

"Welcome everyone," he began, "to the first Dudley Short Film Fest, sponsored by Odeon, Merry Hill..."

I glanced at Craig, who rolled his eyes.

"I'm sure you'll agree it's been an amazing event thus far, with teams coming from all over the Midlands, and as far afield as Manchester."

A clutch of people cheered on the back row.

"Mancs," Craig whispered. "They're all dickheads."

Baz snorted into his drink.

"...In terms of today's format, we'll be screening each of the entries in blocks of five, with breaks in between. When all films have been shown, we'll then announce the winners."

"Can't we just skip to that part?" Craig sneered. "We already know who's won..."

He'd never been short of confidence.

The organiser then signalled the projectionist, then took a seat on the front row.

The lights dimmed, and the first film started to play.

Its title appeared on-screen: *Fatal Five*.

"I think there might be a bit of a theme going on, here," Craig said, nudging me in the ribs. "I bet you ten quid, all the titles have the word 'five' in them..."

The titles faded into a wide shot of a bar, where numerous couples were sitting at tables. The camera panned between each couple smoothly. There wasn't a trace of shakiness.

It looked great.

Really professional.

I glanced at Craig, whose hands were shaking with fury.

I turned back to the screen, then watched as the camera stopped at one of the tables, focusing on the face of the girl. The image was perfectly lit, with light coming in from several angles.

A bell then rang and the man she was with left the table. Another man then sat down in his chair.

I couldn't help but notice how well the film had been cut. The transitions between each clip were seamless. The audio was excellent too, with perfectly balanced dialogue and ambient noise.

It was wonderful.

Brilliant.

It looked like a real film.

I wondered how they'd managed to make something so good in such a short amount of time...

My eyes drifted to Craig, who was staring at the screen, breathing loudly. His face was red with anger.

"You ok, mate?" I asked.

"Yesssss," he hissed. "I'm fiiiiineee..."

He clearly wasn't.

He was massively pissed off.

"This isn't fair," he muttered, grinding his teeth as he spoke. "These wankers are pros..."

I could see what he was getting at.

The team that had submitted this film obviously had a considerable degree of resources to work with. Apart from the twenty or thirty extras they'd hired, they'd also had access to a real-life bar, high-end cameras, professional actors, top-of-the-range microphones, dolly tracks, Steadicams, a full lighting rig, and a full crew to set everything up...

We were rank amateurs in comparison; wannabees, *two blokes with a camera...*

I suddenly felt sick.

I was thinking about the prop design for the *Pleasureatron...*

Maybe it had been a bad idea to scrimp on costs?

"Is he alright?" Baz whispered in my ear.

"He's in a bad mood," I replied. "He thought the competition was for amateurs only."

"Ahh, yeah," Baz smiled. "He thought you were going to win, didn't he?"

He reached across my lap, tapped Craig on the knee, then gave him a thumbs-up.

Craig hissed, then looked away.

I'd never him so pissed off...

* * *

Once all the films had been screened, the organiser stood up to announce the winner. The award, unsurprisingly, went to the team whose film had been screened last. Like *Fatal Five*, it had featured a large cast, good actors, and had been produced by a professional crew with expensive equipment.

"This is bollocks," Craig huffed. "Their film didn't even fit the title. They could have made that last year for we know..."

He had a good point.

The film's title was *Final Five*, but I couldn't for the life me understand how it fit with a plot, which was about a man seeking revenge for a stolen toaster...

"Never mind," I said to him. "We'll do better next year."

"Fuck next year," Craig hissed. "This whole thing is rigged."

I heard Baz chuckling beside me.

The angrier Craig got, he funnier he seemed to find it.

"Come on," Craig said. "Let's fuck off out of here."

He stood up and made his way of the auditorium before the organiser had even presented the trophy. Baz and I followed him, making our apologies to the people sitting behind.

We caught up with him in the car park, kicking a bin.

"Hey dude," I said. "Try not to worry too much about it. Like you said, the whole thing's fixed."

I expected Baz to disagree, but instead he offered words of support.

"Some of the teams were obviously pros," he said. "They were probably film students, using the cameras and equipment from their courses. The extras were probably their classmates too."

"Yeah," I agreed. "There's no way they could afford that kind of shit at their age. They would have had to have had help."

Craig snorted.

"I honestly thought we'd win," he grumbled. "We had a great idea, and we made a great film."

I felt sorry for him. He was truly mortified.

But he was wrong.

We'd made an average film at best. There was no denying it. Compared to most of the other entries, our looked shoddy, cheap, and amateur.

I asked myself why.

After thinking about for a while, I put it

down to three things: the Lighting, the Sound Editing, and the camera movement.

Sadly, none of these things were covered in my books, so I felt a little stuck in terms of what to do.

The way I could learn was by trial and error.

CHAPTER 33: HUNGRY BOY

Several weeks later, Craig had calmed down enough to talk about doing another project.

"I've decided to take your advice," he said. "We can't affect what other people think, so we may as well carry on regardless."

"That's the spirit, mate," I said.

"So, do you have any new ideas?"

"I do, actually," I replied.

I'd been toying with the idea of a recurring sketch, two flatmates, Bill and Fred, who would be played by Craig and Baz, respectively. In each skit, Bill would catch Fred doing something that he'd arbitrarily forbidden, always something, like eating, drinking or sleeping, and would then punish Fred for his indiscretions. Each sketch would always end with Fred telling Bill that he was leaving... Only for him to turn up in the next episode as if nothing had happened.

I showed Craig the outline for the first skit, which I'd provisionally called *Hungry Boy*.

"So, let me get this straight," Craig said, after reading it. "Bill tortures Fred for eating yoghurt?"

"Yeah," I replied. "But it doesn't have to be yoghurt per see, it's the act of eating that bothers him."

"That's mad!" Craig said. "Let's do it!"

I called Baz and explained the idea over the phone.

He was keen to get involved... Especially when I told him his character was a hippy.

"Fantastic," he said. "Can I wear the big brown wig?"

It was the one I'd used for Rhonda.

"Of course, mate," I replied.

"Sweet!"

* * *

The next night, I picked them up and brought them to my house for the shoot. After putting on their costumes, we were ready to go.

The first scene involved Bill's car pulling up onto the drive. Because Craig didn't have a license, we had to cheat the shot by keeping the angle low, so that I could be behind the wheel.

Once I pulled up, I swapped seats with Craig then filmed him getting out.

We then moved inside the house, where I used a tracking shot to capture Craig coming into the Living Room. I then added a reverse shot of Baz sitting cross-legged on the floor, eating his yoghurt. Again, I kept the camera moving to keep things fluid.

It worked nicely, and I immediately felt more confident.

"Ok," I said to Craig, "I wanna go off script and give something a try if that's ok?"

"What?" he replied.

"I reaction shot of you," I said. "But I want to pan from the floor onto your face."

He looked at me confused.

"Why?" he said.

"I just want to try it," I said. "If it looks shit, we'll bin it..."

I called, 'Action', then gave it a go.

It looked great.

Suddenly, I was on a roll.

Before long, I was doing it for every shot. When Craig and Baz cottoned on to what I was doing, they began modifying their performances to catch the angle of the lens.

It all felt fresh and vibrant, as if we were doing something new.

"This is gonna be great," I said, as looked through the rushes. "I've got a really good feeling about this."

"Me too," Baz said.

He seemed even keener than Craig...

* * *

We moved into the bathroom to shoot the harrowing 'punishment' scene, where Bill forces Fred to brush his teeth. After scrubbing for several minutes, Bill remains unsatisfied and tells that he's doing it all wrong. In a fit of rage, he throws Fred aside, grabs his brush, then shows him how to do it....

After several seconds of gum-destroying, high-speed scrubbing, the sequence ends with Bill spitting it all out. ...*Onto Fred's face.*

That last shot proved a little problematic. For some reason, Craig couldn't do it.

"I can't hock in your face, man," he said. "It's disgusting."

"Come on, man," Baz replied. "You gob on the floor all the time."

"Yeah, but his is different... It's dirty."

After several minutes of arguing, I handed Craig the camera and told him to film me doing it instead.

Thankfully, I got in one take.

Craig immediately showed us the rush.

It looked disgusting.

Disgustingly brilliant!

After shooting the finale, we uploaded the footage onto the iMac and started the edit.

It felt like the old days gathered around Colin's PC.

After cutting all the clips, we decided to add some music to the intro crawl and end credits.

Craig picked up the keyboard and began composing a short piano ditty, while Baz wrote some lyrics to. We then recorded it via the narration function, with all of us singing along the tune.

It was hardly a masterpiece, no more than a refrain of, "Hungry Boy," but it worked a treat, and perfectly fit the sketch's style and tone.

After adding a few more sound effects, I added the footage to the DVD image, then burned off a couple of copies for Craig and Baz.

"I can't wait to see this on my TV when I get home," Baz said.

He appeared genuinely excited.

I was excited too.

For the first time in a long time, I felt proud of what we'd done.

Sure, there were still a few issues with the lighting and sound, but the use of camera movement was a huge leap forward.

The story was funny too.

Genuinely funny.

After taking Craig and Baz home, I screened it to my brother, who laughed his ass off. My dad watched it too. He didn't laugh as hard, but I could tell he still enjoyed it.

"What are you making next?' he asked when the credits started rolling.

"The sequel to this," I replied. "*Thirsty Boy.*"

CHAPTER 34:
THIRSTY BOY

A week later, we shot the follow-up.

Like all good sequels, the format was the same, but cranked up to eleven. Instead of Bill catching Fred eating yoghurt, he finds him drinking water.. *From the tap!* Like before, he takes him upstairs to punish him, and it ends with Bill *pissing* on his face.

To keep things consistent, I adopted the same camera style that I'd used in the original. It worked great, as by now I'd figured out that the key to doing it well wasn't so much in the movement of the lens at the start of the shot, but in getting the framing right at the end. By the time we'd finished the first scene, which involved Baz lifting wights in the garage, I'd got it down to a tee.

Before we filmed the 'punishment'

sequence, we emptied out a bottle of lemonade, filled it up with lime cordial then poked a hole in the cap with a pair of scissors. Craig held it over the sink and squeezed its sides. When the liquid squirted out of the hole in a single unfettered stream, we knew we were in business.

When quickly rushed upstairs and started filming it in the bathroom. Their acting was great. It was like watching a live performance of the *League of Gentlemen*.

"Can I stop now?" Baz's character whined, pathetically. "I've been doing this for a fucking hour!"

"Oh, you'll stop all right," Craig, as Bill, sneered. "But only when you've put back what you stole!"

The sequence ended with Baz on the floor, with his back against the bath panel. Craig stood a good five or six feet away, holding the bottle, ready to squeeze. When I called 'Action', he squirted the cordial across the room, directing the stream onto Baz's face.

When the juice hit him, he started screaming, "Oh Lord." It wasn't in the script, but it was hilarious. What made it even funnier was that some of the liquid dribbled mouth while he was yelling, making him gag and splutter.

To this day, it was perhaps the funniest thing I've ever shot.

* * *

After wrapping up we edited the footage and added an updated version of the theme tune to the credits. Once I'd burned off the DVDs, I took them home. They both seemed incredibly pleased with their night's work.

"Have you finished *Thirsty Boy*?" Glen asked, when I came in.

"Yeah," I replied. "You wanna see it?"

He nodded excitedly, and I played it for him on the computer.

"That's even better than the first one," he said afterwards, giggling into his mug of tea.

"Thanks," I replied.

"What's the next one, then?" he asked. "Sleepy Boy?"

"Maybe," I said.

I hadn't got that far. I'd only written two skits.

That night, I went to bed, thinking about the next film. Although *Sleepy Boy* seemed like the logical next step, I didn't know how we could make it work, given the format we'd established in the prequels.

In the end, I realised I'd written myself into a hole and that there was no way out.

"Hey dude," I said to Craig on the phone the next night. "We may have to skip the third sketch..."

"Why?" he asked.

"I can't figure out a reason for Bill torturing Fred."

"I'm sure you can think of something," he replied.

"I'm struggling," I admitted. "I've wracked my brains on this... I'm getting nowhere."

"What about *Sleepy Boy*?" he suggested.

"Already thought of it," I said. "Where's the fun in watching someone fall asleep?"

"How about turning it round?" Craig suggested. "Have Bill force Fred to stay awake. It's the opposite of sleeping, like the pissing thing in the second film..."

"Yeah," I said. "I get what you're saying.. But again, what's funny about keeping someone awake?"

Chris hummed into the receiver.

"All right, mate," he said. "Let's move on and do something else. Something funnier."

"Like what?" I said.

"I dunno," he replied. "Something like *Oh Shut Up, Charlie*. That was hilarious."

"Ok," I said, "I'll have a think..."

CHAPTER 35: RHONDA AND SAVO

I took Craig's suggestion literally, penning a sequel to Oh shut Up, Charlie. The story picked things up where the original left off, opening with a scene at Rhonda's house where she attempts to get Savo involved in the housework. Like the original, I finished the story open-ended, meaning we could carry it on if we wanted to.

After sharing the script with Craig and Baz, we met up at my house to start the shoot. Because I was playing Rhonda, Baz was put in charge of the camerawork.

It went down well, as he was keen to expand his repertoire.

"I've always wondered what it was like on

the other side," he beamed. "I'm gonna film it just like you did in Thirsty Boy."

"And Hungry boy," I noted.

"Yeah," he said, "But that wasn't as good..."

After Craig and I had raided the props bag for our old costumes, we prepped the living room to begin the shoot.

The only additional prop we needed was a vacuum cleaner, so used my dad's. It was heavy, loud, and had seen better days... Perfect for the scene.

I wheeled it out into the middle of the carpet, then Craig and I then got into our starting positions for the first shot.

"You ready?" Baz asked.

"Replied," I said.

My voice was trembling. He could tell that I was nervous.

"Don't worry," he said. "As soon as you get going, you'll be fine."

He pointed the lens at our feet.

"Ok, then," he said. "Go..."

"Woah," Craig said. "The call is 'Action'."

Baz laughed.

"What does it matter? When it's just the three of us?"

"Yeah," Craig said. "But it's all about being professional..."

"Fine," Baz sniffed. "Action, then..."

He panned up to our faces for a two-shot.

"Now, Savo," I said, putting on my strongest

northern accent. "I know you're not used to this kind of thing, so I'll try and make it simple... On."

I switched on the vacuum.

"Off."

I switched it off.

"Ok, cut!" Baz said. "Where am I going now?"

I gestured for him to move to my right.

"We need a close-up reaction shot of Craig," I said. "Then after that, do a reverse shot of me."

"Do you like the way I panned up from your feet?" Baz said, stepping into place. "I think I've managed to capture your leg hair, but I can't be sure until we play it back... It is quite thin."

"Yeah," I said. "I noticed that. I would have done it the same."

It was a lie.

I would started with a wide.

But it wouldn't have been as good.

"Right," he said. "I'm all set. You ready, Craig?"

Craig nodded.

"And... action!"

Craig gurned with confusion.

He looked baffled. It was brilliant.

And I was jealous as fuck.

"Great," Baz said. "Cut..."

We filmed the rest of the scene we went upstairs to edit.

As always, the lighting and sound looked a bit dodgy, but apart from that, the shots were great.

"I could have done better there," Baz lamented, as we watched it back. "I'm shaking a little... I should have had my legs further apart, so I didn't have to stretch."

"It looks fine, Baz," Craig said. "You did a good job."

"Yeah," I sighed. "Not bad at all..."

I hated the fact that he was blessed with such a natural eye. It didn't seem fair. I'd spent months honing my skills... But in the space of an hour, he'd already surpassed me.

It made me feel small and pathetic. Little pieces of me were being chipped away from all sides.

First, my acting... Now it was my camerawork.

If it carried on like this, I'd soon be relegated to 'Team Mascot'.

It was a horrible feeling and didn't like it.

It didn't like it one bit...

"Maybe you should cut that clip a little shorter," Baz said.

He made a moved for the mouse.... I smacked him on the wrist.

"No," I snapped. "I'LL do it. I'm the EDITOR!"

For now, at least...

* * *

The following day, I started writing the

next scene. I didn't have an overall plan in terms of where the story was heading, but I knew that it would have to involve Rhonda's husband, Charlie.

The obvious move would be for him to return to his mother's, but it didn't feel right. At least not at this stage. Charlie vs Mallory would be a showdown best saved for later.

I decided to break things down logically, putting myself in the character's shoes.

So where would Charlie go, I asked myself? Who would he see?

For some strange reason, my thoughts drifted to Sucker 2, and the inclusion of Rhonda as the receptionist.

Maybe I could develop a scene out of that?

I spent the next hour or so piecing together the puzzle, eventually coming up with a simple plot, that involved Charlie being seen in a clinic, receiving hypnotherapy to help him deal with his childhood trauma, which had been alluded to in the original skit. At the end of the session, the Charlie hugs the Doctor as Rhonda enters the room. When she sees them together, she accuses Charlie of being gay, and blaming it for the failure of their marriage.

I was really pleased with my draft.

The dialogue flowed well, and, with the hypnosis segment, there was plenty of scope for visual storytelling.

I also loved the way it followed on from the

two previous scenes. It felt natural and organic; nothing appeared forced.

After giving it a read through, I emailed it to the lads.

"So, the Doctor's gay?" Craig said, when he phoned me later.

"No," I replied. "He's just a complete perv."

"Oh," he replied. "That's ok then. I can do perv well."

"I know," I laughed.

I was thinking of, Damn You, Fred...

He chuckled down the line.

"Cool," he said. "So, when are we doing it?"

"Tuesday?" I offered. "Same as last week?"

"Makes sense," he replied. "Let's make it our filming night going forward..."

* * *

When Tuesday evening arrived, I picked up Craig and Baz then brought them back to mine, where I'd converted the front bedroom into a makeshift treatment room. I hadn't done a lot, just removed the posters from the walls and replaced them with medical diagrams I'd printed off the internet.

"What do you think?" I asked, as I led them in.

"It doesn't look much like a Doctor's room," Craig laughed. "Don't you need a curtain? What happened to the one we used on Mrs Crumpton?"

"It's gone," I admitted. "I had to throw it out because it was covered in mould."

"Shame," Craig replied. "It would have looked good."

"Have you got a copy of the script?" Baz asked.

"Here you go," I said, handing him a copy.

I knew he wouldn't bring one.

"Right then guys," I said. "Are we ready to start?"

"Yeah," Craig nodded. "Let's do this..."

* * *

After staging the scene, we started shooting.

Keen to prove myself after Baz's tour-de-force, I put my heart and soul into getting the camerawork just right.

I also made a special effort with the lighting, using the desk lamp to create more atmosphere. Not knowing quite what I do, I placed it on the floor near Craig's feet, aiming the light upwards onto his face.

To my surprise, it worked perfectly, cutting eerie shadows across his face.

It looked great.

Not that I'd planned it that way.

It had been luck rather than judgment.

Not that I would ever admit it...

As soon as we finished shooting, we started

the edit. As expected, the footage looked superb. To this day, I still rate it as some of my best work.

Craig was happy with it too. He loved his performance as the creepy doctor. He'd done a great job with the character, giving him a sinister, breathy voice, that immediately conveyed his sleaziness.

Baz did great too, slipping back into the role as if he'd played it all his life. He'd also taken time to sort out his character's accent too. In the original skit, it had been a strange Birmingham-Manchester hybrid, but now he was going full-Dudley, and it better suited the part.

Craig and Baz were really pleased with the final cut. So much so, that Craig suggested we pick up the shoot on Saturday, rather than waiting a full week.

"I'm up for that," I said.

"Yeah, me too," Baz added.

"Cool," Craig said. "So, what's the next scene?"

"No idea," I laughed. "You know I'm making this up as I go..."

* * *

The next evening, I penned Scene 3, which involved Rhonda coming home and telling Savo about her day. To add a bit more depth to her character, I decided to make her hyperbolic...

"The two of them were shagging, Savo!" she huffed. "Shagging!"

When I showed the line to Craig, he loved it.

"What do you think?" I asked.

"It's great," he replied. "And it's funny cos it's true."

"What do you mean?" I said.

He didn't answer, responding only with a wry smile.

After reading the rest, he asked about the next scene.

"I'm guessing we switch back to Charlie after this one?"

I gave him a nod.

"Any ideas?"

I'd been toying with the idea of incorporating Craig's character from the *Bastard Son,* thinking I could work him into the script on the basis that he was friends with Charlie, and that Charlie had been staying at his house after being kicked out by Rhonda. I'd pictured it opening with a scene of Colin on the toilet doing a massive, painful, shit, with Charlie bursting in on him and asking him how long he's going to be. Colin then tells him to go away, then we cut to the bedroom, where Charlie asks Colin's son, Christopher, why he didn't tell him that his dad was on the toilet. An argument then ensues between them, and it ends with Christopher telling Charlie to leave.

To crank up the mirth, I thought it would

be good to include some slapstick humour. It had worked well in *Hungry/Thirsty Boy*, so why not give it a go? I'd come up with a sequence involving Christopher spitting a chewed-up banana into Charlie's mouth, figuring we could do it with a fishing line, reversing the clip in the edit.

When we got round to doing it, it looked great. We'd timed it perfectly and the result was hilarious.

"You should write more stuff like this into the script," Baz laughed. "It's funny."

He wasn't wrong.

"I'll try my best," I said. "But I only do it if it's in the right context. We can't just add random stuff for the sake of it. We're telling a story, here, remember..."

My comment was a little mean, but I needed to put him in his place.

Looking back, it was a cuntish thing to do. He was only being helpful, and my words were spoken purely out of jealousy.

"Have you thought about the next scene?" Craig asked, once we were done.

"Yes," I lied. "I'll be writing it up later..."

* * *

After taking them back, I returned home to start writing, but found myself lost for ideas. I knew I needed to take the story back to Rhonda and Savo but didn't know what to do.

In the end, I scratched out a scene that didn't so much expound the plot but develop their characters. It involved Rhonda coming down the stairs, carrying a basket full of washing. While she is doing this, Savo sits on the chair watching TV, ignoring her calls her assistance. After dropping the basket on the floor, she gathers up the clothes and takes them to the washing machine, where she discovers an unusual pair of knickers in the mix.

Once she confirms they're not hers (by giving them a sniff), she angrily confronts Savo in the front room, who lies that he brought them for her as a gift. Rhonda then starts crying, overwhelmed by Savo's apparent generosity. The scene ends with her making a move on him, much to Savo's displeasure.

When it came to the shoot. Baz handled the camerawork. Again, he was eager to impress, and to be fair to him, he did. His shots were excellent and made for an easy edit.

Once we were done, I checked out the runtime. It was 15 minutes, our longest film since *Hunted* (which ran at 20). Even better, was that we still had plenty of scope to progress the story.

"This may end up being feature-length," I said to Craig, while I was driving him home.

"Yeah," he agreed. "It's almost like a serial. We could carry it on forever if we needed to."

I smiled.

It seemed our dreams were finally coming true.

* * *

The next scene picked up Charlie's storyline after he'd been thrown out by Christopher. It involved an outdoor shoot in the park, starting with Charlie waking up, after spending the night sleeping rough. As he makes way back into town, his stomach starts to ache, so he goes behind a bush and takes a shit. After emptying his bowels, Charlie is shocked when his mother starts communing with him via the turd. She implores him to 'return home', and the scene ends with him leaving the park and heading for her house.

At the time of writing, it was late Autumn, and all the leaves had fallen off the trees. It was also cold, wet, and overcast. The location and environment couldn't have been better.

Because it was getting dark around four, and since we all had nine-to-five jobs, we arranged to film to the following Saturday. In the days between, Baz used his artistic skills to create a suitable prop for the talking turd.

"Look what I've done," he said excitedly, when we picked him up on the day of the shoot. "Isn't it wicked?"

He produced the shit-puppet from a bag.

It was the most evil-looking turd I'd ever seen.

"How did you make it?" Craig asked.

"I covered a sock in papier mache," he explained, "then rolled it through the grass and painted it brown and red."

"Why red?" I asked.

"For the blood," he replied.

"Nice," Craig said.

We drove to the park then made our way to the cliffs, where we climbed to the top of the hill for the opening shot. With a vista of the town in the background, Baz lay on the ground, closed his eyes, then pretended to wake up.

Because it was so chilly, Baz had no trouble with the acting. He was only wearing a shirt, a small jacket, and a single glove, so his shakes and shivers were genuine.

"Fuck me, it's cold," he complained, between takes. "Any chance I could lend your coat?"

"Stop complaining," I said. "When we shot *The Banshee*, my forehead was covered in ice!"

Craig laughed.

"Oh yeah," he said. "I remember that. That was funny as fuck!"

"Not for me, it wasn't," I said. "I nearly died..."

We made our way down to the cliff line, then looked around for a suitable location to film the 'shitting' sequence. Before long, we came across a copse of trees. Inside, was a small clearing.

"This is perfect," I said.

"Yeah," Baz said, looking around. "It means I can get my arse out without anyone seeing."

"What do you mean, 'get your arse out'?" Craig said.

"I'm taking a shit, aren't I," Baz replied. "Do you expect me to do it through my pants."

"You really want me to film your arse?" I said.

Baz nodded.

"It'll be funny," he replied.

"Fair enough," I said. "It's your arse..."

* * *

We began shooting the scene, with Craig operating the 'turd'.

It was hilarious.

The voice he did for the shit was terrifyingly sinister, especially after we'd some reverb in the edit. Coupled with the music, a copyright free track entitled, 'Spooky and Kooky', it worked at treat. In the space of thirty seconds, the film's genre had shifted from gross-out comedy to gothic horror.

Steve Pemberton would have been proud...

We were so pleased with the result, we sat around the iMac, watching the sequence repeatedly. It was, hands down, the best work we'd ever done.

After finally calling it day, we congratulated each other with high-fives. As Darius Danesh would have said, "there was a lot of love in the room', and we all excited by the way things were progressing.

"What happens next?" Baz gushed, as I dropped him off.

I'd already mapped it out.

"It's a scene between Rhonda and the Doctor," I replied. "He tries to rape her."

"Cool," he laughed.

We'd hit a point where everything was funny.

Literally *everything*.

* * *

We filmed it the following Tuesday.

Craig was more up for it than ever. It was amazing how easily he could switch between his various roles.

"How do you do it?" I asked. "I struggle getting into character for Rhonda, and it's the only role I've got..."

"Natural talent..." he replied, with a wink.

It made me laugh.

It was his explanation for everything.

To make his character extra-pervy, we decided to use a glass of milk as a prop, which his character would be drinking at the start of the scene.

"Why milk?" Craig asked, somewhat innocently.

"Cos it looks like jizz," Baz laughed.

"Jizz?" Craig replied. "That's fucking disgusting,"

"That's the point said," I said. "Now drink it up like a good little girl..."

"Fuck off," he snorted.

After ribbing each other for several minutes, we finally started filming. An hour later, we'd reached the final shot, which was of Rhonda leaving the room, holding her face, after she'd been punched by the Doctor after refusing his sexual advances.

In the script, the scene ended there, but Baz came up with a twist.

"Why don't we finish with a shot of a patient in the room?" he said. "It can be a random guy who's just sitting there all along?"

"That's fucking awesome," Craig said.

I couldn't disagree.

It was genius.

"Cool," I said. "We can have Craig turn toward the chair and say something like, 'Sorry, that was my receptionist... She has a bit of a crush on me."

The two of them burst out laughing.

"Yeah, that'd be perfect," Craig said.

"Can I play the patient?" Baz asked.

"You're the only one who can," I replied.

"Craig and I were both in the scene."

"Great," he said. "Where's the props bag?"

"In the other room," I said. "Do you need some help deciding what to do?"

"No," Baz replied. "I've got an idea."

He put down the camera and made his way to the door.

"Stay here, both of you," he said. "I want it to be a surprise."

I waited with Craig while Baz put on his disguise.

"What do you think he'll come back as?" I asked.

Craig shrugged.

"Knowing him, it'll be a clown," he sniggered.

Ten minutes later, Baz came into the room and both our jaws dropped in shock.

"What do you think?" he said, pouting like Derek Zoolander.

"Wash it off now," Craig said.

Baz laughed.

"You don't like it?"

"Baz," he replied. "We can't do blackface. It's fucking racist."

"Yeah, but it's funny," Baz replied. "Cos everyone knows I'm white."

"I get where you're coming from," I said. "But no. You can't do this kind of shit anymore."

"Anymore?" Craig remarked. "It was a dodgy back then!"

Baz sighed.

"Spoilsports," he said. "Can I at least have a tan? If I can't be black, can I at least be Spanish?"

"Yes, that's fine," I said.

"Yeah," Craig replied. "That's not racist... *Yet*."

* * *

We filmed the next scene the following Tuesday. It was another weird one... It picked up on Charlie's plotline, with him return to his mother's house. To add a bit of faux drama, we filmed a sequence of Baz stumbling through the streets, as if he was in a daze. I figured that it would make sense, given that in the last scene he'd been having a conversation with a talking shit.

Twenty years later, I wrote a novelisation of the movie called, *Abhorrent*, explained how this had happened. It involved Charlie waking up and foraging for food, and the whole 'talking shit' episode had been the result of him snacking on some magic mushrooms, which he'd found beneath a bush.

The sequence finished with a shot of Charlie collapsing at his mother's door, then being dragged inside. An hour or two later, he regains consciousness, with his mother standing above him.

It was the first and only time Craig had ever

played a female character.

"I'm not happy about this," he said, donning the old woman's wig. "Maybe you should do it? Charlie's mother could be Mrs. Crumpton..."

"We can't," I replied. "You've already appeared as the character."

I was referring to a cut-away we'd shot during the hypnosis scene. It featured Craig, as Mallory, berating Charlie in a flashback.

"Damn it," he said.

"Don't worry mate," I replied. "There's nothing wrong with playing a female part. They do it all the time on *League of Gentlemen...*"

"Yeah, I guess... So, what am I going to wear?"

Because we were shooting at Baz's house, he raided his mom's wardrobe for something we could use. After rooting around in her stuff for a good ten minutes, he produced a long nightgown made from white silk.

"Here you go," he said, handing it to Craig. "Try this on."

Craig worked his arms through the sleeves, pulled it over his head, then went to look at himself in the mirror.

"Bloody hell," he said. "I look like my aunty Jean..."

"Not quite," I laughed. "You're missing the lipstick and blusher."

"Don't push it," he snapped.

* * *

We began filming, starting with the shot of Baz waking up. To better sell the 'horror', I crash-zoomed into his expression of shock.

It worked a treat.

I then reversed the angle to reveal what he was looking at... Craig wearing a nightgown.

"Charlie," he growled. "Where have you been? I was expecting you here two weeks ago!"

"Sorry, mother... I was scared..."

"Scare of ME?"

I called 'cut' before creasing into a fit of giggles.

"That was brilliant," I said to Craig. "Really fucking good! We don't need a second take."

"Thank fuck for that," he replied. "This thing's as itchy as fuck..."

"Are you talking about the wig or the nightgown?" Baz laughed.

"Both..." he replied.

We continued shooting, and in less than an hour, we were.

"Bloody hell," Baz said, "We're getting good at this, aren't we?"

"Yeah," I agreed. "And we're not scrimping on quality either. This footage looks ace."

I wasn't overexaggerating.

Before we started shooting, I set up several lamps around the bedroom to make the atmosphere more sinister.

It had worked a treat.

We quickly headed back to mine for the edit. After cutting the clips, we overlayed the footage with the same music we'd used in the 'talking turd' sequence.

"We'll should always do this whenever the mother is on-screen," Craig said. "It's like she has her own theme tune...."

"Yeah," I said. "I was thinking the exact same thing."

It seemed as if the film was taking on a life of its own; that it was writing and producing itself, irrespective of our input. Normally, this kind of shit would freak me out, but because it was going so well, I was happy ride the wave.

"So, what's next?" Craig asked, once we'd finished.

"Need you ask," I replied. "It's where Rhonda comes home early and discovers the truth about Savo..."

It tied into film's subplot, about Savo using Rhonda's house as a brothel.

"Oh god," Craig said. "Does it involve a sex scene?"

"Yes," I admitted.

"Well, I'm not playing no prozzie," he rasped. "I'd had enough of wearing skirts..."

I laughed.

"It's ok, mate," I said. "We can't use you anyway. Savo's in the scene."

Craig hummed.

"So, who are we using? I hope that doesn't mean us having to use the tit-girl?"

He was referring to Kathy, from *My Last Fiver*.

"Hey," Baz said. "What's wrong with Kathy?"

"She can't act," Craig replied.

"Yeah," I added, "And wouldn't want to risk you shagging her for real. We're making a comedy, not a porno!"

"So, who then?" Craig asked.

"I was thinking maybe Mary?"

"You reckon she'll do it?"

I nodded.

"It's only a short shoot," I replied. "Plus, it's on a weeknight, so she can't give us any bullshit about going to the zoo..."

* * *

After writing the next part of the script, I gave Mary a call to see if she was interested in the part.

"What's the role?" she asked. "Is it something meaty that I can get my teeth into, like a woman who's been cheated on and takes revenge on her husband? Or is it something dramatic, like someone's who dealing with grief? One of my uncles died recently, so I know exactly how that feels and I can channel my real-life emotions into the part..."

"It's a prozzie," I replied.

"A prostitute?" she said. "Ok... So, I'm guessing she's guessing she's an addict, or has a baby or something, and she's only doing because she's come from a broken home...?"

"If you like," I said. "But none of that's in the script..."

"Oh..."

She sounded disappointed.

"It's more like a Carry-On-type thing," I said. "Like Babs Windsor in stilettos?"

She suddenly perked up.

"Babs Windsor? I love her!"

"Cool," I said. "Can you do the voice?"

"Not arrrf!" she replied, in a broad cockney tang.

"Great," I said. "That's exactly what we're going for."

* * *

The following Tuesday, I picked her up and brought her back to mine for the shoot. Baz had recently bought his own car, a massive Volvo, so he drove himself over, picking up Craig on the way.

"Is what I'm wearing ok?" she asked, while I set up the camera in the bedroom.

I looked her up and down.

She was wearing a short skirt, knee-high

boots, and a little purple top.

"Yeah," I replied. "That's fine."

"What about me?" Baz asked.

He'd just been in the bathroom, getting changed, and had entered the room wearing a mesh T-Shirt, which exposed his nipples.

"What the hell's that?" I asked.

"My costume," he replied. "What do you think?"

"It's a bit G.A.Y," I said. "But it'll do."

"Perfect," Craig said. "You look like a proper ponce."

"No," I said. "He's a punter... You're the ponce. 'Ponce' means Pimp."

"Does it?" he replied. "I thought 'punters' and 'ponces' were the same thing?"

"No," I replied. "A 'ponce' is the pimp. A 'punter' is a customer."

"So, what's a 'nonce' then?"

"A paedo," I replied.

Craig laughed.

"How do you know these things?" he asked.

"Believe me," I replied. "I wish I didn't..."

After Craig and I had donned our Savo and Rhonda costumes, we staged the scene for the first shot, which involved Rhonda coming in and catching Baz's character having sex with Mary on the bed.

I handed Craig the camera and told him what to do.

"When I open the door," I said, "Catch my

reaction then pan round onto the bed. We'll then cut to a close-up of their faces for a reaction."

"Yes, master," Craig sneered. "Whatever you say..."

Mary climbed onto the bed, then lay on her back with her legs akimbo. Baz positioned himself between them, then pulled up the sheets.

"Shall I pull my top down a little?" Mary said. "...So, it looks like I'm naked?"

"No need," Craig said. "This is a family show."

Suddenly, Baz started giggling.

"You ok, mate?" I said.

My tone was sharper than it needed to be.

"Yeah," he chuckled. "Just a bit of rubbage... Give me a sec to adjust..."

He reached down and moved his junk.

Mary baulked theatrically.

"Bloody hell," she laughed. "What are you packing down there? A fresh fruit salad?"

Baz smiled proudly.

"Ok," I said, shaking my head. "Can we make a start now?"

Baz turned his head and nodded.

"Right," Craig said. "Starting positions..."

I stepped back and closed the door.

"Action!"

I turned the handle, came inside, then looked towards the bed. Craig followed the movement of my eyes onto the bedsheets, which were moving up and down.

"Cut," Chris said. "We need more volume... You're shagging too realistically. We need more grunting and groaning."

"What, like this?" Baz said.

He began yelling, "Oh Lord" at the top of his voice, ramming his hips into Mary's gusset like a Porn Star. It immediately set her off, and she started laughing and joining in, with a series of 'ooohs' and 'cooohs', ad-libbing lines like, "Fuck me" and "Harder, Daddy, please!"

For a second, I wondered where she was getting it from. Back in those days, *Pornhub* and *YouPorn* hadn't been invented.

"Ok," I said. "Maybe tone it down a little. Too much filth and we lose the laughs."

Baz responded by checking his thrusts and quietening his moans. Mary did the same.

"Lose the words," Craig said. "I only want the groaning."

Baz laughed, then did the same thing again. This time, the words, "Oh Lord" were barely audible.

"Bloody hell," I rasped. "We're not gonna get anywhere if you don't take this seriously."

Baz stopped and grinned at me.

"Chill out, Dom," he said. "We're having a laugh. Is this what it's all about?"

"No," I said. "We're making a film."

"Ooooh," he mocked. "Someone got out of the wrong side of the bed this morning..."

I stood there and huffed.

"Come on," Craig said. "Stop pratting around now. Let's get this done this done before Dom has a coronary..."

* * *

A good two hours later, we finally wrapped. Of all the shoots we'd done, this had been the worst. The footage however, looked great. Despite all the larking around, we'd all delivered some solid performances, hitting the right notes in all the right places.

After the edit, the timeline stood at 28 minutes. It was far and away the longest film we'd ever made, and there were still a few more scenes to do.

The first of these involved the resolution of Charlie's storyline with his mother. After giving it some thought, I decided it would be best to kill off Mallory so that Charlie could return home to Rhonda and save her from Savo.

I originally conceived of him hitting her over the head with a vase, but after further thought, I rejected it on the grounds that Charlie was the hero of the story, and that matricides couldn't be heroes.

In the end, I opted for Mallory dying from natural causes - a heart attack, triggered by overexerting herself whilst whipping Charlie's arse...

It made a lot of sense.

We'd already established that she was a psychopath who liked to torture on her son. What better way for her to die, than in the very act itself?

It was deliciously ironic.

And with her out of the way, I figured the final scene would write itself. Charlie would return home where he'd find Rhonda being held hostage by Savo. He'd then fight Savo, defeat him, and win back her heart.

Simples.

The next night I bashed out the scene on my PC and emailed it over to Craig and Baz, entitling the message, 'Penultimate Scene'.

Craig immediately phoned me.

"Only two scenes left?" he said.

"Yeah," I replied. "We're nearly there... This time next week, we'll be done."

"How's long do you reckon it'll be in total?" he asked.

"We're probably looking at around 35 minutes," I replied. "But we could probably stretch it to 40, if we do a '*They Live*' on the fight scene."

They Live was one of favourite films. It starred Rowdy Roddy Piper as an American everyman, who one day discovers that aliens have been living among us. It was infamous an extended fight scene between the protagonist and his disbelieving friend, and had garnered a cult following amongst fans, for how long and ridiculous it was. It had been parodied several times in TV and Film, most notably in the *South Park* episode, *Krazy Kripples*, where they produced a shot-for-shot remake involving the characters, Jimmy and Timmy.

"Yeah, we defo need to do a *They Live*," Craig chuckled. "We should probably we choreograph it out first... We don't want to end up with the kind of shit fight we had on *Hunted*."

"Definitely," I said. "I've already been thinking about that. I've got a few ideas."

"Cool," he replied. "I can't wait."

"Me neither," I said.

It was true.

I couldn't.

CHAPTER 36:
DISASTER

Four days before the shoot, my cousin, Curt, called me from Plymouth. He'd heard about my films through the family and wanted to hear how I was getting on. He was also a big fan of Apple computers.

"Is it true you got yourself an iMac?" he asked.

"Yeah," I replied. "It's great. I love it."

"What OS have you got? Is it the latest version?"

"Probably not," I replied. "I'm not connected to the internet, so I can't download anything."

"You need that update," he said. "The latest OS is amazing. Everything is faster."

"What, like applying effects to video clips?" I said.

It had been only bugbear with the software.

Rendering took ages. If you were applying an effect to a whole scene, it could easily take an hour or more.

"Yeah," he gushed. "Everything."

"Including effects?" I pressed.

"That especially," he replied. "Up to twice as fast, I hear."

"Wow," I said. "That'd be really helpful."

"You should get yourself on the internet, mate," he said. "Download it."

"How big is the file?" I asked.

"A couple of hundred meg," he replied. "But it's well worth it."

"Will it wipe my movie files though?

I asked the question because I'd heard stories of people upgrading to the latest version of Windows and losing all their shit.

"No," he laughed. "It's a system upgrade. It doesn't affect the software."

"Are you sure?" I asked.

"Yeah," he replied. "Positive."

"Ok," I said. "I'll give it a go..."

* * *

After burning off a DVD of the footage we'd shot so far, I brought the iMac into my brother's bedroom then plugged in the ethernet cable. Following the instructions on-screen, I connected it to the web, then searched Yahoo for the Apple website. When it opened, I found the link to the upgrade then started the download.

The next morning, I found the *dmg* file sitting proudly on my desktop. I took a breath to steel myself, then launched the file.

The loading bar popped up and the software began installing.

So far, so good...

I sat watching, as the progress bar ticked away. When it reached 100%, the iMac's base unit pinged and a message appeared on the screen saying, *'Software Update Successful. Preparing to Restart'.*

A moment later, the screen faded to black. A second after that, the restart tone sounded.

When the desktop reappeared with iMovie in the dock, I beathed a sigh of relief.

Everything was ok.

And then I loaded the program...

To my horror, all my videos were gone!

My heart skipped a beat.

This wasn't supposed to happen!

Frantically, I opened the Finder and typed in the word, 'video'.

I tried it again, using the extension .mov.

Again, nothing appeared.

The movie files weren't there.

"Oh god, no," I whimpered.

I couldn't believe what was happening.

With an angry roar, I stormed out of the room, connected Glen's PC to the internet, then switched it on. Loading up Yahoo, I searched for the Apple website. Beneath the 'Download Update' button was a link named, 'User Notes'.

I clicked it and it brought up a list of common issues.

Second from top was an article named, 'Loss of Video Clips in iMovie'.

I bit my lip.

Jesus Christ...

I clicked on the link, and it opened text file containing a paragraph, which warned that installation of the new OS may result in the unintentional loss of data files.

"Fuck!" I swore at the top of my voice.

I immediately rushed downstairs and called my cousin.

"For God's sake, Curt," I yelled. "You've fucked up everything!"

"What are talking about?" he replied.

"That new OS," I snapped. "It's deleted my movie files."

"Did you not check the installation notes?" he said, finally.

"Only afterwards," I said. "You told it would be ok."

He went silent.

"I'm guessing you made backups, right?"

"I burned off a DVD," I said.

"Then you're ok," he replied. "All you need to do is rip the video and reinsert it into the timeline."

"How?"

He explained that there was a piece of software I could buy called *Toast*, which could be used to convert DVDs into video files.

"You think it'll work?" I asked.

"Yes," he replied. "Definitely."

* * *

The next morning, I drove to PC World for a copy of *Toast*. After parking up, I rushed inside to the Apple section then looked for it in the software stand.

It wasn't there.

"Can I help you?" a voice said.

I turned and saw that it was Phil.

"Hi Phil," I said. "Remember me? I bought an iMac off you a few months ago."

He gave me a blank look.

"Yeah," he lied. "What are you looking for?"

"A copy of *Toast*," I replied. "I need it urgently."

He blew out his cheeks.

"Sorry, mate," he replied. "We don't stock it. You'll have to order it online."

"Can't you order it for me?"

"We can," he replied. "But it'll take four weeks to get here."

"Why?" I asked.

"That's just the way it is," he said. "You'd be better off ordering it direct."

At this point, I'd never bought anything off

the internet. I'd heard too many stories of people being conned.

"Is there no way you can get it quicker?" I said.

Phil shook his head.

"If you're desperate to get it," he said, "you might want to try one of the Apple stores. There's one in the Bull Ring..."

* * *

I left the shop, got in my car, then drove through the Christmas traffic to Birmingham, where I parked up then made my way to the store. It had been a long time since I'd last braved the Bull Ring and didn't even know there was an Apple store there, let alone know where it was.

After wandering around the huge mall for three quarters of an hour, I eventually happened upon it, near the Corporation Street entrance.

Its frontage looked like the screen of my iMac, made from glass and brilliant white plastic panels. Embossed above the double-panelled door was the Apple logo. There were no words beneath it.

It looked a little pretentious.

As did the people inside...

I saw them mingling through the glass, a multitude of hipsters and creative types. Stepping in, I noticed that many of them weren't even shopping, they were simply sitting around desks, chatting to each other or drinking lattes.

I went inside and made my way to the counter, where I was greeted by young man in a black T-Shirt, whose eyes were made up with mascara. He wore a name card on a badge around his neck. It said, 'Tarq'.

"Greetings, traveller," he said to me. "What can I do for you today?"

"I looking to buy a copy of *Toast*," I replied. "Do you sell it?"

"Sorry, no," he replied. "*Toast* is a third-party product. We only sell licenced software here."

I groaned.

I'd come all this way for nothing.

"Do you know where I can get a copy?" I asked.

"Have you tried online?" he said.

"But I need it now," I said, shaking my head. "I can't wait a month for delivery."

Jez hummed.

"In that case, you may be a bit stuck..."

I snorted through my nostrils.

"Can I ask why you need it?" he said. "There may be an Apple product that does the same thing."

"I need to rip the video off a DVD," I replied.

"Oh," he said. "Well, here at Apple we don't endorse that sort of thing."

"It's my own DVD," I clarified. "It's a film I made with my mates, on iMovie."

"Oh," he said. "In case, you might want to talk to one of our iGeniuses..."

"iGeniuses?" I said.

"Yes," he replied.

He pointed to one of the tables, where several clerks were demonstrating products.

"They're members of staff who know everything about Apple Products. I'm sure if you had a session with one of them, they'd be able to find you an alternative solution."

"Ok," I said.

I turned and made my way over.

"Wait," the young man said. "You can't just go over. You'll need to book an appointment."

"How do I do that?" I said.

"Well, first, we'll need to register you on the system..."

I followed him to one of the computers that was sitting on an empty table.

"I'll need to take your details," he said. "Name, address, Date of birth, Credit Card details..."

"Credit Card details?" I said.

"Yes," Jez nodded. "To access the iGenius service, you'll need a subscription with the store. It's £5 a month, but for that you'll get unlimited access to iGenius services. You'll even be able to book yourself into an iGenius session up to *two weeks* in advance."

I nearly choked on my own spit.

"Hang on," I said. "So, what you're telling

me is that I'll need to pay five quid a month in order to book myself a session with an advisor, who may or may not be able to help me, and even then, I'll have to wait up to two weeks before I'm seen?"

The young man smiled nervously.

"Yes," he said.

"No thanks," I replied. "This is fucking con."

With a loud huff, I turned on my heels and left the store.

* * *

As I made my way back to the car, I wondered how I'd break the bad news to Craig...

There were two approaches. Soft and Hard. The former involved apologising profusely, admitting my mistake and asking him for forgiveness. The latter involved blaming everything on Curt.

I chose the latter.

"It's all Curt's fault," I groaned, after summoning the courage to call him. "He told me everything was going to be fine; that installing the updates wouldn't affect the files. That fucking idiot has cost us our film..."

"He didn't force you to do it though, did he?"

"No," I said. "But he said it would be ok."

"Yeah, whatever," he replied.

He wasn't buying a word of it. He knew me

too well. He could see through my lies.

"Maybe we should re-film it...?" I suggested. "We can shoot it again from the start?"

"Nah," Craig said. "I aint going through all that again."

"Then what are we going to do?"

"*You* can do whatever you want," he rasped. "But I'm out. I've had enough disappointments this year."

"Are you still pissed off about *My Last Fiver*?" I said.

The line went dead.

He'd hung upon me.

Bastard!

I called him back, but he'd turning his phone.

Blowing out my cheeks, I reached for my car keys.

It couldn't end like this. We just couldn't.

I got in my car, but before I could turn the key, a devilish voice inside my head started speaking to me...

"What are you doing?" it said. "Are you just going to let him win? Be his footstool forever? Think about it... You have the camera, the means to edit... Everything you need to make films for yourself. Films that *you* want to make... And in the way *you* want to make them. No more relegations, no more being brushed aside... This is chance. Your chance to be the boss. Your chance to take control... Do it."

I removed the key from the ignition and went inside.

Looking back, it was the biggest mistake of my life...

CHAPTER 37:
OBSESSED

I called up Baz and told him what had happened. I gave him the same story that I'd given Craig. Unlike Craig, he didn't take it too badly.

"Ahh, these things happen," he said. "Don't let it get you down."

I told him that Craig was out, that he'd had enough and was quitting filmmaking.

"Seriously?" he replied.

"Yeah," I said. "He doesn't want to do it anymore."

"But you still want to, yeah?"

"Yeah," I replied. "More than ever. Maybe you and I should carry it on from here?"

"Yeah," he said. "I'm up for that. I've got loads of ideas."

"I know you do," I replied.

Not that we'll be doing any of them...

"We'll need a new name, too," Baz said. "We can't use Shadowbright anymore."

It was true.

The name Shadowbright had been Craig's idea.

"Yeah," I agreed.

It made sense. After all, we were making a fresh start.

"How about *Wakatar*?" he suggested.

It sounded awful.

"What does it mean?" I asked.

"It doesn't mean anything," Baz replied. "But it's memorable, isn't it? Plus, it kind of fits the crazy shit we'll be doing."

I wanted say 'no, that's a terrible idea, let's think of something else,' but I needed to be diplomatic. I'd only just brought him on board. I didn't want to piss him off from the get-go...

"Yeah," I said. "Why not?"

"Cool," he replied. "So, you want to hear my ideas?"

"Yeah, go on then..."

* * *

I listened the best I could to what he had to say but I wasn't impressed. Most of his ideas were little more than concepts, or descriptions of things that he thought would look good on camera.

He'd always been obsessed with Tim Burton films, in particular *Mars Attacks*, and was keen to do something involving flying saucers.

"I've made an UFO with two paper plates," he said. "We can hang it out of my window on a fishing line to make it look like it's flying."

"That's good," I replied. "But what's the story?"

"I dunno," he said. "But I was thinking of what we could do for the aliens too. My dad's got these boiler suits. We could put them on then chop ping-pong balls in half to use for the eyes."

"Yeah," I said, "but we still need a story...."

It quickly became obvious that was he wasn't getting it, and that all he was interested in was videography for his art projects.

"Dude," I said. "I love your ideas, but we can't do anything until we've got a script."

"Ok," he hummed. "So have you got one?"

"Yes," I lied.

"What's it about?"

I quickly glanced around the room, looking for something to say. To my left was a bookcase.

"Feng Shui," I replied, reading one of the titles.

"Feng Shui?" he said.

"Yeah," I repeated

Baz started chuckling.

"Feng Shui," he laughed. "I never understood that shit."

"I know," I said. "It's weird, isn't it?"

"All right, mate," he replied. "Sounds like fun. Let's do it..."

As soon as I hung up the phone, I realised what a ball ache I'd created for myself. I'd put myself under needless pressure. I knew that whatever I produced next would probably fall under the scrutiny of Craig, who would find any reason to criticise it.

Whatever I made had to be good.

Very good.

If it wasn't, he'd use it as a stick to beat me with... I pictured him watching the finished film with Baz, slagging me off as a talentless nobody who could achieve nothing without him.

Feng-fucking-Shui!

I cursed myself for even breathing the words. How the hell would I be able to write a story about that? I knew hardly anything about it, only that it came from Japan and had something to do with furniture.

What had I been thinking?

It crossed my mind that I should phone Baz and tell him we'd go with his alien idea instead.... But then I realised it would mean handing him control.

And I couldn't have that.

I just couldn't.

This was about me now.

This was my time to shine.

Glory or death...

"Come on," I told myself. "You can do this.

You can make this work. You're as talented as Craig and Baz... You know you are..."

* * *

After wracking my brains for next two hours, it soon became apparent that to write a cogent story about *Feng Shui*, I would need to know more about it, so took the book from the shelf and started reading.

Before long, I realise that *Feng Shui* was weird. Really weird. Full of hipster, spiritualist shite about chi, energy flows and positive thinking.

It didn't sound like it was about interior design at all. It sounded like a lifestyle. A philosophy. A religion.

With this is mind, I started working on a plot, involving and a recently divorced man, who turns to *Feng Shui* to bring order to his life. Things take a tragic turn, however, when he starts taking its teachings literally. At the end of the story, he becomes so obsessed with maintaining 'harmony' that he locks himself in a cupboard, where he eventually dies from starvation.

I spent the next three days writing it up. When it was finished, I emailed it to Baz.

"I love it, mate," he said, after reading it. "It's hilarious!"

"Thanks," I replied.

I expected nothing less.

I'd put a hell of lot of work into it, drafting and redrafting it several times over.

"Are we going to use Mary for the girl?" he asked.

He was referring to the wife of the lead character, who was the story's antagonist.

"Yeah," I replied.

"Cool," he said. "I'll give her a call."

"It's okay," I said. "I'll do it."

"Are you sure?" he said. "I really don't mind."

"I'll call right away," I said. "It's already on my list of things to do."

It wasn't, but I didn't want her thinking that he was in charge.

"All right," he said. "But I'll call her too, just in case. When are we going to film it?"

"Next Tuesday," I said. "As usual."

"Cool," he said. "I'll pick her up on the way over..."

Shit, I thought. *I'd forgotten that he had a car...*

* * *

The following Tuesday evening, he turned up at mine with Mary. She'd made a special effort to look the part, decked out in a trouser suit and specs, and had slicked her hair back to make herself look more uptight.

"How do I look?" she asked.

"Perfect," I replied.

"Thanks," she said. "I met with Baz last week and we had a chat about my character..."

I glanced at Baz, who responded with a grin.

"...He told me I needed to look frigid."

"Well," I said, "That's one way of interpreting it. Shall we make a start?"

* * *

Things went well from the off. Over the weekend, I'd storyboarded extensively and knew exactly what shots were needed for each scene.

Their acting was good too. They worked well as a pair, complementing each other's performances.

After wrapping up, Baz took Mary home while I made a start on the edit.

A few hours later I'd cut all the clips and had added a basic score, which I'd composed on my keyboard.

The next night, Baz came over to record the narration.

Sadly, this it didn't go so well. Although his voice was great, he struggled with some the lines.

"I don't speak like this," he said. "This isn't my natural patter..."

"I know," I replied. "But it's the voice of the

character, not *you*."

He gave it a few more tries but couldn't get it right.

"Can't you just change the script?" he asked. "Take out all the long words?"

"No," I said. "It needs to be said as it's written, otherwise it won't make sense."

"But I can't do it," he moaned.

Craig could, I thought. *He'd have nailed it first time...*

"Don't worry," I said, finally. "I'll do it myself."

I clicked the 'record narration' button then started reading the lines from the script.

When done, I added it to the timeline, and played the footage. I noticed, straight away, that it didn't sound right. The pitch was off. The voice didn't look like it belonged to the character.

"Is there any way of deepening the sound?" Baz asked.

"I dunno," I replied. "Let's see what we can do in *Garageband*."

Garageband was another program that came free with the iMac. It allowed you to record music tracks and burn them on CDs. It also allowed you to modify sound clips in a variety of different ways.

I opened it up, created a new file, then dropped the narration into the timeline.

"Click *Effects*," Baz said, pointing to one of the buttons in the toolbar.

I did as he said and a menu appeared, showing several different options. One of them was 'Pitch Changer'.

"There you go," Baz said, spotting it. "Lower it down."

I selected the option and a dial appeared on-screen. On one side was a plus sign; on the other was a minus.

"Click on the minus," Baz said.

I clicked the button, lowering the pitch by 20%. I then played the track.

To my surprise, my voice now sounded exactly like Baz's!

"Bloody hell," he exclaimed. "You sound just like me!"

"I know," I said. "This is great!"

I exported the narration, dragged it into the iMovie timeline then pressed play.

It was a perfect fit.

"That sounds really good," Baz said. " That *Garageband* is ace!"

"Yeah," I said. "It's pretty good, isn't it?"

"It sure is," he replied. "Maybe we should also use it record some songs? I've written loads on my guitar. Maybe we could use them in our films?"

"I suppose we could," I replied. "...Providing they fit..."

"Yeah," he replied, mulling it over.

CHAPTER 38:
DAN LIZARD:
ROCK LIVES ON

I was really pleased with my work. Obsessed was great little film. The story, the camerawork, the editing, the acting, the pacing, had all come together perfectly.

The only reservation I had was the lighting. It wasn't the best, but there was little I could do about it.

Baz and Mary were overjoyed by the final cut.

"It looks great, mate," Baz said, when I next saw him. "I love it."

"Onwards and upwards from here," I replied.

"Yeah," he said.

"Now all we need is a script for the next

project..."

Baz scratched his chin.

"I've been thinking about that," he said. "Maybe we don't need one?"

My heart stopped in my chest.

"Why do you say that?" I said.

"I was thinking we could do a fake documentary," he said.

"A fake documentary?" I replied. "What about?"

"A rock star," he said. "Called Dan Lizard."

I laughed.

I couldn't deny that it was a good name.

"I love the idea, but it'll be too hard to do," I said, bringing him back down to earth. "Rock Stars go on tours and play concerts. We won't be able to do anything like that without a budget."

He looked glum.

"Unless," I added. "We make him a washout? Or someone who isn't that famous? Or maybe he's not famous, but thinks he is?"

"That's great," Baz agreed. "I like that!"

"Cool," I said.

"Yeah," he replied, "And we can do songs and music videos for it too!"

Ahh, I thought. *It suddenly makes sense...*

"Is this just an excuse to promote your music?" I sneered.

"No," he laughed. "All the songs for this will be new. I'll write them specifically for the character, stuff about trees and nature, cos I see him as being a bit of a hippy..."

"So, you haven't already wrote these songs, then?"

"Well," he said. "I've written a few... Do you want to hear one?"

He picked up his guitar and started strumming away.

"*Ooooh, Eeeeeh, Ooooh,*" he sang, "*...Cre-ate the waves.*"

I recognised the tune.

It was something he'd written years ago.

The lying git...

"So, what do you think?" he asked once he'd finished.

"I like it, mate," I lied.

His mouth parted into a wide grin.

"You wanna hear the others?"

I didn't.

I really didn't.

"Ok," I said. "Go on..."

* * *

After serenading me with several other numbers (most of which I'd heard before), he put down his guitar and asked for my opinion.

"Do you think we use any of these in the film?" he said.

The devilish part of my personality came to the fore.

"Yes," I said, "let's use them all."

"Fantastic!" he replied.

What he didn't know was that while he was singing away, I'd been hatching a plan in my head to make him look as ridiculous as possible. If Baz wanted to showcase his songs in a film, he'd only do so after I'd turned into a parody. Dan Lizard would be a joke. An idiot. Someone to laugh at. Not the loveable hero that Baz had in mind.

"It's gonna be great, mate," I said, smiling wickedly. "I can see it all now."

"Great," Baz replied. "When shall we start?"

"No time like the present," I replied.

It was a Saturday afternoon, and we still had plenty of light.

"Cool," he said. "Let's crack out the wigs!"

He took the long-haired wig out of the props bag and plonked it on his head. After wrapping a multi-coloured scarf around the neck around the neck of his guitar, we then made our way to the park to shoot an intro sequence.

While we were walking, I suddenly had an idea.

I took out the camera then asked him to talk into the lens.

"Pretend I'm the documentary camera crew" I said. "I'll ask you some questions, then give answers in character."

"Cool," he said.

"So why are we going to the park?" I asked.

"I saw this tree," he replied, putting on his best hipster accent, "Realised it was alive..."

"Are you going to show us this tree?" I said.

"Yeah," he replied. "I'll show you the tree..."

We carried on walking and talking, my questions becoming increasingly bizarre.

When we got to the entrance to the park, I noticed an empty can lying on the floor and asked him to comment on it.

"Oh God, would you look at that?" he yelled. "There's mud, life; a rock, life..."

He then picked up the can.

"This is... Is not LIFE!"

He threw it into the bushes.

"It gets to me..."

Straight away, I realised I'd totally underestimated Baz's intelligence. He could tell that I was shooting this as a parody and was playing up to it.

Once again, I felt outplayed.

Not only was he a gifted artist, actor, musician, and singer, but also an astute satirist.

Was there no end to his talent?

But by now it was too late now to throw in the towel. We'd already started making the film. I had no option but to see it through...

* * *

After shooting the opening sequence, which involved Baz talking about his love of nature, music, and love itself (deftly explained with a monologue which took the piss out of

Hipster Fuck Bois), we headed back to mine to start the edit.

While he sat and watched me arranging the clips, he made a great suggestion.

"Why don't we cut a song into this?"

"What do you mean?" I said.

"Start with me playing the intro to *Create the Waves*," he replied. "Then cut to that first clip, then cut back to the first verse of the song, then that second clip, and so forth..."

I imagined what he was saying in my mind.

Fuck me, I thought. *It was genius.*

"Ok," I said. "We'll need to film you playing it live. Can you do that?"

He smiled.

"Sure..."

* * *

He sat on my bed with the guitar while I got out my old karaoke machine and set up the mic. I turned it on, added a bit of reverb, and he sung a few notes to so he could hear what he sounded like.

"I like this," he said, fiddling with the volume. "I might have to get one of these myself."

"If this film goes well, mate," I replied. "You can have it."

I'd been done with Karaoke since 1999.

"Cool," he said, giving me a grin.

"Ok," I said. "Are you ready to go?"

"Sure am, Chief," he replied.

I held up the camera and called 'action'.

He began singing into the mic, while I did my best to make the footage look interesting.

Luckily, I didn't have to try too hard.

I'd heard the song enough times to know it's structure, so moved the camera in time with the chords.

I'd also struck it lucky with the lighting. Since my bedroom was south facing, and because it was late afternoon, his outline was perfectly sheened with a glow of cold sunlight.

It couldn't have looked better.

Once he was done, I imported the footage into the timeline, then cut in the clips as he'd described.

It looked brilliant.

Really brilliant.

"This is ace," Baz said, grinning at me like a Cheshire Cat. "I've got a good feeling about this, Dom."

"Me too," I replied.

You talented bastard...

* * *

Buoyed by the success of the opening sequence, we decided to do some more filming the following night.

"I've had another idea," Baz said. "I think you should be in it."

"Me?" I said. "But I can't act."

I was acutely aware of my limitation in front of the lens. I'd done a half-decent job as Rhonda in the last film, but that was only because I'd been ripping off Mel B from Bo-Selecta.

"I dunno," I said. "You were so good in the last scene, I wouldn't want to lower the standards..."

"Don't be daft," he said. "You're an ace actor. And I've got the perfect role for you.... *Billy Guana.*"

"Billy Guana?" I replied.

"Yeah," he said. " Billy Guana... Dan Lizard's bandmate."

I pondered the role.

Maybe it would offer me some creative input?

I'd contributed nothing so far.

"Ok," I said. "Give me two mins to think about my character..."

While I was at University, I'd watched *Spinal Tap*, so decided to draw some inspiration from the character, Derek Smalls, who had a softly spoken demeanour that would perfectly contrast with Dan Lizard's brashness.

"Ok," I said. "I'm ready to give it a go."

"Cool," he said.

After putting on a wig, a cap, and a dodgy T-Shirt, I was ready to start.

"Let's do it as a vox-pop," I said. "I'll talk

directly into the lens."

I handed Baz the camera, then asked him to press record button.

"Rolling," he said. "So, Billy, where did you first meet Dan Lizard?"

My mind went blank.

I'd never done improvisation before. Without lines, I felt completely lost.

"Errr..." I stuttered.

Baz started laughing.

"Don't worry, mate," he said. "We'll go again."

He clicked play.

"Action!"

I froze again.

"Shit," I said. "I've gone blank..."

He turned off the camera.

"Have a think about what you're going to say," he said. "...Then, when you're ready, we'll go again."

"Ok," I said.

I started thinking about my character. The only things I knew about him were his name and where he came from. Other than that, I had nothing

"I might need a few minutes," I said.

"No worries," Baz replied, with a grin. "Take your time..."

I wasn't used to thinking on my feet. When it came to creating characters, I liked to mull things over, create backstories, however brief, that would explain their motivation and foibles.

I sat back and began imaging the kind of life that Billy Guana had, and how he had come to find himself in the company of a man like Dan Lizard. Because their personalities were so different, I thought it unlikely that they would have been friends at school, reasoning that they'd probably met each other through music.

But if that was a case, I thought, why would someone as self-obsessed as Dan Lizard burden himself with the annoyance of Band mates?

In the end, I decided that their initial meeting had occurred by accident during a family holiday to Morocco.

"Ok," I said. "I'm ready."

Baz pressed record, then gestured for me to start.

"So where did you first meet Dan Lizard?" he asked.

"Danny Lizard?" I replied. "Tangiers, Morocco. I was on holiday with my nan, and we were in the Bizarre. At the centre on the crowd, sitting on a box, was a white Caucasian male. He looked a little out of place, in Morocco, so I turned to my nan and said, 'Nan, what's wrong with this picture?'. 'What picture?' she replied. 'The man on the box,' I said. 'That's the picture you should be looking at...'"

"Dom," Baz said. "What are you doing?"

"What do you mean," I said.

"This story..." he laughed. "It's not going

anywhere. It needs to be snappier."

I scratched my head.

He was probably right. I had been mostly waffle.

"Ok," I said, "I'll wrap things up."

"Cool," he replied. "Action!"

I carried on with my monologue, recounting the story as best I could.

After a while, Baz started chuckling.

"Bloody hell, dude... You're so boring," he said.

"Boring?" I replied.

"Yeah," he said. "But don't worry... We can work this into the film."

He handed me the camera then put on his wig.

"Shoot me," he said.

I did as he told me.

"Billy Guana?" he began. "Yeah, despite him being one of the most boring people in the world, I love him like a brother... Unconditionally. As in, I have no choice, if you know what I mean?"

I bit my lip.

It was brilliant.

In a single sentence, he'd not only salvaged my piss-poor performance, but had established a foible of my character that we could use going forward.

Talented bastard...

When we pieced together the two interviews in the edit, it worked a treat.

"I think we need another song," Baz said, once I'd saved the file.

I was in no position to disagree.

It was clear he knew what he was doing. He had the minas touch.

He pulled out the karaoke machine and set up the mic.

"Ok," he said, as I pointed the lens in face. "This one's called, *Australia*..."

* * *

We persisted with the vox-pop/music video format for several more shoots, but it soon became stale.

"Dude," I said, after watching our footage one night, "we need to introduce a narrative here. We can't just keep doing talking heads and music videos. Something needs to happen."

"Yeah," he agreed. "I was thinking the same thing. That's why I've asked Blakey to help us out. He's gonna play Danny's manager, Bryan Clarkson."

Blakey was going out with Baz's sister. I'd only ever met him a couple of times, so didn't know much about him.

"Can he act?" I said.

"None of us can act," Baz laughed. "But he's willing to give it a go."

"All right," I said.

I didn't bother arguing.

It was clear who was running the show.

* * *

The next night, Baz brought Blakey to mine to film his first scene.

"He's gonna need a wig," Baz said. "Can I have a look for something in the props bag?"

"Sure," I said. "Knock yourself out."

"Thanks for letting me in on this," Blakey said to me, while Baz was rooting around in the cupboard. "I've seen some of the films and it looks like a right laugh."

"No worries," I replied.

It wasn't like I had any say in it...

"Here you go," Baz said. "Try this."

He handed Blakey the short brown wig that Craig had used in *The Magical Entrance.*

He put it on.

Surprisingly, it suited him.

"Ok," he said. "Where do you want me?"

We told him to sit in the armchair by the wall, while Baz set up the camera.

"What do you want me to say?" he asked.

"It'll be like an interview," I explained. "I'll ask you some questions and you'll answer in character."

"All right," he nodded.

I then gave Baz the signal to roll the tape.

"So, how did become Danny's manager?" I asked.

Blakey hit the ground running, describing in detail how he'd met Dan Lizard whilst working as a Roadie for *Motley Crue*. It was every bit as longwinded and overly detailed as my own account as Billy Guana, but not nearly half as boring.

"How was that?" he asked, after Baz had called 'cut'.

"Brilliant," I said. "You're a natural."

Another one, I thought.

I instantly felt crap.

We took the action downstairs to start filming the story. Now that there were three of us, it was much easier to do, as it allowed me to pick up the camerawork while they improvised their scene.

Before we'd met, Baz and I had discussed where would go with the narrative, finally agreeing that it would focus on the breakdown of Dan Lizard's relationship with Bryan. The catalyst for change would be Bryan's suggestion that Danny involve himself in a local protest to stop the creation of a new bypass. After turning up at the site, the two of them find that they are the only people there, that the protest occurred a year earlier, and that they'd actually travelled on the new bypass to get there.

The revelation sickens Danny, who blames Bryan for the mistake. He then writes a song about it, which Bryan hears. Taking it personally, he goes to the woods, where he drinks himself into a stupor, and is eventually found by Danny, who deals with the issue by having Bryan sectioned.

The film then ends with Dan Lizard pondering his future as an artist.

As far as storylines went, it was a strong one, which offered a lot of scope for conflict.

Baz loved it.

"It's just brilliant," he said, after we'd sketched it all out. "It's all about one man's descent into madness..."

"Yes," I agreed, "And there's something markedly Shakespearean about the fact that it was all caused by his best friend's arrogance."

He gave me a confused look.

"Yeah," he said. "That too..."

* * *

Once Blakey had had a smoke, we started shooting the scene where Bryan broaches the subject of the protest.

I kept the camera loose in my hand. It meant I could move it as fluidly as possible, allowing me to follow the action as the improvised dialogue switched between Danny and Bryan.

I was a little worried about how it would turn out, given the fact that they were working without a script, but the two of them pulled through, delivering masterful performances, which not only progressed the plot but also foreshadowed the ending.

"Brilliant work, both," I said, after finally calling 'cut'. "That was excellent. Truly excellent."

"Thanks," Baz said. "Shall we do the next part too, while we're all here?"

I couldn't see why not.

It was still early afternoon, and it wasn't like we were working off a script.

"Yeah," I said. "Why not?"

We jumped in the car and drove to the park. Once there, we got out and started shooting the sequence where Bryan discovered he'd made an error with the dates.

It was excellent.

Their performances were even stronger than in the previous scene.

Once we were finished, we returned to my house, surfing on a wave of positivity.

"I've got a really good feeling about this," I said, as we pulled up on my drive. "I can't wait to edit it."

"Me neither," Baz said.

We went in, transferred the video onto my iMac, then spent the next two hours editing everything we'd done.

Despite there being no script, it was easy. For the first scene, there was hardly any cutting at all. Their improvisation was so strong and interesting to watch, there was no need to chop it up.

When the final clip had been inserted into the timeline, I noticed that the total length of the project was greater than 20 minutes.

I couldn't believe it.

We'd nearly equalled the run time of Savo and Rhonda in just three shoots.

"I definitely think improvisation is the way forward," Baz said, as he watched the footage on-screen. "It's more realistic when you don't have to worry about lines."

He was right.

Without a script, the performances came across as more natural.

"I agree," I said. "But we you also need structure. What we've done today proves that."

Baz nodded.

"So, when are we filming next?" Blakely asked.

"Are you free tomorrow?" Baz replied.

* * *

The next day, we went to the park to film the next two scenes. The first one involved Danny's search for Bryan, who had gone missing following their argument at the protest. The second involved shooting a music video for a song I'd written for the film, called *The Whore of War*.

Both were a lot of fun to shoot.

For the music video, Baz put on some combat trousers and wrapped a cord of red ribbon around his head like Rambo, and I got a load of shots of him rolling around the grass and climbing up trees.

When we got back, we recorded the song together in my bedroom, with Baz singing and Blakey playing rhythm guitar.

He was surprisingly good.

Once we'd finished, I extracted the audio, inserted it into the timeline, then wove in a bunch of clips that we'd shot at the park.

It looked fantastic.

Much better than I ever expected.

The song sounded great too, perfectly complimenting the video.

All in all, it was an incredibly successful day.

I felt great afterwards. It was nice to finally make a significant contribution to the project.

I was happy that I'd received a bit of praise, too. Not only from Baz, but from Blakey, who complimented my song writing skills. To this day, I'll never forget what he said to me: "You're like one of these people who are good at everything, aren't you?"

It was first and last time anyone had ever told me that.

* * *

The final scenes of the film involved Danny calling Bryan's wife to tell him that he'd been sectioned and had been admitted to a mental health hospital.

It was an easy shoot as it only involved Baz.

"Why don't you start it," I suggested, "...by saying, 'Hi Virginia, I'm just calling for two things: First, to say what a nice day it is and ask if you're enjoying the weather, and second, that I've had your husband sectioned...'."

Baz laughed out loud.

"Yeah, mate" he chuckled. "That's hilarious!"

I couldn't help but smile.

Two for two, I thought.

He said the line exactly as I'd said it, but his comedy timing was much better. As was his acting.

Not that it mattered.

It was my joke.

And probably the best in the film.

"You know what," Baz said, after we'd finished shooting. "It'd be great to get my sister in to play Virginia."

"Yeah," I agreed. "We do a vox pop of her, commenting on how what you did fucked up their marriage."

"Unintentionally..." Baz added.

I started chuckling.

Sometimes it sounded like he and Danny

were the same person.

"Yeah," I said. "But he's just too stupid to realise it."

* * *

He drove me down to his house, then went into back garden, where we set up a deckchair on the grass.

"Kaci!" he called up to her bedroom window.

The curtains parted and her face appeared at the glass.

"Wanna be in a film?" Baz shouted.

She opened the window.

"What?" she said.

"Wanna be in my film?" Baz repeated.

"What have I got to do?" she asked.

"Pretend to be drunk and pregnant," I said.

She pondered my word for a few seconds.

"Ok," she said. "I'll be down in a sec..."

A few moments later, she came outside holding a wine glass. By the looks of it, she was already half-cut.

"Have I got to learn any lines?" she asked.

"No," Baz explained. "It's all improvised."

She came onto the grass and sat down on the deckchair.

"Do I need a bump?" she asked.

"It would be good," I said. "Unless we just shoot your face... But if we do that, we'll lose a bit of impact."

"Here," Baz said, handing her a pillow. "Shove this up your top."

She lifted her blouse and stuffed it under.

It looked lumpy and rubbish.

"A balloon would be better," she said.

I looked at Baz.

"Do you have one?"

He shook his head.

"Who keeps balloons?" he replied.

"I can go to the shop and get one," I said.

"Nah," Baz said. "We'll stick with the pillow and keep the shot high."

"Fair enough," I replied.

I handed him the camera and he pointed the lens at her face.

"Ok," I said to her. "You're expecting triplets, but you've just had a phone call from your husband's best friend telling you that he's had your husband committed... How do you feel?"

She started giggling.

"What kind of film is this?" she tittered.

"A comedy," Baz said. "It's funny."

"I know what a comedy is," she sneered.

"Ok," I said, "Let's do a take..."

Baz pressed record.

"How do you feel about the man who committed your husband?" I asked.

Kaci laughed.

Straight away, I assumed she was corpsing. But then I realised it part of her act.

"Danny Lizard..." she slurred. "...Is a bad man... A bad man, who took my husband away from my three babies... Yes, I'm having three. Three beautiful babies..."

She started snorting through her nose, half-laughing, half-crying.

"...What if one of them is deformed?" she suddenly crowed, downing the rest of her wine. "Deformed... And without a dad?"

"And 'cut'!" Baz said. "That was great, nice one."

"Great?" I said, "It was amazing. Where did that come from?"

I wasn't being glib.

Her performance, though short, had been something else.

In two short sentences, she'd managed to the convey both the comedy and the tragedy of her situation.

It was wonderful.

All I could do was stand there and clap.

* * *

We went back to mine, uploaded the footage then added it to the timeline.

"There we go, mate," I said. "All finished."

We watched it through. All thirty glorious minutes of it.

I felt proud at what we'd achieved in such a short period of time. Its total runtime was longer than that of *Savo and Rhonda*, but it had only taken a fraction of the time to shoot.

"I can't believe what we've managed to do," I said, as the credits started to roll.

"I know," Baz said. "It's really good."

It felt like a huge leap forward. The film was proof that we could achieve something that was genuinely worthy of TV. And the fact that we'd turned it around so fast was testament to our production skills.

I started thinking about Craig.

This had all happened without him.

I wondered whether it would have happened at all if he'd had part of the project? It would have certainly taken longer to shoot. Being married, he had less time on hands to commit to filmmaking. He was also incredibly critical. Would he have allowed Baz to run away with his ideas if he was leading the project?

Probably not.

"See," my inner Devil whispered. "I told you. All he ever did was hold you back..."

Yes, I thought. *But he was still my best mate. And I was missing him like crazy...*

CHAPTER 39:
REVENGE
IN MIND

Rock Lives On proved what could be achieved when you combined a simple format with a strong idea. I put its success down to three things: good characters, good acting, and a good story. The first made the audience care. The second made the audience believe. The third kept their interest.

Everything else, the lighting, the sound, the cinematography, etc., were all just peripheral. They could enhance or degrade a piece, but they couldn't make or break it.

Reflecting on my previous work, I realised that the best films I'd made all had these three core elements. The worst films had failed in at least one of them.

Man on the Edge, for example, was a pile of tosh because the acting and story were crap, not because of the shoddy camerawork. Similarly, *Mrs Crumpton* worked, despite its bad lighting and sound.

I discussed this theory with Baz while we were talking about our next project.

"What do you think?" I asked. "Am I right?"

"I think you need good camerawork," he replied.

"Yes," I said. "But the audience are more likely to forgive it if the characters, acting and story are good."

He laughed.

"Why are we even talking about this?"

"Because I want to know what makes a good film," I replied. "For years, I've been obsessed with improving the quality of what we do, making it as perfect as possible. At one point, I thought it was all about getting the technical stuff right, but now I know there's more to it than that. It's the other things that matter the most, not this stuff."

He smiled and shook his head.

"You're taking this way too seriously," he said.

I sighed.

He didn't care what I had to say.

Craig would have.

He and I used to talk about this sort of stuff for hours. In his bedroom. Whilst drinking his mom's tea...

"Yeah," I said. "Maybe I am..."

"Let's just concentrate on the next film," he sighed. "We should do a sequel to *Rock Lives On*... What do you think?"

"I'd be up for that," I said.

"Great," he replied, "But we'll have to put it on hold for now, pick it up in a few months' time..."

"Why?" I asked.

"I'm going to New York," he replied.

"Cool," I said. "Who are you going with?"

"Just some friends," he replied.

It was code for the Grebo gang.

"Oh," I said. "So, when are you getting back?"

"The middle of next month," he said. "But then I'll be busy prepping for Glastonbury... I'll be working on a float for the parade."

"A what for the what-now?"

He laughed out loud.

"Don't worry mate," he said. "I'm not ditching you... We'll do more films in the Autumn, I promise."

* * *

The weeks rolled by very slowly. Without a project on the go, I was incredibly bored, and I found myself yearning for something to get my teeth into.

After parting ways with Craig, I thought this would be my chance to branch out and produce more projects. It seemed ironic that I was now doing less than ever.

After several weeks on sitting on my hands, the creative yearning got too much to bear, and I started phoning around, asking friends, friends of friends, and friends of friends of friends, if they wanted to be involved.

I wasn't expecting it to work. Most of them weren't creative types. They were normies, whose lives revolved around going out on a weekend and getting pissed.

However, I did find one person.

His name was Ant. We used to be friends in Year 7, before I'd ditched him for the Grebos. He wasn't cool. He wasn't hip. And he spoke funny... As if he was posher than he was.

"Hey dude," I said, speaking to him on the phone. "Long time, no speak. How are you?"

"Yeah, good thanks," he replied.

"What have you been up to since we last spoke?"

"Hmmm," he said. "When was that, exactly? 1991?"

"Probably," I chuckled.

I told him about the filmmaking and asked him if he'd like to help out.

"What's the film about?" he asked.

"I don't know," I replied. "But I was thinking we could meet up and discuss ideas?"

"Cool," he replied.

* * *

We met at the Merry Hill Wetherspoons, where I told him about my previous projects.

"I used to do stuff with Craig," I explained.

"I know," he replied. "I've seen a few of your films."

"Which ones?" I asked.

"The one where you're the old woman..." he replied.

"Ahh, yes," I said. "That was Mrs. Crumpton. What else?"

"I've seen the werewolf one," he replied. "...Oh, and the one with Allan where you're the vampire."

"*Bite?*" I said.

"Yeah, that's the one."

"What did you think?" I asked.

"I liked them," he said. "I'm not a big fan of horror, though... I'm more into Sci-Fi."

"Oh yeah," I replied. "You're into Star Wars, aren't you?"

"Just the OT," he clarified. "The news ones suck Bantha Ass."

I agreed.

They *were* shit.

"Ok," I said. "Maybe we should do a Sci-Fi then?"

We put our heads together and soon came

up with a story involving a man who is left in a coma after being attacked by an intruder. To save his life, a doctor performs an experimental procedure on him, which sees the contents of his brain being transferred onto a computer. He wakes up, seeing things through the lens of the computer's built-in camera, and discovers that the man who attacked him is his wife's secret lover and that the two of them had conspired to kill him so that they could elope. Enraged, he man exacts his revenge by tricking his cuckold into hooking himself up to the computer's base unit, and the transferring the contents of his mind into his body. In the final scene, he confronts his wife, with... *Revenge in Mind.*

"What happens now?" Ant asked, once we'd agreed on the plot.

"Now I need to write it," I said. "Then we'll need to look for someone to play the wife."

"Who's going to play the man?" he asked.

"Why don't you do it?" I suggested. "Because you'll be in a coma for most of the film, there won't be many lines."

"Ok," he replied. "I'll give it a shot."

* * *

I returned home and started penning the script. A couple of hours later, I'd written the first draft.

When we'd discussing it in the pub, I'd

been wondering how we'd do the special effects sequences involving the brain transfer, toying with the idea of creating slides in PowerPoint, running screengrabs, then creating animations in iMovie by inserting single images into the timeline. I'd watched *Rolf's Cartoon Club* as a kid, so I had a fair understanding of how to it. The concept was simple, it just required a lot of patience.

The next morning, I called my go-to actress, Mary, and asked her if she'd like to play the role of the wife.

"Sorry," she replied. "I can't. I'm going on holiday this weekend. I won't be back for a fortnight."

"Where are you going?" I asked, half-expecting her to say 'New York'.

"Benidorm," she replied. "Cheap and cheerful."

"Sounds nice," I replied.

I hadn't been away in years.

After finishing the call, I wondered what to do. I needed an actress, and I needed one in time for the shoot, which we'd arranged for the following Saturday.

Thinking fast, I called up Becky and asked her if she was willing to take part.

"But I've moved," she said. "I live in Oxford now... And in any case, I wouldn't be able to do it as I've just bought a coffee shop on the High Street."

"Very swanky," I said.

Very annoying, I thought.

Starved of options, I called up Ant and asked if he knew any girls.

"There is someone I know," he replied. "Her name's Nat."

"Does she live locally?" I asked.

"Halesowen," he replied. "She's got her own flat."

"Cool," I said. "Can you ask her if she's up for being the wife?"

"Does that mean she'll have to kiss you?"

I'd written in a scene where the comatose man sees his wife getting it on the intruder.

"Yeah," I replied.

"I might need to send her a pic of you," he said. "She's very fussy when it comes to men."

"Fine," I said. "I'll ping you a photo.."

I combed my hair, took several selfies, and sent him the best one. Half an hour later, he texted me back.

"She's agreed to do it," he said. "She also wanted to know how tall you are, so I told her six feet."

"Thanks mate," I replied.

I was only 5'11".

"What does she look like?" I asked.

It was purely a cursory question. If she was willing to act in my film, I didn't care if she looked like *Jabba the Hut*.

"I'll send you a pic," he replied.

A few minutes later, I received it on my phone. She was tall, slender, with straight dark hair that came down to her shoulders. She wasn't the prettiest of girls, but she wasn't a troll.

"She looks good to me, mate," I said.

"Cool," he responded.

I suddenly had a brainwave.

"Dude," I said, after calling him up. "Can you call her again and ask her if we can use her flat to shoot in?"

"Yeah, sure," he replied.

"Excellent," I said. "It'd be good to break the monotony of shooting at my house or in the park.

* * *

The following week I picked him up then drove over to Nat's flat, which was new-build near the college.

As soon as I saw it, I knew it would make for the perfect location.

"I've got a good feeling about this," I said, as we left the car and made to the door.

Ant rung the bell. a few second later she answered.

"Hi Natalie," Ant said, playfully. "We're here for your close-up."

She giggled down the line then buzzed us in.

Ant open the door then held it as I squeezed

inside with the camera, and the iMac, which we were using a prop. He then led me up the stairs to her flat, where Nat was waiting for us at the door.

"Hi Ant," she said.

"Hello, my dear," he replied, using an old man's voice. "This is Dom."

We exchanged hellos and she beckoned us inside to the lounge, where I placed my stuff on the floor.

"Thanks for letting us use your flat," I said.

"No probs," she replied, with a smile. "Saves me having to drive anywhere... Do you two want drinks?"

I set up the iMac and camera while she headed to the kitchen to make us some tea.

"She seems nice," I said to Ant, as he helped me lift the base unit onto the table.

"Yeah, she has her moments," he replied.

* * *

While we drank our tea, I explained that we'd shoot the film using a tripod whenever I was on-screen, meaning that neither of them needed to do any of the camerawork.

"Thank god for that," Ant said. "I've not used a camera since High School."

I could believe it.

He'd never been into tech.

"So, what are we filming first?" Nat asked.

"We'll shoot it in chronological order," I

replied. "...Starting with the pre-title sequence. You know, the part where you come into the house and get attacked."

"Nice," Ant said.

"Cool," I replied. "Shall we make a start?"

* * *

I explained to Ash what I wanted him to do. It was very simple... He would open the front door, come inside, then act like he'd heard a noise.

"Just don't do anything until I call 'Action'," I said.

"Ok, mate..."

When went into the hall, where he opened the door, stepped outside, then closed it behind him.

So far, so good...

"Action!" I called.

He slid the key into the lock, turned the latch, then came forward into the hallway...

Like a robot.

"Cut," I said. "Can we do it again mate?"

"Why?" he asked. "What did I do wrong?"

You're wooden as fuck, mate... I'd since Conifers with better screen presence.

"Nothing," I lied. "I just need to get it again... For safety."

He performed the scene again.

Again, he was stiff and jerky. All his actions

seemed forced and unnatural.

Had he never opened a door before?

"Ok," I said. "Do it one more time, but with a bit more emotion."

"More emotion?" he replied.

"Yeah," I said. "Give me more... *feelings*."

"Ok," he said. "I'll give it a try."

He repeated the process, this time adding a snarl.

"What was that?" I asked.

"You said more emotion," he replied. "I'm angry."

"Why angry?"

"Because someone's broken into my flat..."

"Yeah," I said. "But you don't know that yet."

He looked at me, confused.

"So, what emotion do you want exactly?"

I suddenly got his meaning. When I'd said more emotion, I'd meant, 'more fluidity'. He was following my direction perfectly... I'd used the wrong wording.

"Sorry, mate," I said. "I meant to say, 'be more fluid'... Less robotic."

"You're saying my acting is robotic?" he snorted.

"A little, yeah."

"He's right," Nat said.

She was standing over my shoulder.

"You're a bit wooden."

"How can I be wooden opening a door?" Ant sniffed.

"You can, believe me," I replied.

"Let me see..."

I rewound the tape and showed him the rushes.

"Oh yeah," he said. "I see what you mean..."

We shot the take again. This time, he removed the gurn.

"How was that?" he asked.

"It'll do," I replied.

It was still as wooden as fuck, but we were running out of time.

"Let's do the next bit..."

* * *

The next bit was the fight sequence, which consisted of a single shot of Ant being hit on the back of his head.

Once we'd filmed it, I breathed a sigh of relief. For the rest of the shoot, his character would be in a coma, meaning the only acting he'd need to do would be to close his eyes.

"Where are you putting those wires?" Ant asked, as he lay on the couch with half a roll of Andrex wrapped around his forehead.

"It needs to look like it's attached to your brainstem," I said, threading the cable behind his ear.

I tucked the cable beneath the toilet paper, but it wouldn't hold.

"Why don't you put it up my nose instead?"

he suggested, after failed several attempts. "Then it won't fall out."

I gave it a try, but it looked stupid.

Nat liked it, though. It made her laugh.

"You should go with that," she chuckled, giggling into her hands.

After faffing around for a few more minutes, I eventually managed to get it stick.

"There," I said. "That'll do... Just don't move."

I picked up the camera and told him to act like he was in a coma.

For some bizarre reason, he started wiggling his eyes under the lids.

"Dude," I said. "Stop moving your eyes. It looks as if you're having a bad dream."

"But I am," Ant replied. "I'm watching my wife cheat on me."

"Yeah," I said. "But that hasn't happened just yet. We're filming it chronologically, remember..."

* * *

Fifteen minutes later, I finally got the shot. To save a bit of time, I decided to stuff the plan and do the rest of his shots too.

"Stay there," I said, "I'll get all the footage of you in one go."

"Eh?" he said. "I thought you said we were doing everything in order?"

"Yeah," I replied. "But I'm the Director, and I've changed my mind."

I started filming him from various angles, trying to get as much variation as I could. I asked him to keep his eyes still, move them, do the same thing in close-up, then from different angles; every possible shot I could think of so we wouldn't have to re-shoot anything later.

Five minutes later, I was done.

"All sorted, mate," I said. "You can open your eyes now."

"That's it?" he replied. "Are you sure you've got everything?"

"More than enough," I said. "Now I just need to film the sequence between me and Nat."

I glanced at her, and she smiled.

"Are you ok with the snogging?" I asked.

"I think I can manage," she replied, giving me wink.

I fixed the camera to the tripod, then set it up on the table in front of the iMac, giving the illusion that his mind was inside the computer, looking out.

"Ok, Nat," I said. "Stay where you are while I frame the shot."

She froze on the spot while a flipping the viewfinder, then zoomed in to medium, leaving enough room for me to come into shot from on the right.

After setting the auto-focus, I pressed record, then moved to my mark.

"Right," I said. "I need you to look at him on the sofa, give him a cruel smile, then look over toward the door. When you do, I'll come forward, give him a filthy look, then we'll kiss each other to rub it in."

"Sounds good," she replied.

"Ok, then," I said. "Action."

She looked at Ant, curled her lip, then turned her head towards the door. I strode forward confidently, gave him an evil look, but before I turned to face her, she grabbed me by the cheeks and pulled me in for a snog.

"Woah," I said, pushing her away. "I'm the one kissing you, remember?"

"Sorry," she said. "We'll have to do it again..."

"Yeah," I replied. "And less the tongue, too, if that's ok... We're not kissing for real."

"I'll try," she giggled.

* * *

Five failed takes later, I realised something was going on. Nat was deliberately messing up the scenes. After a while, I called 'cut' and suggested that we take a break.

"Maybe we should all stop for a cuppa?" I said.

"Sure thing," Nat replied. "I'll get the kettle on..."

She left the room, and I looked at Ant, who responded with a smile.

"What's going on?" I said. "She's fucking up

these takes on purpose."

"Yeah," he replied. "It's pretty obvious."

"Why?" I asked.

It was a stupid question. I already knew.

"She likes you," he replied. "She told me so after she saw your pic."

I shook my head.

"So, she's just doing this to snog me?" I said.

"She's lonely," Ant replied. "She's really wants a boyfriend."

"Yeah, but I'm here shoot *Revenge In Mind*," I replied. "Not bloody *Blind Date*!"

"You seemed like you were enjoying it," he scoffed.

"It's called acting, mate," I replied. "I don't even fancy her!"

"You don't?"

I turned around and saw her standing at the door.

"Sorry," I said. "You're not my type."

Her cheeks flushed red, and she glared at Ant.

"You told me he liked me," she hissed.

"I said he thought you looked ok," ant replied.

"What's the difference?"

With an angry snort, she turned on her heels then went back into the kitchen.

"Well," ant said, finally. "This is awkward...."

* * *

After drinking our tea, Nat calmed down and agreed to finish the shoot. To save further embarrassment, I decided to skip the kissing scene.

"I'll just cut together what we have," I said. "I'm sure we've more than enough footage."

It was a big fat lie.

Without even seeing the rushes, I knew that none of the takes were any good, and that I'd have to salvage things in the edit

It wasn't ideal, but there wasn't a lot I could do about it...

* * *

Once we'd wrapped, I dropped off Ant, then returned home, where I transferred the footage onto my Mac.

To say I was disappointed was an understatement.

It was horrible.

All of it.

All three fundamental ingredients were missing.

The acting was wooden, the characters came across as unsympathetic, and the story was too drab to retain the viewer's interest.

It had been an abject failure.

I sat back in my chair, deflated.

Though my camerawork had been good, it hadn't been enough to carry the film. Like lighting and cinematography, it was something that could only *enhance* a project, not make it good.

I let out a long sigh.

My dream of 'going it alone' had failed.

CHAPTER 40:
MOON MEN
FROM MARS

I sat on my hands for the next two months, waiting for Baz to return from his long summer break. During this period, I reflected on my new role as the 'junior' partner of our duo; the Garfunkel to Baz's Simon; the Ant to Baz's Dec, the Taupin to Baz's Elton..

I found it hard to square. I'd always seen myself as being 'the man', the 'boss', the 'alpha'...

But I wasn't. And, truth be told, I never had been.

For the past two months I'd been living a lie.
It made me feel small and pathetic.
Again.
In later July, Baz called me up.
"Hey dude," he said. "You'll never guess

what?"

"What?" I replied.

"I've only gone and got myself an iMac and camera!"

My heart sunk but I tried not to show it.

"Cool, mate," I replied.

"You'll have to show me how to edit," he said. "I've got some footage of New York that needs doing."

I really wanted to say 'no'.

If I said 'yes', it meant that he wouldn't need me anymore. I'd already consigned myself to the role of *Henchman,* I didn't want to drop down to *Dogsbody*...

"Ok," I replied, belatedly. "When are you free?"

"Tonight," he replied. "Wanna come down?"

I was too weak to refuse.

* * *

I drove to his house, and he welcomed me inside, then took me upstairs to his room. He'd set up a desk in the corner. Upon it sat a brand-new iMac with a huge screen. Glued to edge of the table was the headpiece of a tripod. Beside it was a Firewire cable that had been attached to a cable-tie, which had been duct-taped to the panel.

"It's to stop the wire falling down the back," he said.

He picked up his new camcorder from the bed, fixed it to the headpiece, then plugged in the wire.

"What do you think of this?" he asked.

"It keeps things neat," I remarked, wishing I'd thought of it myself.

He sat down, turned on the Mac and opened iMovie, where several clips had been added to the timeline.

"I've been having a play already," he said, with a grin.

"I can see," I replied.

I sat down on the edge of his bed as he dragged the marker to the start of the project and pressed play.

To my astonishment, the footage had already been edited. Not only that, but it was beautiful. He'd taken his home video clips and turned them into an epic montage, a tour de force of imagery... A veritable feast for the eyes.

He'd also added a soundtrack, comprised of songs he must have recorded on Garageband. All of them fit the footage perfectly. They sounded great too, almost professional.

At once I wondered why he'd brought me here.

It hadn't been for editing lessons, that was for certain. What he was showing me proved he already knew everything he needed to know.

"What do you need me to show you?" I asked, somewhat mutedly.

"Oh yeah," he said. "How do you cut audio clips?"

"Apple and T," I replied.

It was the keyboard shortcut.

He knew this already because it was the same as cutting video.

"Ahhh, yeah," he said, pretending he'd learned something new.

He selected one of the clips then pressed the buttons.

"There we go," he said. "All sorted."

"So, is there anything else you want to show me?" I sighed.

He looked me in the eye and smiled.

"Well," he replied. "I've been playing around with a few other things..."

He opened a project, which was entitled, *Moon Men from Mars*.

"Have a look at this," he said, clicking play.

A Titler appeared on-screen. It looked like the *Shadowbright* logo, but with white lettering against a black background. The only thing that had been changed were the words, which now read *BozGoinOn Productions*.

"What's that?" I asked.

He stopped the tape.

"It's my new name," he said. "Do you like it?"

"I thought we were going with *Wakatar*?" I replied.

"Yeah," he said. "But that's only for when it's me and you. *BozGoinOn* is for my side projects."

"Do you have many more in the pipeline?" I asked.

"Just this one at the moment..." he said.

He pressed play, and the screen faded into a shot of the night sky, peppered with stars. Suddenly, there was a humming sound, and then a silver flying saucer came into shot.

I assumed it was the prop he'd been telling me about.

"That's your UFO, isn't it?" I said.

"Yeah," he grinned. "That shot's from the kitchen window. Blakey was hanging it from my bedroom on a fishing line."

I remembered him telling me about his UFO idea before we'd started filming Dan Lizard.

"I cast Blakey and Bob as the Aliens," he said excitedly. "You'll see them shortly."

Lo-and-behold they appeared on-screen. Both were playing aliens, with ping-pong balls for eyes. His sister, Kaci, played their victim, a random girl who was walking through the park.

It was undeniably artistic; the kind of thing that would have gone down great with the Grebo crew.

But it was all just facade.

There was no substance to it.

It reminded me of an episode of Jackass: watchable, but trite. All the elements that had made Dan Lizard work were missing. After a short while, I realised it was nothing more than the husk of a film, empty and hollow.

At the end, he asked me what I thought.

His smug look suggested I would shower him with praise and tell him how great he was.

But I didn't.

And I didn't need to lie about it either.

"It's ok, mate," I said. "But there's not much to it."

He seemed shocked, as if he couldn't believe what he was hearing.

He looked into my eyes, searching for signs of dishonesty.

But he couldn't find any.

"You don't like it?" he said.

I shook my head.

"I think it's ok, mate," I repeated. "But compared to Dan Lizard, it's a bit crap."

The colour drained from his face.

He was mortified.

"You really think so?" he said. "Why?"

I told him about the three essential elements.

"I remember you talking about this before," he said, turning back to the screen. "You know what.. I think you may be right."

Something inside me stirred.

Was he was giving me kudos?

Yes.

Yes he was.

But not as an artist, but *as a critic.*

"This *is* crap, isn't it?" he said, tutting at the monitor.

I felt oddly elated. Suddenly, my opinion seemed to matter.

"Don't worry, mate," I said. "The last thing I did was crap too."

I told him about *Revenge in Mind*, and how it had been a disaster from the off.

"It just goes to show that we only make good stuff when we're working together," he said.

"You're right," he agreed.

"Yeah," I said. "When it's you, me... and Craig."

He looked at me.

"Craig?"

I nodded.

"We both know he's a great actor," I said. "But he also knows what works. Probably more than the two of us combined."

He hummed and nodded.

"I really fucked things up after *Savo and Rhonda*," I continued. "I never told you what really happened."

"You said he quit," Baz said.

"He didn't," I replied. "Not really. He was just feeling down, deflated. He just needed picking up, but instead of talking him round and being a good friend, I left him to it."

"Shit," he said.

"I think I need to talk to him," I said. "I need to tell him I'm sorry."

Baz nodded.

"It's not just him I need to apologise to," I